**Two wounded hearts that had never really mended...**

"I've missed you, Anna."

"I've missed you, too." A tear rolled down her cheek.

Matt lifted his hand and brushed it away with the pad of his thumb. "Five weeks," he said softly. "Give me five weeks to get to know you again."

"Five weeks to break your heart," she said.

"Five weeks that will last forever."

Her chin quivered. "I can't stay."

He gave her a lopsided grin, his eyes glassy. "I never asked you to."

The longing in his eyes sucked her breath away. But could she survive walking away from him?

# ALWAYS YOU

# ALWAYS YOU

## DENISE GROVER SWANK

FOREVER
NEW YORK  BOSTON

Copyright © 2017 by Denise Grover Swank
Excerpt from *Only You* copyright © 2016 by Denise Grover Swank
Cover design by Elizabeth Stokes
Cover copyright © 2017 by Hachette Book Group, Inc.

Forever
Hachette Book Group
1290 Avenue of the Americas, New York, NY 10104
forever-romance.com
twitter.com/foreverromance

First edition: November 2017

Forever is an imprint of Grand Central Publishing. The Forever name and logo are trademarks of Hachette Book Group, Inc.

The publisher is not responsible for websites (or their content) that are not owned by the publisher.

The Hachette Speakers Bureau provides a wide range of authors for speaking events. To find out more, go to www.hachettespeakersbureau.com or call (866) 376-6591.

ISBNs: 978-1-4555-3981-9 (mass market), 978-1-4555-3983-3 (ebook)

Printed in the United States of America

OPM

10  9  8  7  6  5  4  3  2  1

# ALWAYS YOU

# Chapter One

~

Standing at the edge of a grass soccer field, Matt stared into the sea of parents' faces and resisted the urge to groan. Obviously, word had spread after last season that Coach Matt was relatively good looking, somewhat successful, loved kids, and most important, was single.

Maybe he should rethink his decision to coach his five-year-old nephew's soccer team. But when he looked down into Ethan's adoring face, he knew he'd never quit. He'd swim through shark-infested waters for the kid—what were a few single moms? Well, more like a half a dozen...

"This is the five- and six-year-old peewee division," Matt said, continuing with his introduction while the kids fidgeted behind him, "and we don't keep official score. The goal is to learn the rules and have fun. Any questions?"

A redheaded woman with a toddler at her feet shot her hand into the air. "Is it true that you're single?"

Matt forced a laugh and rubbed the back of his neck. "Any questions about *soccer*?"

A few of the women giggled, and some of the others

looked downright sheepish. He noticed there was one lone man in the group. He stood at the back and seemed to be ogling the women's asses. Matt planned to keep an eye on the creeper.

A familiar brunette lifted her hand and Matt relaxed. Phyllis, thank God, was very happily married. "I'd be more than willing to coordinate the snack schedule, Matt."

"Thanks." He held her gaze, trying to convey how much he meant it.

Her grin told him she knew exactly what she was doing. He spun around to face nine excited faces. "Okay. Who's ready to play soccer?"

"We are!" the children shouted, jumping up and down with excitement.

Nine faces. There were supposed to be ten. He pulled the folded printout of the team roster from his back pocket and studied the list. Sure enough, he was missing one. He started calling out the names he didn't recognize, trying to figure out which kid was missing.

"Trevor Millhouse. Billy Houser." Both kids raised their hands. "Toby Robins." No answer.

He scanned the group. "Toby Robins?"

Ethan's hand shot into the air. "He was at school today, Uncle Matt. He said he was coming. But he's never played soccer before, and he's scared."

Matt squatted in front of his nephew. "Scared enough to miss his first practice?"

"Nah," Ethan said as though Matt had said the most ridiculous thing in the world. "I told him that you'd teach him *everything*." The boy beamed up at him with a grin showing his missing front tooth.

"Then maybe Toby's just running late," Matt said. "We'll get started and catch him up to speed when he gets here."

Ethan nodded. "I'll help him."

He rubbed the boy's head. "I'm sure you will."

Matt lined up the kids and passed out a miniature soccer ball to each of them, keeping one for himself. He rested his foot on the top of the ball. "Now, the important thing to remember is that you can't touch the ball with your hands. If you touch it with your hands, you lose it to the other team. But," he said with an exaggerated grin, "you can touch it with any other part of your body." He scooped up the ball with his toe and tossed it into the air, bounced it from his knee to the top of his head, back to his knee, and then down to the top of his foot before letting it fall to the ground.

The kids released excited oohs and ahhs. He tried to ignore the appreciative murmurs from the women behind him.

"You probably can't do that now," Matt said, "but if you keep practicing, you can learn how. Some soccer players can even make goals with the tops of their heads." He tossed the ball up with his foot again and then bounced it off his head, this time aiming it toward the goal behind the kids.

"Your uncle's so cool…" Becca said to Ethan with awe in her voice.

Ethan's grin stretched from ear to ear. "I know."

"Okay," Matt said as he jogged over to pick up the ball, but one of the mothers, Miranda Houser, had already run over to pick it up and toss it to him.

"Here you go, Coach Matt," she said with a grin.

"Thanks," he said, catching it with his hands.

"You're out!" one of the boys shouted. "You touched the ball with your hands."

"Good job, George," Matt said. "You were listening."

"Look at me, Coach," Remy, one of the new boys, called out. "I can kick the ball just like you!" Then the ball at his feet flew through the air and slammed into the nose of one of the new mothers.

"Oh, shit," Matt muttered as the woman screamed.

"Coach Matt said a bad word!" a girl shouted.

The injured mother covered her face with her hands, then looked at the blood covering her fingers and started to wail.

He dashed for his bag and grabbed a clean hand towel and a bottle of water before running over to the still screaming woman.

The other mothers had circled her, offering sympathy and telling her to lean her head back and pinch her nose. Matt pushed between them as he glanced at Phyllis and mouthed, *Do you know her name?*

"Amy," she whispered in his ear. Phyllis's daughter Becca had been on his team last fall, and he'd come to rely on Phyllis more than once for advice on handling the little ones. And for running interference with the overeager single mothers. After his last serious girlfriend had turned out to be a bank robber using an alias, he was in *no* hurry to start a relationship.

"Okay, Amy," Matt said, guiding her to a folding chair. "Let's have you sit down, and I'll take a look."

She quieted and sat down, watching Matt with rounded eyes. "I think my nose is broken." Her words were muffled by her hands.

He offered her a reassuring smile. "I suspect it's fine. Kids this age don't have enough power to cause that much damage." He pulled her hands down and examined her face. A slow trickle was dripping from her left nostril, but just as he suspected, it didn't look broken. He grabbed her hand and guided it up to pinch her nose. "Just give it a bit of pressure and it will let up in a minute."

She did as he instructed, the fear in her eyes fading.

Her face and hands were still covered in blood, so he opened the water bottle and poured some onto the clean towel.

As he gently washed the blood off her chin, the look in her eyes changed again.

The women around him began to murmur among themselves.

Oh, shit. He'd treated her like he would have any kid on his team, but he could see how the women might misconstrue his intentions. There was a wedding band on her left hand, but he wasn't sure whether he should find that reassuring.

*Shit.*

He tossed the towel to her as he got to his feet.

"You should be fine," he said, then hurried over to the kids, who were watching with open mouths and wide eyes.

"I want to learn to kick a ball like that," one of the boys said. "I want to give my brother a bloody nose."

"Not me," one of the girls said with a lot of attitude, putting her hands on her hips. "I want to hit Mitchell Blevins in the balls!"

Matt lifted his hands. "Okay! We don't kick the ball to hurt anyone. We only kick the ball to make a goal."

"But that's not what Uncle Kevin said last week at your house," Ethan said, tilting his head back to look at him. "He said he was going to kick Uncle Tyler in his balls, and he wasn't even playing soccer."

He was going to kill his best friend. "Then Uncle Kevin needs a time-out, and I'll ask Aunt Holly to give him one."

"Your uncle has balls?" Becca asked. "You're so lucky. My uncles only have cell phones."

"Not those kind of balls," the feisty girl who wanted to kick Mitchell Blevins in his private parts said in a condescending tone. "Those balls." Then she pointed at the crotch of the boy next to her.

What the hell was happening?

Matt grabbed her arm and pushed it down. "No more talk about balls."

One of the little girls started to cry. "I wanted to learn how to kick a ball hard enough to give someone a bloody nose."

"But Uncle Matt," Ethan asked insistently. "How can we play soccer without balls?"

Matt shot an exasperated look at Phyllis, but she was too busy laughing to offer help.

"Everybody listen up!" Matt shouted, and the children gave him their attention. "There are lots of different kinds of balls, but we're just going to talk about soccer balls today. Okay?"

The kids nodded, looking eager to please him, probably so they, too, could learn self-defense with a soccer ball.

"Oh!" Becca said in excitement. "I get it now. Boys have golf balls."

Matt leaned back his head and groaned.

"There he is!" Ethan shouted. "There's Toby!" He took off running toward the street, where the parents had parked their cars.

"Ethan!" Matt shouted. "Come back!" He liked to think Ethan was smart enough not to run into the street, but he'd learned over the last six months that five-year-olds sometimes did stupid things for no good reason.

The boy ignored him, but Matt felt better when he saw a small boy running toward his nephew. The woman standing at the car looked like she'd come straight from work. The skirt she wore hugged her curves, and from what he could see of her as she turned to fish in the backseat of the car for something, she wasn't at all dressed for the field.

"Toby!" she called after him. "Wait for me!"

Thankfully, Ethan had changed directions. He was running back toward Matt with Toby on his heels.

Ethan stopped in front of Matt, panting with excitement. "He's here, Uncle Matt! He's here!"

Ethan's excitement was infectious, and after glancing back at the other kids—they were happily kicking their soccer balls in a dozen different directions—Matt grinned at the boy standing behind his nephew. He was a cute kid, with dark blond hair and bright blue eyes. Matt noticed his pale complexion and made a mental note to make sure he was slathered with sunscreen when they played their soccer games under the midday sun.

"Hi, Toby. I'm Matt. Glad to have you on the team." Matt held out a hand to shake with the boy.

Toby giggled as he shook his hand.

Matt glanced up at the woman making her way toward them. Something about her felt…familiar. Or maybe it was the stirring he felt down deep that was familiar.

"Is that your mom?" he asked the boy, trying not to sound too interested.

"Yeah," Toby said with a scowl. "She was late. *Again.*"

Was that a British accent? Ethan had mentioned that Toby "talked funny," but Matt had figured the kid probably had a lisp. Ethan had one, too, after his front tooth fell out the weekend before.

"That's okay. You haven't missed much."

"I don't know how to play football," the boy said with a frown.

Ethan chortled. "I told you it's not *football*. It's *soccer*. Uncle Matt says I'm too little to play football, isn't that right, Uncle Matt? But he played in high school, and I'm gonna play, too, when I'm big like him."

Toby's frown increased, and Matt wanted to put him at ease. "Ethan says you're new. Where did you live before?"

"London."

Matt squatted in front of him, balancing on the balls of his feet. "Well, there you go," he said with a grin. "We call it soccer here, but you call it football in the UK."

The woman was closer now. She was pulling her heels out of the ground like she was doing leg lifts, and he couldn't help noticing that her legs were sexy as hell. And the way her golden blond hair fell across her face as she stared down at her shoes sinking deeper with each step made him think of after-sex bed head. *Focus.*

"Toby," she said. "I told you to wait. We don't know if it's your team or not."

Her voice sounded familiar, too. That stirring feeling inside him turned a bit uneasy. Surely he was just hearing things…

"Mum," Toby groaned. "Ethan's on my team! I had to hurry or I was going to miss practice." His worried gaze met Matt's.

"Don't worry." Matt patted Toby's shoulder as he stood to get a good look at the woman's face. He smiled down at the boy. "We're all learning the basics right now. Ethan, get Toby a ball and we'll get star—"

A ball walloped Matt on the back of his head with enough force to make him lose his balance. Before he could right himself, he fell forward. Ethan and Toby scrambled out of his way as he landed in the damp grass, his hands breaking his fall.

"Coach Matt!" the kids shouted.

"You killed him!" one of the girls cried out.

Another girl screamed.

Matt tried to sit up, but another ball hit the back of his head with enough force to make his teeth rattle.

"Remy! Stop that!" one of the mothers shouted. "Quit kicking balls at your coach!"

"It's just like Angry Birds!" the boy said as another ball sailed over Matt's head.

"If you don't stop," Becca snarled, "I'm gonna kick *your* balls."

Remy screamed.

Matt rolled onto his back, wondering how practice had gotten so out of control. Maybe he should just call it and start again on Thursday night.

The kids huddled around him, looking down with curious glances.

"Uncle Matt?" Ethan asked, sounding worried. "Are you still gonna teach Toby how to play soccer?"

Matt closed his eyes and groaned, and when he opened them, Toby's mother was leaning over him. Her hair had fallen into her face again, but she tucked it behind her ear. While it promptly fell back, he had seen her face for a few brief seconds. Sucking in a breath, he told himself he'd been wrong to think these kids didn't have enough force to do serious damage.

He must have a traumatic head injury that included hallucinations, because he was staring up into the face of the only woman who had ever broken his heart.

# Chapter Two

❧

They'd met during their junior year of college in a business class at the University of Missouri in Columbia. He'd noticed her—and vice versa, she later told him—but he hadn't known how to approach her. It had seemed like kismet when they were assigned to work on a group project together. They'd completed the project, getting to know each other during several late-night study sessions, and it was during one of those sessions they'd discovered they had both grown up in Blue Springs, Missouri. They'd graduated the same year, although Matt had attended Blue Springs High School and Anna had gone to Blue Springs South. They even shared a few mutual friends. After the project was finished, Matt asked Anna out. Their first date had been magic, and when he dropped her off at her apartment that night, he kissed her good night and knew she was the one.

He'd never told anyone that. His two best friends, Kevin and Tyler, had still been very single at the time—and vocal about their belief that only a fool would tie himself down to one woman, and of course he hadn't told Anna either...not until the next year. Matt had fallen hard, and so had Anna, but the closer they got to graduation, the more evasive she became about what she wanted for their future.

Two weeks before graduation, Matt took Anna out to dinner and proposed, offering her a one-third-carat diamond solitaire engagement ring. It had taken him eight months and two jobs to save up for it, but when he showed it to her, her eyes filled with tears.

"Tell me those are happy tears," Matt said, giving a nervous laugh.

Her blue eyes rose to his and he knew.

He set the ring on the table. "Anna?"

She shook her head. "I can't."

"You can't marry me? Why not?"

"I don't want to get married."

"To me?"

"To anybody."

He blinked in shock. "Since when?"

Her chin quivered. "I know we discussed marriage, but every time the subject came up, I started to panic. I thought it was because I've been so focused on school and worried about my grades. I was sure after everything died down, I'd want to get married after we graduated. But the closer we've gotten to graduation..." She paused as tears filled her eyes. "I love you, Matt. I love you so much, but I don't want to get married."

He stared at her in disbelief. This was like his worst nightmare come true. "I don't expect us to get married right away, Anna. Hell, you haven't even gotten a job yet."

"I have," she whispered, her eyes pleading with him to understand.

He sat back in his seat, feeling gutted. "You took a job? Without telling me?"

"I didn't want to hurt you."

"You mean like you're doing now?"

Her top teeth scraped her bottom lip. "I'm sorry."

The silence hung between them, and he asked in a raspy voice, "Where are you going?"

"London."

*"England?"*

"I'm sorry," she whispered.

"So we're over just like that?" he asked in dismay.

"We can still see each other." She sounded so hopeful, he almost believed it was possible.

But while Kevin and Tyler might have accused him of being the romantic of the trio, he could also be a realist. "How long are you planning to stay in London?"

"I don't know. Maybe a year. Maybe five."

Just like that, Matt's whole life had been shattered to bits. His dream was to return home to run his father's construction business, to settle down and start a family. With Anna. "You want me to wait five years. Then you'll be ready to get married and have a family?"

Tears filled her eyes. "No. That's not what I want. I want a career in international finance... and, Matt, I don't think I want kids."

His gaze drifted around the restaurant as he tried to make sense of what was happening. They'd never discussed when or how many kids they planned, but he'd made no secret that he saw kids in his future. He turned to her with a sad smile. "But I do."

She started to silently cry. "I know."

He flagged the waitress and asked for the check. The ring lay on the white tablecloth, mocking him. How had he gotten it so wrong? She'd talked about a future... with him. Had she lied to him? Changed her mind? No matter the reason, he felt like a fool. He wanted to spew hateful, accusatory words at her, but he couldn't. She'd ripped his heart to pieces, but he still loved her.

The moment the waitress placed the black folder on the table, he grabbed his wallet out of his back pocket. He started to remove his credit card, then changed his mind. It would be torture to stay there, stuck in the middle of this humiliating moment, any longer than necessary. He tossed down all the cash in his wallet, thankful he had enough to cover the meal and a generous tip since he didn't want to wait for the change.

Then he stood, barely able to look at Anna.

"Matt," she said, her voice breaking, "the ring."

It still sat there on the table, glittering in the candlelight, mocking him. It represented his hopes and dreams. The life he had imagined with Anna. "Leave it. I don't want it."

Better to leave it on the table along with his bloodied heart.

She called out to him, but he ignored her and headed toward the door, leaving her to follow. He got six feet before stopping. His father had taught him better than that. Turning slightly, he waited for her to catch up and then walked slightly behind her to the exit, pushing the door open so she could walk out into the warm April night.

They were silent during the ten-minute drive to her apartment. He pulled into a parking spot and Anna had the door open before he turned off the engine. But he climbed out and quickly caught up to her.

She turned to look up at him, pain in her eyes. "Matt. You don't have to—"

"I'm walking you to your door." His tone was rough and brooked no argument.

She started to protest then stopped. Hanging her head

with defeat, she continued walking up the steps to her second-floor apartment and stopping outside her door. After she unlocked the door, she spun and wrapped her arms around his neck and pressed her lips to his.

This was good-bye.

Her tears coated his cheeks, and he knew if he stayed a second longer, his own tears would be added to hers. Grabbing her hands, he slowly pulled them down and took a step back.

"Good-bye, Anna. I hope you find what you're looking for."

*       *       *

Anna gasped and took a step back, stumbling into a small child behind her, but she righted herself—only for her three-inch stilettos to sink into the ground *again*. She should just take them off, but then her feet would freeze. However, at the moment, she had something bigger to deal with.

*Get a grip.*

It had been hard enough coming home for the first time since her mother's funeral, and she'd known full well she might run into Matt, but the chances had seemed slim. Over fifty thousand residents lived in the suburb, so it should have been easy to get lost in it. Even so, she'd envisioned running into him at the grocery store. At the movies. Or maybe at Quick Trip while pumping gas. She'd never once pictured him as her son's soccer coach.

He sat up, staring at her like he was seeing the Ghost of Christmas Past, but why wouldn't he? As far as he was concerned, she was.

He got to his feet, blinking and shaking his head slightly. "Okay. Who kicked that? Remy?" he asked, scanning the children crowding around him.

One of the boys hung his head, his chin touching his chest, and mumbled, "Sorry, Coach Matt."

Matt tousled the boy's head and chuckled, although it sounded strained. "You've got quite a kick, Remy. We just need to train you to use your power for good, not evil." He shot Anna a questioning glance, as if confirming she was in fact there, then turned back to the kids. "But first we're going to learn to dribble a ball around those orange cones I set up. Ethan, you stand behind one cone. Becca, you stand behind the other, and everyone else pick a line." He followed the kids as they shuffled to line up.

She watched her son run after the other blond boy—Ethan—but her gaze was drawn back to Matt like a magnet. He was just as good-looking as he'd been in college, maybe more so. He'd been built back then, but now he seemed even more ripped. She used to tease him about being a stereotypical construction worker since he looked so good when he took his shirt off. She found herself wondering what his chest would look like now.

Anna shook her head. No. She had no right to think about Matt like that. Not after what she'd done to him. Still, she couldn't help searching for a ring on his left hand.

She couldn't see his ring finger, but he had to be married. He'd always wanted a family. One of those kids on the team had to be his.

She wasn't proud of it, but she'd tried to Facebook stalk him multiple times over the years. He either rarely posted or his posts were all set to friends only. She'd never had the guts to send him a friend request, and stalking his two best friends' posts had yielded even less information.

Matt turned to the side, but his arms were crossed over his chest, his hands tucked under his arms. Why was she even looking? It wasn't like anything would come from him being single. He hated her and he had every right. How long had she hated herself for hurting him the way she had?

Her heart lightened when she saw Toby smile—a genuine, full-of-happiness smile. He'd always been such a happy child, the one true bright spot in her life, but his light had dimmed after the move to Blue Springs. Not that she could blame him—she'd taken him from the heart of London, his private school, and his part-time nanny, and brought him to the Midwest to live with his cranky grandfather in the small house she'd grown up in. Talk about culture shock.

But his new friend had helped him with the transition. Ethan made her son happy, but she wondered if it was too late to switch to another coach? Was it fair to Toby if she moved him? Was it fair to Matt if she didn't?

*Calm down. He's married and over it by now.*

Obviously, he was probably still angry with her, but surely time had healed his wounds, not to mention his new family.

*Her* wounds had gotten in the way of her relationships, even with Phillip. She'd never met anyone she could love as she'd loved Matt.

No. Phillip's philandering had ruined them soon after Toby was born, but now she wondered if Phillip had realized she held part of herself back. Was that why he had strayed?

Still, she wondered what would have happened if she'd answered Matt differently that day, if she'd followed him back to Kansas City and built the life he'd so desperately craved. But twenty-one-year-old Anna Fischer was a different person than thirty-three-year-old Annaliese Robins, and she liked who she was now. Despite the pain and heartache she'd suffered, she was a strong, confident woman who loved her career and loved her child. She was successful and respected by her colleagues, adored by her son.

But sometimes it wasn't enough.

Seeing Matt now was a reminder of what she could have given her son. What she could have given *herself*.

Wiping a tear from the corner of her eye, she scanned the team, trying to figure out which child belonged to Matt. The way he handled the kids proved that he was an awesome dad, not that she was surprised. He'd always been filled with infinite patience. It was his quiet strength that had drawn her to him back in college. He had been this tall, well-built, sexy guy, sure of himself without being cocky. Like he knew who he was and made no apologies for it, but didn't need to broadcast it either. Her roommates had thought she was the luckiest girl in the world, and she'd agreed, even if something hadn't felt quite right.

There was no doubt his confidence had drawn her in like a moth to a flame. She had been inspired by his certainty about what he wanted for his life, partly because she had been so uncertain about her own.

Toby caught her attention and gave her a tiny wave as a smile lit up his face. She gave him a small wave back. For the first time in over a month, he was happy. There was no way she'd take this from him. She'd find a way to make it work.

"Does your son have an accent?" a woman asked, shaking Anna out of her thoughts.

"Yes," she said, turning toward her. She was a twenty-something mother, dressed in jeans, a T-shirt, and an over-sized cardigan. Her dark hair was in a ponytail. Waves of condescension rolled off her as she curled her lip at Anna's heels. Anna knew they were out of place, but in her defense, she hadn't planned on her business lunch with her boss lasting four hours. He'd flown to Kansas City to see a client and insisted Anna meet him for a long lunch. Not that it had done much good. But she'd worry about that later. "British."

"You don't have one," the woman said. "Are you his mother?"

"Hi," another woman said, quickly approaching her. "I'm Phyllis and my daughter is Becca. The one with two braids. Welcome to the Tigers."

The woman gave off a laid-back vibe, and Anna instantly relaxed. "I'm Annaliese, but call me Anna. And I'm sure you've all figured out that my son is Toby."

"Ethan's friend. He was worried that Toby hadn't shown up yet," Phyllis said.

Anna took a half second to scan for a dig at her tardiness, but the smile on Phyllis's face seemed genuine. She gave her a tentative smile in return. "I came from downtown. The traffic was a nightmare. Toby would have killed me if he'd missed practice. He's been looking forward to it all week."

"Is Toby your only child?" Something in her tone set Anna on edge, but Phyllis grinned. "Sorry. No offense meant. Becca is my fourth child."

"Four?" Anna asked in wonder. "I can hardly handle one." Judging from the disapproval that immediately washed over Ponytail Mom's face, it wouldn't be a good idea to admit that she'd had the help of a nanny in London.

Phyllis laughed. "Trust me. You get more adept at juggling them, along with their activities and everything else, with each new kid." She gave Anna a conspiratorial grin. "Just don't drop over at my house unexpectedly. I usually need forty-eight hours' notice."

Anna laughed. "Duly noted." If the other mothers were like Ponytail Mom, at least she had one ally on this team.

"I take it you moved back from the UK," Phyllis said, and the other mothers cast their attention toward the conversation with interest.

Anna hesitated. She'd never been good at small talk, but

something told her she needed to study up now that she was back home.

"My widowed father got sick and needed help, so I've moved back for a few months to help him convalesce."

"Then you're going back?" another mother asked. "What part of the UK are you from?"

She ignored the first question. "London."

"That must be so exciting!" a blond woman said with a sigh. "I'd kill to visit London, much less live there."

"Well," Anna said with a cautious grin. "It definitely has its drawbacks. It's expensive and crowded and the weather is dreary. It's not for everyone."

"Oh!" the woman said excitedly. "I heard a bit of an accent when you said 'dreary.'"

Anna forced a smile. She'd gotten this in reverse when she'd first moved to London twelve years ago. Her American accent had made her a novelty and, strangely enough, had seemed to give her an edge over her British female counterparts. But now poor Toby was constantly confronted with people who were fascinated with his accent. Since he was shy and hated attention, he'd started talking less and less in public.

"What do you do there?" asked the one lone father, standing at the back to the group. "Are you a model?"

Every woman turned to glare at him.

"What?" he asked with his hands flung wide. "She looks like a model."

Anna wasn't impressed. The guy was most likely married. "No. I'm something far less exotic. I'm in international finance."

"So you're a bank teller," Ponytail Mom said, making "bank teller" sound synonymous with "homeless person."

"Not really," Anna said. "It's a little more involved than that."

"So if you're moving back," Ponytail Mom continued, "will you finish out the soccer season?"

"I'm not sure," Anna admitted. There were a lot of uncertainties in her life at the moment.

She put her hands on her hips. "I see."

Anna suspected Ponytail Mom was looking for a reason to be disagreeable.

"Calm down, Tina," Phyllis snorted. "This is peewee soccer, and they play three kids at a time. If Toby leaves the season early, your Billy will get more time on the field." Then she winked at Anna.

Anna decided that Phyllis was her new favorite person.

Turning to the other women, Phyllis said, "I still have two gaps on the snack schedule." She glanced back at Anna. "And one of them is for the second game."

The hint was obvious. "I'll take it."

Tina scowled. "I'm not sure how they do things in *London*, but we prefer healthy snacks. Organic and gluten free is preferable and nothing with peanut butter."

Anna gave her a pointed stare. "While this is Toby's first organized sport, we've heard of healthy snacks. It shouldn't be a problem." She paused and tapped her chin. "You *do* have blood pudding here, don't you? I'm certain it's gluten free."

Tina's eyes filled with horror, but Phyllis burst out laughing. The other mothers hesitated and then laughed, too, which only seemed to irritate Tina more.

"I'll take the other game," the blond woman said.

"Perfect, Lisa," Phyllis said, marking down her name. "We're all covered now."

When Anna returned her attention to the kids, Toby was trying to kick a ball around several orange cones while his friend Ethan cupped his hands around his mouth and shouted, "You can do it, Toby."

Matt stood to the side, watching Toby and another girl weaving in and out of the cones. His gaze rose to hers and Anna couldn't ignore the zap of awareness that shot through her. But his gaze was perfectly emotionless. She had no idea what he was thinking, but if she were to guess, he was probably trying to figure out the best way to get rid of her.

Maybe she shouldn't have signed up for the snack schedule.

She spent the next forty-five minutes answering the other women's questions about her life and where she'd gone to school. It turned out that she'd graduated high school with Phyllis's younger sister. As she talked to the mothers, she tried to determine if one of them could be Matt's wife. Matt had given Billy some extra attention after he'd done well with the cones. But if he was Matt's son, that meant Matt was married to Ponytail Mom. He wouldn't marry her, would he? She couldn't see him with someone like her. But she had married Phillip, so who was she to judge? Finally, she couldn't deal with the uncertainty and decided to be bold and ask, "Which child belongs to the coach?"

"Ethan," Phyllis said. "Matt's Ethan's uncle."

Anna tried to hide her surprise.

Phyllis leaned in closer and whispered, "Matt's single, but he coaches Ethan's sports teams."

"Oh."

Matt was single.

Matt was *single*?

How was that possible? Then a new horror hit her. This changed *everything*. If Matt was still single after all these years, her showing up with her son after she'd claimed she hadn't wanted children was bound to make things worse. What if he took out his grudge on her son? She was going to have to pull Toby from the team.

"Okay!" Matt called out. "Everybody huddle around."

When the kids gathered in front of him, he said, "That was a great practice! Everybody showed a lot of hustle and you're learning to control the ball. If you have your own soccer balls, practice at home, and feel free to bring your own balls to practice. Parents," he said, looking over at the mothers and the lone father, "we're using a size three ball, so it would be helpful to get your child one in that size. I hope to have the completed game schedule by next Tuesday. Any questions?"

The parents were silent.

He grinned. "Okay. Everyone put your soccer balls in the mesh bag, and Ethan, help me pick up the cones. I'll see everyone on Thursday!"

Toby nearly tripped on his ball as he tried to kick it toward the bag, but Matt grabbed his arm and held him upright. "Easy there, bud. You almost did a face plant just like I did when you got here."

Toby looked up at Matt with adoring eyes. "How did I do, Coach Matt?"

Matt stared down at the boy for a moment before his face lit up with a soft smile—almost like it was in spite of himself. "You did great for your first practice, Toby. And you'll do even better next time."

Anna's heart shattered into pieces.

"Thanks, Coach Matt!" he said, then took off running for Anna. "Mummy! I did it!" He threw his arms around her legs and hugged her.

"You were wonderful, Toby," she said. A lump formed in her throat as she saw Matt watching them. She and Matt were adults, and he obviously could put aside his feelings to be kind to her son. Maybe they could work this out.

His eyes held hers for a second, the bitterness and hurt sucking her breath away, then he turned on his heels and walked toward the empty field.

# Chapter Three

Toby talked more on the short car ride home than he had in the past several days, giving her little time to think. "I kicked the ball around the orange cones, Mummy. Did you see me?"

She smiled at him in the rearview mirror. "Yes, I saw you. You were amazing."

"I can't wait until the next practice. Can I get some balls? Coach Matt said I need three balls."

She pulled up to a stoplight and caught his gaze. "He said you need a size three ball, pumpkin. Not three of them." It would devastate him when she told him that he was going to have to switch teams, but the look on Matt's face convinced her there was no other choice.

"Oh." He was silent for a moment. "Coach Matt says my shin guards are too big. He says I need to get smaller ones."

"Okay," she said. Coach Matt. How could he already adore his new coach? Then again, why was she surprised? Toby was always drawn to kind men who paid attention to him. "We'll get you a ball tomorrow, along with smaller shin guards. Right now we're going home and starting dinner."

He scowled. "That's not home. It's Grandad's house."

"Well, Grandad's house is ours for now."

His frown deepened and he looked down at his lap.

Anna's heart sank. "Is living at Grandad's so bad?"

He lifted his face with a smile that looked forced. "No, Mummy."

But she knew he was lying, and it killed her even more that he was trying to make her feel better. "I know Grandad can be grumpy—"

His gaze held hers. "Why doesn't he like me?"

A car honked behind her—the light had turned green—and she had to look away. Why were they having this conversation in the car? Then it occurred to her that he was opening up *because* she was partially distracted. She knew her father scared him at times, but she'd hoped Toby would get used to her father's rants. "What are you talking about? Of course Grandad likes you. How could he not? He's just hurting from his broken leg." And his wounded pride, but no need to mention that to the boy.

Toby didn't answer.

"Hey, I know," she said in a cajoling tone. "After tea, how about you and I watch TV snuggled up on the bed? Just like we do back home."

He looked unsure. "Grandad won't like it. He doesn't like when we watch TV in our room."

Toby had a point. "Well..." she said with a grin, "Grandad can get over it."

A smile spread across his face. "Okay."

Anna sighed. Albert Fischer had never been an overly pleasant man, but age and widower-hood had made him downright cranky. His schedule was precise: he was up at six, by six fifteen he was drinking his coffee and reading the *Kansas City Star* at his kitchen table, he liked his dinner promptly at five thirty, and he was always in bed by ten. Her mother's death seven years before had made him even more set in his ways, and anything that threw him off-schedule made him a bear to live with. A five-year-old boy underfoot had sent Albert's whole world careening off its axis.

In fairness, her father's world had already been upended when he'd broken his femur. Albert was fiercely independent, so having his thirty-three-year-old daughter move in with her son to care for him had filled him with shame, which only exasperated the problem. But the doctors had told Anna that if someone didn't move in with him for the next few months, he would have to go to a nursing home. Since Anna was an only child, that left the sole responsibility to her. She'd considered hiring him a full-time nurse, but it would have been difficult to make decisions about his care from across the ocean. So she'd taken a semi-leave of absence, packed up her son, and moved back home.

Her firm hadn't been supportive, not that she blamed them. Being gone for three months was a burden to her as well. But even though she wasn't in the London office, she was still working at her father's house, juggling her clients with e-mails and international phone calls and the occasional client meeting when they happened to come through Kansas City— a more common occurrence than she'd expected. But they still weren't happy, as Anna's boss had made perfectly clear this afternoon as they'd gone over her accounts.

This wouldn't end well. She could feel it.

"Can we have fish fingers and chips?" Toby asked.

She had a package of fish sticks in the freezer, but her father always complained that the house reeked of fish when she heated them up. Let him complain. She was going to make her baby boy happy before she broke his heart with the news he had to switch teams. "Yes, baby. You can have fish fingers and chips."

Several minutes later, she pulled into the driveway of the 1960s ranch house and turned off the engine. She got out and opened the back passenger door as Toby finished unbuckling his booster seat. Grabbing his backpack, she slung it over her shoulder. "Let's go make your fish fingers and you can tell me about your day. Who did you play with at recess?"

He gave her a look that suggested she'd lost her mind. "Ethan. Duh."

"Duh?" she asked, amused. "That's a new term."

He shrugged as they walked to the front door. "Ethan says it." He reached the front steps and hesitated. "Maybe we should just watch TV with Grandad."

Damn her father. He'd been on a rant that morning that had been louder than usual, and while Anna had dealt with worse as a child, her sensitive son had taken it personally.

Anna brushed past Toby and opened the front door. "I'll deal with Grandad. What should we watch tonight?"

"*Ninjago.*"

She laughed. "You've seen every episode. Twice. You don't want to try something new?"

"I like it," he said quietly.

He stood on the doorstep, hesitating.

Why did her father have to be such an ass? She'd hoped things would ease up after he'd adjusted to having house guests, but if anything, they'd gotten worse. What was she going to do? Her father's answer would be to tell Toby to toughen up—the Albert Fischer who'd raised her had no patience for weakness—but she refused to do that. And she couldn't continue to traumatize her son, but she couldn't leave her father alone either. Maybe hiring a nurse wasn't such a bad idea after all. She could find a short-term place for them to stay—close enough to check on him, far enough to give them all some space.

She grabbed Toby's tiny hand and squeezed. "Come on."

They entered the dark living room and Anna turned on a lamp. "Dad, we're home." When she didn't see him in his chair, her breath stuck in her chest. "Dad?"

"Back here," he said, his voice faint.

How had he gotten to the back of the house?

Anna handed Toby his backpack and cupped his cheek. "You go into the kitchen and get out the fish fingers, okay?"

"Yes, Mummy."

He headed to the back of the house while Anna walked down the short hall. "Dad, you're in your room?" She stopped in the doorway, surprised to see him sprawled on the bed and his walker several feet away and tipped on its side.

"I wanted to lay down. Can't a man do what he wants in his own damn house?"

She didn't answer his question. He'd asked it multiple times over the last four weeks, and in many different forms.

It was definitely time for a *Come to Jesus* chat.

"I thought you were going to lunch in downtown Kansas City, not Chicago," he grumbled. "You said you'd be gone a couple of hours."

"I'm sorry. It took longer than expected, and then I didn't have time to come back before I picked up Toby from school and took him to his first soccer practice."

He frowned. "Isn't he too young to be playing soccer?"

"They start kids as early as three," she said, picking up the walker and moving it next to the bed. "And since Toby turns six in a few weeks, he's more than old enough. Besides, I told you before I left for my meeting."

"Where's he at? I don't hear him making a ruckus."

Her jaw clenched. "Toby's in the kitchen. I'm making him fish sticks and French fries for dinner, but I'll be happy to heat up some leftover casserole from last night if you would like."

"More damn fish sticks. The house is gonna stink to high heaven."

She stood next to the edge of the bed. "They make Toby happy, and that little boy needs some happiness in this house, Dad."

"What the hell does that mean?" he asked, his eyes flashing with anger as he stared up at her.

"Toby's hungry. I'll get his dinner started, then we'll discuss it later."

"Your son has had your attention for nearly six years," her father said. "You can spare me two damn minutes."

Was that what this was about? That she'd stayed in London after her mother had died? He'd been the one to run her off, not that she'd been eager to return since. Her mother had always been her anchor growing up. While her father had been a better parent when she was younger, he'd never been like all the other dads. But he slowly changed, and by the time she'd hit middle school, he'd gone from cantankerous to emotionally distant.

After she left for college, her mother had been the reason she'd come home and her grief had resurfaced the moment she'd walked through the front door. She missed her mother, and her father's surliness only made it worse.

Anna shook her head. "Later. I'm going to heat up your dinner. Do you want me to help you up before I go?"

He hesitated, then gave a rough nod.

She helped him slide his feet to the side of the bed and positioned his walker in front of him. "You got out of your chair in the living room without any help," she said. "That's great."

"Took me ten minutes."

"You'll get faster as you get stronger."

"Hmm..." he grumped.

Stepping back, she watched him balance his hands on the walker and then slowly rise. While he was still as difficult as ever, it was hard to see him so vulnerable. When she was younger, his strong physique and sour attitude had made him an intimidating force, but now his weak and frail body wore his surliness like a hand-me-down coat. She felt guilty for being gone so long, but he hadn't made it easy. Still, her mother would have been disappointed in her, and that was reason enough. "I'm going to get dinner started. Holler if you need anything."

When she reached the kitchen, Toby had the box of fish sticks and a bag of crinkle-cut French fries out on the kitchen table.

"I turned on the oven," he said with a proud smile. "And it's the right temperature. Four twenty-five Faren... Fahrenheit. What's that number back home, Mummy?"

Toby had been confused by Fahrenheit versus Celsius and was constantly asking the difference. "Two hundred, but you know you're not supposed to play with the oven."

His head drooped down. "But I've seen you do it, Mummy. I know how to turn the knob. I wanted to help."

"Four twenty-five is very hot, my love," she said. "You have to be careful when you turn on an oven."

"I *was*," he insisted. "I turned the knob *very. Slow.*" He mimicked the movement with his hand.

Anna squatted in front of him and gave him a soft smile. "I very much appreciate your help—you are such a thoughtful boy. But your safety is more important than anything, okay?"

He nodded, his eyes serious. "Yes, Mummy."

She stood and grabbed a cookie sheet from the cabinet next to the stove. "Why don't you help me put the fish fingers and chips on the sheet? Enough for the both of us."

Toby took his chore seriously, his mouth set in determination as he lined ten fish sticks in two rows. By the time he got the fries situated, the oven was ready.

Her father appeared in the doorway, the thump-shuffle of his walker announcing his presence long before he arrived at his destination.

Toby moved closer to Anna and stood partially behind her, still on edge from this morning.

She slipped an arm around her son's back and held him close to her side. "Dinner's not ready yet, Dad, so if you want to watch the news, I'll let you know when it's time to eat."

"Dinner's already forty-five minutes late. How long does it take to heat up a damn casserole?"

"Dad." Her tone was brisk. "Language."

"I've said 'damn' around you since you were a baby," he grumbled. "I never censored myself around you."

"I'm raising Toby differently."

"I'll say," he grumbled. "You're raising him on the other side of the damn world. What? The US of A's not good enough for him?"

Anna moved to the back door and pushed it open. "Toby, why don't you go play in the backyard while I talk to Grandad?"

He looked up at his grandfather with big, wide, round eyes before shifting his gaze to her.

"It's okay," she said softly. "We're going to have a chat while we wait for your fish fingers."

He nodded, then headed out the back door. Once it was shut behind him, she turned to her father.

"Do you purposely want him to be afraid of you or is it an unconscious effort?"

"What the hell are you talking about?" he asked as he took a step into the small kitchen.

"You scare him."

"I can't help it if he's like a damn church mouse." He plopped in a kitchen chair. "Ain't that what you say over there in England?"

"Any child would be scared of you. Half my friends were scared of you growing up."

"I just tell it like it is."

That's what he'd told her too many times to count when she was younger, that he was entitled to his bluntness because he was telling it like it was—other people's feelings be damned. Hers included. Even her mother wasn't completely spared.

"No, you never think of anyone else or their feelings. Only your own." How many times had she seen her mother bow down to her father's wishes? Too many times to count. "Maybe it would be better for all of us if I found somewhere else for Toby and me to stay for the next month and a half."

A sneer curled his upper lip. "Is this house not good enough for ya? Not as fancy as your *London* apartment?"

She sighed, too tired and frazzled to fight with him. "This house is just fine, and if you took the time to get to know your grandson, you'd realize that Toby could live in a paper bag and be happy as long as he's surrounded by people who love him."

A strange look passed over her father's face, and when he spoke again, it was quieter and with less venom. "You said you came back to take care of me. Falling through on your promise, I see."

She opened the refrigerator and pulled out a plastic

storage container. "No. I'll still be around to take you to your physical therapy and doctor's appointments, and you'll have a full-time nurse, but I think we'll all do better with a little more space between us."

He pointed a bony finger at her. "I never asked you to come."

"Look, Dad," she said, brushing a strand of hair from her face with the back of her hand. "I realize you're not the most demonstrative person in the world, and I don't even expect you to thank me, but I do expect you to be civil and not to scare my son."

"I never tried to scare the boy."

"You haven't been very nice to him either." She pried the lid of the container open, then grabbed a plate. "Do you hate me that much for leaving?" she asked quietly as she scooped some casserole onto a plate.

"Don't be so dramatic, Annaliese."

She put the plate in the microwave and turned it on. "Dramatic? I've held my tongue for too long, Dad. He's miserable here, and it has everything to do with your attitude."

Her father waved a hand in dismissal. "I ain't that bad."

"You're no Sunday picnic."

The corners of his lips twitched into a grin. "Sometimes I can be an ass."

The fact he could see some humor in the situation was a good sign. Her eyebrows rose. "*Sometimes?*" She sat in the chair next to him. "I know you're mad at me. I know you think I should have been here when Mom was first diagnosed, and you're probably right, but it all happened so fast. I thought we had more time." Her voice broke with regret and grief.

He lowered his gaze to his hand on the table. "She hid how bad it was from all of us." But then his eyes hardened as he lifted them to hers. "You were too busy getting knocked up by that British dick."

"Dad."

"I knew you were pregnant when you came home for the funeral. Even if I couldn't do the math, all that barfing gave you away."

"What's done is done, Dad." She had many regrets when it came to Phillip, but Toby had never been one of them.

His lips pinched shut for a moment. "Life is full of regrets, Annaliese. You got any?"

"A mountain of them." One man in particular was her biggest, and it wasn't Phillip.

"Your mother was always the one to keep me in line." Her father rested his arm on the table and sighed. "I'll try to be more civil."

Anna knew this was the closest he'd come to an apology. She'd never heard him offer her mother one, and she would have been far more likely to get an apology than anyone. "Is this your way of saying you don't want me to move out?"

"Go if you want," he said in a short tone. "Go back to England for all I care."

And here she had thought they were making progress. "Dad. If we stay, you have to make an effort. I know you're in pain. I know it's awful to be stuck in this house, but this is hard for us, too."

"Fine."

"And I want you to get to know Toby."

He lifted his gaze to hers, but she couldn't read what he was thinking. "I'll be nice."

"Really nice, not Albert Fischer nice."

A real grin lit up his face. "Fine."

Maybe this would work out after all.

# *Chapter Four*

$\sim$

Anna was back.

Somehow Matt had kept his shit together during practice, but his gaze had kept drifting to the woman on the sidelines. Anna was just as beautiful as he remembered her—and affected him just as she had twelve years ago. However, not only was she back, but she had a five-year-old son. *That* was a kick in the gut.

Part of him was pissed beyond belief at her hypocrisy, and a lesser man might use her son to punish her, but he would never do that. And even if he'd entertained the idea, one look into that innocent, oh-so-eager face and every ounce of animosity toward the boy would have vanished.

He'd wanted to approach her after practice and ask what had made her change her mind about kids...or rather who. When she'd said she didn't want kids, apparently she'd meant she didn't want to have them with *him*. But it had come as a small relief when she'd left immediately. He couldn't have handled talking to her in front of the other mothers. Several of them had surrounded him, offering to help with everything from ordering T-shirts for the parents to bringing him dinner on practice nights. He'd quickly nixed the dinners, assuring them he was capable of feeding Ethan and himself, and then put Phyllis in charge of delegating all parent projects.

He'd always wanted a family, but after Sylvia, he'd sworn off women. Initially his two best friends, life-long womanizers, had sworn off women after breaking up with crazy exes, too, and they'd jokingly formed the bachelor brotherhood, vowing to remain bachelors and staying away from women indefinitely. Kevin had been the first to bail, sleeping with his now wife the day after they made the pact. Surprisingly, Tyler was next, falling hard for his wife, Lanie, only two months later. Which was a surprise to all three of them. If there had been a Most Likely to Get Married and Have Kids First award, they would have handed it over to Matt soon after high school graduation.

Some days Matt found it difficult to believe that his two friends had each found the love of his life so easily after they made the pact, especially when Matt had always been the one who wanted that the most. He'd been sure he'd found her and he'd been so, so wrong. Nevertheless, Matt was thrilled Kevin and Tyler were so happy. He just wanted to find the love of his life, too.

Ten minutes later, everyone else was long gone, and Ethan was helping him load the equipment into the back of his pickup truck. He checked his phone after he got inside and saw a text he'd missed from his sister.

Just found out I have a study group tonight and have to miss my Skype call with Ethan. Tell him I'm sorry and that I love him.

He glanced over his shoulder at the boy. Abby's deadbeat

husband had left her two years ago and she'd decided to pursue her dream of going to medical school. Unfortunately, Abby hadn't been accepted at her first pick, a school close to home. Instead, she'd been accepted to a school on the West Coast. It quickly became obvious that the original plan was a bust. There was no way Abby could move in with her mother and count on her full-time child care. But it also became equally clear she couldn't take Ethan with her. Even if Abby could afford to pay for round-the-clock babysitters when he wasn't at school, he'd be miserable. So, last August, Abby had loaded up a small U-Haul and headed out West, while Ethan had moved in with Matt's mother. And that's where he'd stayed for a few months until Matt's mother had taken a week-long cruise after Christmas with her new boyfriend, and Ethan had stayed with Matt.

Ethan had fit so seamlessly into Matt's life and vice versa, he'd never gone back.

Matt loved taking care of his nephew, but he worried about Ethan. Abby had been calling less and less. This wasn't the first Skype call she'd canceled... it wasn't even the third, and each time Ethan was hurt. Matt worried that Ethan thought his mother had abandoned him. Sometimes Matt wondered the same thing.

Matt put a smile on his face and glanced back at Ethan. "How about we go out to eat at Red Robin? You can get a balloon."

"We can't," he said, practically bouncing in his seat. "Mommy's gonna call me. I want to tell her about Toby coming to soccer practice."

"Actually..." Matt paused and watched him in the rearview mirror. "She sent a text and said she's busy. She has to go to a study session. She's really sorry."

Ethan's face fell. "She's not going to call me?"

"Not tonight. Maybe she'll call tomorrow."

A deep frown covered his face. "She can't. Today is Tuesday. She has class on Wednesday night."

There was something pathetic and sad about a kindergartner learning the days of the week because of his mother's availability to talk to him.

"So what do you say about Red Robin?" Matt said, forcing a cheerfulness into his voice he didn't feel.

Ethan didn't feel it either. He shrugged, a sure sign that he was upset. Red Robin was his favorite restaurant.

"We can talk about Toby and come up with a plan to help him get better."

That perked him up. "Isn't he cool, Uncle Matt?"

"Totally cool. And he seems nice."

"He's the nicest boy in Mrs. Brown's class. Even Mrs. Brown says so."

Matt grinned. "You don't say?"

"Can we really go to Red Robin?"

"You bet."

Ethan dove into a tale about a kid who'd thrown up at lunch, delving into enough detail that Matt was having second thoughts about dinner by the time he pulled into the restaurant parking lot.

"How come we get to eat out on a school night, Uncle Matt?" he asked as Matt waited for him to unbuckle his booster seat.

"I thought we'd celebrate your first soccer practice."

Ethan giggled. "It wasn't my first practice, sillyhead. I played soccer last year."

"Okay, you got me. The first soccer practice *this year.*" *And distract you from thinking about your mother*, but he obviously kept that part to himself.

They went inside and got a table. The hostess had brought

over a kid's menu for Ethan, crayons included, and he immediately began to color on it. "Play a game of tic-tac-toe with me, Uncle Matt."

"Okay, but I'm not holding back," he teased as he picked up a crayon.

Ethan giggled.

Matt let Ethan mark down an X before he put an O in a corner. "So tell me more about your friend, Toby." It was probably an asshole move to use his nephew to spy on his ex-girlfriend, but desperate times called for underhanded measures. He'd been tempted to look her up on Facebook, but he couldn't bear the thought of seeing photos of her happy in the life she chose without him.

"He's awesome."

"That much is apparent." Maybe this would go more smoothly if he asked questions. "Did his dad get a job here?" He was going to hell for this, but at least he'd go informed.

"Toby doesn't have a daddy."

"Oh?" Matt hated the way his heart tripped at that piece of information.

"His mommy is divorced. Like my mommy."

"Does his dad live in England?"

Ethan gave him a questioning look. "I don't know."

"So his mommy got a job here?"

"No."

Matt waited for him to continue, and when he didn't, he asked. "So why did they move here?"

Ethan's face screwed up in confusion. "Why are you asking so many questions about Toby?"

Shit. "Because he's new. And he's your friend."

"My *best* friend."

Matt forced a grin. "I had no idea you two had moved to the next level."

"Huh?"

"Never mind." Considering how much time Matt spent with Ethan, this wasn't the best news. Matt had hosted several playdates, and his nephew was sure to request one with his new best friend. "So what else do you know about Toby?" he asked as he purposely put his O in a box that would let Ethan win the game.

"He lives with his grandpa, but Toby says he's mean."

The hair on the back of Matt's neck stood on end. "How so?"

"What?" He looked up and blinked. "Toby says he's just grumpy. And yells. A lot. It scares him."

Matt had met Anna's parents several times while they were dating, and Anna's father had always come across as stern and cranky. It sounded like the man hadn't softened over the years. "How about his grandma?"

"She's dead."

"Oh." Of Anna's parents, he'd always preferred her mother. Her patience had softened her husband, which meant Albert Fischer had to be a total bear now.

"But Toby's here so he can help take care of his grandpa."

"He's sick?"

"Dunno." He looked up at Matt. "So are you gonna teach Toby how to play soccer?"

"That's what we do at practice. I thought I'd set up some drills for the new kids who are just learning the rules."

"But I told him you'd help *him*. Just him. I promised."

Matt pushed out a sigh. "You really shouldn't have promised that, Ethan. You can't promise that someone else will do something unless you ask them first."

Tears welled in his eyes. "Are you mad at me, Uncle Matt?"

He shook his head and took the boy's hand. "No, Ethan,

but even if I was mad at you, it wouldn't change how much I love you."

"But Daddy got mad, and he didn't come back."

Matt would love to string that bastard up. "I'm not your father. I'm here no matter what, and you can always count on me. *Always.* Got it?"

Ethan nodded, but he didn't seem convinced. Abby's husband had left a lot of damage in his wake, and now she was wreaking her own havoc, even if she hadn't meant to. Matt realized more than ever that he needed to be the one constant his nephew could count on, and he was more than willingly to be Ethan's stopgap. He loved the little guy.

"So you won't help Toby?" Ethan asked with a sniff.

"I'm not sure his mother will let me."

Ethan's mouth dropped open. "Why not?"

The last thing he wanted to explain to a five-year-old was that he'd once been in love with his best friend's mother. "Some moms are too protective to let their kids hang out with their coaches."

"But all the moms on the team really like you. I heard one of them say she'd like to bring you home for a playdate, and the other mom said she had some toys for you to play with. So why wouldn't Toby's mom like you?"

Matt choked on his water, and Ethan patted Matt's hand. "Are you okay, Uncle Matt?"

"Yeah." It was obvious his nephew wouldn't let this drop without a fight, and the earnest look on Toby's face after practice didn't make his protest any easier. "Okay, Ethan. I'll talk to his mom."

"Tonight?"

"I don't know, bud . . . how about at the next practice?"

"He's going to think I'm a liar."

Matt's heart sank. "You told him I'd call his mom? What exactly did you promise him?"

Ethan looked down at the tic-tac-toe game. "That he could come over to your house and we'd play soccer in your backyard."

Matt reminded himself that his nephew was trying to be a good friend, a character trait to be proud of. Besides, if Toby was living with his grumpy grandfather, he might need a positive male in his life. His past with Anna muddied things. But if he let that interfere with helping the boy, that made him no better than Ethan's father. "I'll call her."

His face jerked up. "Tonight?"

"Yeah." He suspected this would *not* go well.

# Chapter Five

Toby snuggled into Anna's side, and she leaned closer to smell his damp head. There was nothing like his little boy smell.

This was her favorite time with him. Back in London, after a long day at the office and a lengthy commute home, she wouldn't get home until after six, usually later. Toby's nanny was also their housekeeper and cook, and she usually had dinner waiting by the time Anna got home. She would leave and Anna and Toby would eat dinner together at the kitchen island. Afterward, she'd give him a bath and then they'd pile onto her bed and snuggle while they watched TV.

But when they'd continued their routine at Anna's father's house, he hadn't understood why she and Toby always disappeared into her room to watch TV. He definitely hadn't liked it and made no secret of letting them both know.

"There's a perfectly fine television out here," he would grumble.

"It's just what we do."

Now, as she lay with her sleeping son in her arms, she thought about how wonderful it had been these past few weeks to be able to spend more time with him, cooking dinner together, taking him to his first soccer practice. She'd missed so much of his short life. While parts of this trip had been hard on them, at least they had more time together here.

Her cell phone vibrated on the nightstand and she reached for it, surprised at the local number she didn't recognize. "Hello?" she said tentatively.

The line was silent for several seconds before she heard, "Anna."

One word and her stomach clenched. It was him. "Yes."

"This is Matt. Matt Osborn."

"I know who you are, Matt," she said softly.

"I wasn't sure if you remembered."

"I couldn't forget you if I tried."

"I'm not calling for a trip down memory lane," he said, his tone short. "I called about your son. Toby."

And here it came. He was going to ask her to move Toby to a new team. She'd intended to call him—to tell Matt she was requesting a new team—she just hadn't summoned the will to make herself do it yet. "I understand."

He paused. "Understand what?"

"That you want Toby to go to another team. I had no idea you were the coach when I requested that Toby be on Ethan's team, otherwise I would have switched as soon as I realized it." She tried not to sound breathless, but her racing heart made it difficult.

"Why would I want him to switch teams?"

"Because…" Was he really going to make her say it? "Of us."

"What happened twelve years ago is in the past. It doesn't interfere with my ability to coach your son. Is it a problem for *you*?"

He was good, she'd give him that. "No. Not at all."

"I noticed Toby's shin guards were too big. You should consider getting another pair by practice on Thursday, but if you can't, Ethan has an extra pair Toby can use."

"Toby mentioned it on the way home from practice. I can manage getting him a pair and a size three ball, too. Thank you." Her tone was short and she sat up straighter as though ready to defend herself. Her motherhood felt more tested here in her hometown, where she was working from home, than it ever had been back in London, only making her question her life choices even more.

"I'm not sure if you're aware," he said, his voice cool, "but Toby is good friends with my nephew. Ethan is worried about Toby's soccer skills—not because he isn't good enough to play, but because he's so unsure of himself. Apparently, he told Toby that I'd privately coach him to help catch him up to speed. I'm just calling to let you know that I'm here if he needs help."

"We come from England, the country that practically invented soccer." What had possessed her to say that?

"If that's your way of telling me to mind my own business, messaged received," he said.

She panicked, suddenly terrified he would hang up. "No. I'm sorry. It's just…this is hard."

"It doesn't have to be. This is for the boys. You and I are ancient history. I can keep it in the past," he said. "Can you?"

"Yes, definitely."

"Ethan wants Toby to come over for a playdate. I can practice with them then. Are you open to this?"

"Yeah," she said, thrilled that Toby had been invited to

a playdate. If nothing else, it would get him out of her father's house for a few hours. She'd have to deal with her discomfort.

"If this is your cell phone, I can text you the address. Would Saturday from one until four work?"

"Yes, Toby will be there. Thank you. I can't tell you how much this means to me."

"This isn't about you." Then he hung up.

She didn't know how she'd find the courage to face him.

She'd definitely been put in her place. Not that she deserved any less.

*       *       *

Anna dreaded Thursday's practice, but to her relief and Toby's disappointment, it was rained out. Matt had sent a group text, telling the parents they could practice on Sunday afternoon at a local church, but it was optional. Anna considered saying Toby couldn't go because they had plans, but Toby would see through her deception—they never had plans here. She'd lost touch with most of her high school friends, and while her best friend, Ashley, still had an apartment in Blue Springs, she was gone over half the year with her wildlife photography job. She'd deal with it. Just like she'd dealt with everything else.

On the bright side, her father must have had some sense scared into him because he was less gruff on Wednesday and Thursday and downright pleasant on late Friday morning when she helped him walk out to his car so they could go to his doctor's appointment.

"Maybe you'd like to stop somewhere for lunch after your appointment," Anna said as she backed out of the driveway.

"Don't you have some important conference call to make?" he asked, but his voice lacked his usual gruffness.

"No. I got up early and dealt with all my calls," she said. Being seven hours ahead was equally a pain in the ass and an asset, depending on the moment. But it meant she often went to bed with Toby and was up and working by 3 a.m.

Anna pulled up to the doctor's office entrance and parked. Her father had already opened his car door and swung his legs onto the pavement by the time she had his walker set up.

"You're getting faster," she said with a smile.

"I don't plan on using this thing forever," he grumped. "The sooner I get rid of it, the better."

"Your therapist is working on it."

He shot her a frown as he put his hands on the handles and tried to pull himself to a standing position, but the car seat was too low, and he fell back onto his bum, letting out a loud gasp of pain. He looked so frail and small, he hardly seemed like the man she'd left after her mother's funeral.

"Dad, let me help you."

He started to protest, then closed his mouth and hung his head in defeat.

She hated to see him like this, but she wasn't sure what to do. While he was making tremendous progress, she understood why the staunchly independent man was frustrated. Without saying a word, she wrapped an arm around his back and hauled him to a standing position, making sure his head didn't hit the roof of the car.

Once he was standing, he began his shuffle toward the entrance.

"Do you want me to open the door for you?" she asked.

"I can push the damn handicapped button."

Sighing, she parked the car then found him in the waiting

room, sitting in a chair with his walker in front of him, his mouth taut.

After she made sure he was checked in, she sat down in a chair beside him. "Would you like some ibuprofen? I have some in my purse."

"No." He kept his gaze on the far wall.

He was obviously in pain, and this had been an issue when he'd first come home from the hospital. He'd refused to take his pain medication and had been in too much pain to fully utilize his therapy. Finally, Dr. Martin had intervened and convinced him to take his medication as prescribed. Anna planned to address it again with the doctor today.

When the nurse appeared at the open doorway and called out his name, her father pulled himself to a standing position and shuffled over to her.

"Looking good, Mr. Fischer," the nurse said with a grin.

He harrumphed as he hobbled past her and stopped in front of the scale.

Anna took his hand to help him climb up. He tried to shake her off, but the nurse put her hand on her hip and shook her head with a disapproving stare.

"Mr. Fischer, if you try to climb onto that scale without support, I'll snatch that walker away and convince Dr. Martin to put you back in a wheelchair."

Her father scowled as he let Anna offer her support. The nurse looked at the numbers with a frown. "You haven't gained any weight since your last visit."

"I ain't hungry."

She remained silent as she wrote on his chart then led them to an exam room, where she took his blood pressure. When she'd finished, she handed Anna a gown. "Help him put this on so Dr. Martin can examine his incision. He can leave his shirt on."

The nurse walked out of the door and humiliation covered her father's face. "I ain't taking off my clothes in front of you."

"Dad," she said, giving him a sympathetic look. "I helped you to the bathroom when you came home from the hospital."

Shame covered his face and he started to unbuckle his pants.

"Wait." She helped him put on the gown over his button-down shirt, then turned her back to him. "Undo your pants and let them drop to your feet, and I'll help you step out of them." She could at least give him this dignity.

He didn't answer, but when he said he was done, his shoulders didn't sag as much as they had before. He'd always been a proud man. She knew this was hard on him.

After she helped him out of his shoes and pants, she held his arm as he climbed up on the table. Moments later they heard a knock, and a middle-aged man in a lab coat opened the door with a warm smile. "You ready, Albert?"

"Does it matter?" he asked, staring at the floor.

Dr. Martin took that as permission to enter the room. "How are we feeling?" he asked as he shut the door behind him.

"Ready to be rid of that damn contraption," Albert muttered, pointing to the walker.

Dr. Martin sat in a chair at the desk and pulled up a screen on the computer. "It looks like your therapy is going well. You should be able to move to a footed cane within a few weeks. How's your pain?"

"Good."

The doctor swiveled his chair to face him. "Good as in you enjoy your pain, or good as in you don't have any?"

Anna couldn't help smiling. When she'd first met Dr.

Martin in the hospital, she'd liked that he didn't tolerate her father's crap, instead dishing out a healthy dose of sarcasm to counteract it without insulting him.

Albert's brow furrowed. "I don't have much."

The doctor turned to Anna. "Is that the truth?"

Anna smiled. "Mostly. But sometimes he aggravates his leg and refuses to take any ibuprofen to counteract the pain."

Dr. Martin rested his hands on his knees. "Albert, soreness is fine and expected; any sharp or outright pain is counterproductive. Anti-inflammatories aren't the same as narcotics. They actually *help* you heal. You'll move to the cane faster."

"I hate taking medicine."

"I know, but it's necessary." He glanced at the computer screen. "Are you taking your blood thinner?"

"Yeah."

The doctor glanced at Anna with an inquisitive look.

"I'm giving it to him, but he grumbles."

"Albert, with your history, you know I'm worried about blood clots. You don't want to go back to the hospital with a clot in your leg, or God forbid worse if you have a pulmonary embolus."

Her father didn't answer.

"Okay," Dr. Martin said, rising to his feet. "Let's look at your incision."

Her father shot him a glare. "The surgeon looked at it last week."

"I know, I saw *his* report, too, but he was worried about a pucker in the skin. I want to see it for myself."

Her father lay down on the table, and Anna looked away as the doctor performed his examination then helped the older man back to a sitting position. "Keep up the great work, and I want to see you in two weeks."

"All I do is go to doctors and clinics," he grumbled.

"What can I say?" Dr. Martin said with a grin. "We can't resist your charming personality."

Anna laughed for the first time in she didn't know how long.

Dr. Martin turned to her. "Annaliese, can I talk to you for a minute in the hall?"

Her heart skipped a beat. Had he found something bad? "Of course."

Her father didn't look happy as they both left the room.

"Is everything okay?" she asked as soon as he shut the door behind them.

"Your father is healing, but I'm concerned about what's going to happen after he's finished with his therapy."

"Do you think he'll have trouble getting around?"

"No, he's progressing fairly well with his therapy, in spite of himself, but nevertheless, I'm worried about him living alone. Are you still planning on going back to England in six weeks?"

She stared at him in surprise.

"I have a pretty good memory," he said with a grin and shoved his hands into his lab coat pockets. "But it helps that your father is one of my favorite patients."

"*My* father?"

He laughed. "Albert Fischer is an acquired taste, but I've been his doctor since I got out of residency and joined this practice. I was your mother's doctor, too. I was so sorry everything progressed so quickly. She was a good woman."

"Thanks. She really was." Anna was surprised at the tears that filled her eyes. It had been easy to pretend that her mother wasn't gone while Anna was living in London. But the constant reminders hurt more than she'd expected and added to her guilt. Her mother's illness had been short and devastating. Anna still remembered her mother's call, as she explained in a calm soothing voice that she had cancer but she was having surgery in a week and there was no need to come home, only to sit around in a hospital waiting room. She'd encouraged Anna to wait until she was a few days out of surgery. But they'd determined her cancer inoperable and closed her back up, giving her only weeks to live. When she heard the news, Anna changed her flight to the next day, but her mother had died before Anna's plane ever landed.

"Your father hasn't handled your mother's passing very well. His health and mental state have deteriorated over the last few years."

She gasped. "Do you think he has Alzheimer's?"

"No," he said softly, removing his hands from his pocket and letting them hang at his sides. "I think he has a broken heart."

That was the last phrase she ever expected to be used describing her father. But Anna had to admit that he'd loved his wife, even in his own gruff way.

"I know you have a life in England you need to get back to, but as much as it pains me to say it, I think you should consider moving him to an assisted living center before you go back."

*"What?"*

Dr. Martin lowered his voice. "He was lucky he fell in his front yard and was discovered by a neighbor. If it had happened inside his house, I have no idea how long he would have lain there before he was discovered. He broke his femur this time. Next time could be worse." He paused. "I know this is difficult. Albert values his independence. If you like, I'll go in and be the bad guy and break the news to him."

She shook her head and clasped her hands to her chest. "No. Don't tell him yet."

"The longer you put it off, the harder it will be. He needs time to prepare himself. He's lived in that house most of his life." When Anna's eyes widened in surprise, he gave her a wry grin. "Like I said, I've been his doctor for a long time . . . plus he talked to me a lot after your mother died. I've suggested moving before, but he refuses to leave. He says he feels your mother there."

Tears welled in her eyes. Her father had never shown any signs of sentimentality to her. "Are you sure he has to move? What about if we hire him help? Or what about those alert necklaces?"

"Annaliese, the man won't take ibuprofen. Do you really think he'll wear an alert necklace?" He gave her a sad smile. "And trust me, I've already tried to get him to wear one."

"Okay," she said, worrying her bottom lip. "Give me some time."

"If you want me to break the news to him, I'll tell him at the next appointment. But even that is pushing it. You'll only have four weeks to get him moved and his house cleaned out before you go home."

## Chapter Six

M att was nervous. It killed him to admit it, but there was
no denying it was true. His hands were sweating, and he was
nauseous. Toby was going to show up soon, and Matt wasn't
ready to see his mother.

Matt was no slob, but he'd gone on a cleaning spree that
even Ethan commented on.

"Why are you scrubbing the floor, Uncle Matt?"

"It's called spring cleaning, bud."

"Oh."

He put Ethan to work, giving him a wet rag and having
him wipe the baseboards. Matt had made it a game in the
beginning, but the five-year-old quickly lost interest, so he'd
let him loose on a clean load of towels, a job that always
seemed to keep the boy's interest.

"Mommy never let me fold towels," Ethan said as he
folded a bath towel into a wadded mess. "She says I don't do
it right."

"There's no such thing as folding towels a wrong way in
a bachelor house," Matt said with a grin. "Anything goes."

"A bachelor house?"

"A house where single guys live."

"Just like us, Uncle Matt!"

"Yeah," Matt said, not nearly as excited as his nephew. "Just like us."

"Have you ever had a puppy, Uncle Matt?"

"A puppy? Yeah, when I was a kid."

"Like me?"

"Yeah. I think I was seven when we got him. His name was Pepper because he was all black." Matt hadn't thought of his childhood pet in ages.

"Did you have to feed him?"

Matt laughed. "I had to feed him and walk him, not that I minded most of the time. I loved that little guy. But your mom had to take turns with me to clean up his poop."

Ethan giggled. "Eww!"

"Dogs poop. You don't want to step in it, do you?"

"Do you like dogs, Uncle Matt?"

"Yeah. I love them."

"Then how come you don't have a dog now?"

That question had a difficult answer. "I was waiting."

"What for?"

A family. When he thought about being married and having a family, he always pictured the dog. He'd loved having a dog when he was growing up, and taking care of Pepper had taught him responsibility. He wanted his kids to have a dog, too. But the sad truth was he was thirty-four years old and things hadn't worked out the way he'd planned. Sure, he didn't have the family he'd hoped for, but he had Ethan. And he had a house. Maybe it was time for him to stop waiting for what he'd hoped for and embrace what he had.

Matt tilted his head and gave Ethan a long look. "You know, come to think of it, I'm not sure what I'm waiting for."

"Mommy won't let me have a dog. She says she doesn't want to take care of the mess."

"Dogs are a big responsibility," Matt said. "Your mommy's busy learning how to be a doctor. That's a big responsibility, too."

Ethan frowned. "I guess..." Then a hopeful look lit up his face. "Can we get a dog, Uncle Matt? *Please?*"

The way Ethan included himself in the decision with his *we* warmed Matt's chest. "Since dogs are a big responsibility, I think we should give it serious consideration first."

Ethan's eyes narrowed. "What does 'serious consideration' mean?"

"It means we need to think long and hard about whether we want to take on the responsibility of a dog. Once we get one, we can't return it. We have to promise to be his owner no matter what."

"No matter what," Ethan parroted, but he seemed to be pondering Matt's words with a frown. Was he thinking about the father he hadn't seen in nearly two years?

Matt glanced down at the towels, which were now piled into wads, and grinned. "Good job folding. Now let's put them away."

After they'd put the towels in the linen closet, Ethan ran in place as he asked, "How much longer till Toby gets here?"

Matt pulled out his phone and his throat constricted. Twelve fifty-eight. "Any time now."

Ethan let out an excited squeal and ran into the living room, then pressed his nose into the window overlooking the front yard.

"That's not going to make him come any sooner," Matt said with a nervous laugh as he put the clothes basket in the laundry room.

Jesus, he was a mess. Why was he letting this woman

have so much control over him? He had to stop obsessing over the fact that Anna Fischer was going to be standing on his doorstep any minute. No, she went by Annaliese Robins now, according to Toby's registration paperwork. Had she started using "Annaliese" after she'd moved to London? She'd told him she thought her name was pretentious. Had she lied about that, too? He still couldn't wrap his head around the fact that she'd gotten married and had a kid.

But one thing was certain—her recent reappearance had made him take a long, hard look at his own life.

It was hard to admit he'd put part of his life on hold, especially when it was obvious Anna hadn't. Maybe he *should* give serious thought to getting a dog. He worked long hours with his commercial construction business, but he could install a pet door so the dog could let itself out during the day to go outside and do his business. Plus, Matt was home most evenings and weekends. Now that Tyler and Kevin were married and he had Ethan full-time, he saw his best friends even less. There'd been a lot fewer nights out at the Power and Light District and hanging out on Sunday afternoons to drink beer and watch whatever game was on TV.

"He's here, Uncle Matt! He's here!" Ethan shouted, and Matt heard the front door open.

Crap. He hadn't locked the deadbolt.

"Ethan! Don't go outside." But when Matt rounded the corner, the front door was standing wide open, and Ethan was already in the middle of the yard, hugging Toby.

Matt descended the front porch steps and walked toward the boys as Anna got out of the car. She stood a foot away from her open door and watched the boys with a frown.

A wave of defensiveness washed through Matt. He hadn't let their past bleed into his feelings for her son; could she do the same with his nephew? But then he noticed that sadness filled her eyes, not disdain. Did she have regrets? Or was she sad that her son was friends with someone tied to Matt?

She glanced up at him and every nerve in his body became tightly strung. Her blond hair was loose and hung in soft waves that rested just above her shoulders and framed her face. She was dressed in jeans and a gray scoop-neck, long-sleeved T-shirt that showed off her curves, and damn did she have curves. He forced his gaze up to her face before she realized he'd been checking her out.

Toby and Ethan broke up their hug fest and Ethan asked, "Did you bring your soccer ball and shin guards?"

Toby's smile fell.

Anna looked worried. "I can go home and get them."

"No need," Matt said as he moved closer and put a hand on Ethan's shoulder. "I doubt we'll need shin guards, and I've got plenty of balls." Remembering Tuesday night's practice fiasco, he added. "*Soccer* balls."

A smile ghosted her lips. "Thanks for clarifying." Then just as quickly, her smile disappeared. "Thanks again for letting Toby come over. He's been so excited he could hardly sleep last night."

"Ethan, too."

He could see the questions in her eyes. Why did he spend so much time with his nephew? Why wasn't he married with kids of his own? He wasn't about to go there. Not now. Not ever.

"Do you want to come in and look everything over?" he asked. "Did you do a background check?" He was partly joking, but the mother of one of Ethan's pals had gone overboard with her paranoia when she brought her son over for his first playdate. "I really don't mind."

Her face softened. "I trust you, Matt."

Somehow that was even worse.

She sucked in a breath, making her chest rise, and he resisted the urge to watch more closely, forcing his eyes to remain on her clear blue ones. Watching her now, all he could think about was the life he'd imagined for them, and how she'd just thrown it away.

"Do you still want me to pick him up at four?" she asked.

"Yeah."

She hesitated then crossed her arms over her chest. "You have my number so feel free to call me if you need me to come early or something comes up or..." She paused and Matt could sense she was anxious. "This is the first time I've left him since we came back."

Matt was pissed all over again about what she'd done to them in the past, but this was the present and she was a worried mother. He wanted to put her concerns at ease. "If Toby asks for you before four, I'll give you a call. I'd hate for him to not want to come back. Ethan's already planning their next playdate."

Relief washed over her face. "Thank you. I was worried you would...I can understand how this would be difficult."

Anger burned in his gut. He glanced over to make sure the boys, who had moved closer to the door, were out of earshot. "The past is in the past, Anna. I sure as hell would never hurt or traumatize your son to get back at you."

She looked stricken, and he regretted being so harsh.

He ran a hand over his head, suddenly wondering if this was a bad idea after all. "I'm sorry. You didn't deserve that."

Tears welled in her eyes. "I do. And so much more. I trust you, Matt. Toby wouldn't be here if I didn't." Turning on her heels, she got into her car and shut the door.

Matt realized she hadn't told Toby good-bye, and when she started to back out of the driveway, Toby's eyes widened. He glanced up at Matt.

"Do you want to tell your mom good-bye?"

Toby watched her pull out into the street then she stopped and rolled down the window, giving Toby a warm smile. "You have the bestest afternoon, okay?"

He nodded. "Yes, Mummy."

"I love you," she said as her smile lit up her entire face.

Toby's shoulders relaxed, but Matt's gut tightened. She used to smile at him just like that years ago.

* * *

An hour later Matt was in his backyard, watching Ethan and Toby run around the orange cones while kicking their miniature soccer balls. Poor Toby lacked some coordination, but he'd been concentrating hard as he tried to control the ball.

"You're getting better, Toby," Matt said. "Are you sure you haven't played before?"

Toby got to the end of the line of cones then glanced over at him. "This is only my second time, Coach Matt."

"Wow. With improvement this quick, next thing you know, you'll be trying out for the Arsenals."

Toby scrunched up his nose. "Who?"

Matt shook his head. "Never mind. Who's ready for a snack?"

"Me! Me!" both boys shouted.

"Then leave your balls there and let's head inside. Ethan, show Toby where he can wash his hands."

"Yes, sir," Ethan said then ran inside with Toby on his heels.

Matt followed them through the door to the kitchen, then paused as he grabbed an apple from the counter. He hadn't asked Anna if her son was allergic to anything. He considered calling her, but decided to ask Toby first.

The boys came barreling down the hall in their excitement, and Matt couldn't hide his smile. He hadn't seen Ethan this excited in months, and it warmed his chest to see him so happy.

"Toby, are you allergic to anything?"

He shook his head. "No."

"I was going to cut up some apples and give you peanut butter to dip them in. You're sure you're not allergic to peanut butter?"

"Of course he's not, sillyhead," Ethan said with a laugh. "He'd have to sit at the peanut-free table if he was."

"There's a peanut-free table at school?"

"Yeah," Ethan said like he was a fool for not knowing. "Duh."

Matt's eyebrows rose. "Saying 'duh' isn't polite. We've discussed that before."

Ethan's chin dropped to his chest. "Sorry, Uncle Matt."

"It's okay. Now let me cut up those apples."

"How come we can't have chips like Wesley's mom gave us at his house?"

"Because chips aren't healthy. They don't make you grow."

"That's not what Ms. Peterman said to Ms. Murphy at recess," Toby said, taking a drink from the cup of water Matt handed him. "She says too many chips will make you fat. Only she was talking about the other kind."

"What other kind?" Ethan asked. "Tortilla chips?"

Toby shook his head. "No, not the kind that come from bags. The other kind."

Ethan looked confused. "You mean the ones in the cans?"

Toby looked frustrated, but Matt put a plate in front of him and said, "Ethan, I think the problem is that 'chips' mean something else in England. I suspect Toby's talking about what we call French fries. Is that right?"

Toby nodded with relief.

"That's just dumb," Ethan said. "Why would they call it the wrong thing?"

"Who says it's wrong?" Matt asked. "I'm sure they think we're wrong. And we don't tell our friends that something's dumb."

Ethan scowled but pressed on. "If they call French fries chips, what do they call real chips?"

"Crisps."

Ethan laughed and looked at Toby. "You say things weird there."

Matt was about to intervene but Toby laughed. "*You* say things weird *here*."

They spent the next five minutes discussing different words in England versus the United States while Matt cut up apple slices and scooped peanut butter onto their plates. His mother would have tossed the boys a bag of chips and cans of soda, turned on the TV, and been done with it. But that's not how he would have raised his kids, so that wasn't how he was going to raise Ethan.

He paused, his spoon still on Ethan's plate. He wasn't Ethan's father, yet he'd been deciding a lot of rules for raising Ethan and it made him uncomfortable. Those decisions were supposed to be made by Abby, but she wasn't around and someone had to make them.

"Uncle Matt makes the best spaghetti," Ethan said as he scooped his apple slice into his peanut butter. "Maybe you can eat over sometime."

"Yeah," Toby said, looking down at his plate.

Was he missing his mother? While Ethan was full of bravado now, Abby had left last summer and then again after Christmas, Ethan went through some separation anxiety. Talking about Abby and reminding him she still loved him had seemed to help. "What's your favorite dinner?" Matt asked. "What's your favorite thing that your mother makes you?"

"Nanny Maureen makes my favorite dinner," Toby said. "Bangers and mash. But when Mummy cooks, she makes me fish fingers."

Anna had a nanny?

"Fish fingers?" Ethan giggled. "Fish don't have fingers."

Toby stuck out his bottom lip. "Some fish do."

"No they don't," Ethan said. "They have *fins*, not fingers."

"Ethan," Matt said in a stern voice.

Ethan stopped and realized Toby was unhappy then looked up at Matt in confusion. "But it's true."

"We just had an entire discussion about people in England having different names for things. Maybe that's the case here."

"Oh."

"In fact," Matt continued, "I bet fish fingers are the same things as fish sticks."

"That's what my grandad calls them," Toby said. "He says the house stinks to high heaven when Mummy cooks them."

Matt waited for Ethan to comment on the fact Toby called his mother Mummy, but thankfully he let it pass.

"So your favorite food is fish fingers—"

"And chips," Toby added before he took a bite of his apple. "Fish fingers and chips. The hot kind, not the crispy ones. Mummy lets me line them up on the baking sheet. Nanny Maureen won't make them. She says they are *processed* food."

"Is your nanny like the ones in the movies? Is she mean?" Ethan asked. "Does she live in the attic of your house?"

"I don't have a house," Toby said. "We live on floor

twenty-one. I can see the river from my bedroom because we're so high."

"You live in an apartment?" Ethan asked. "Like on those shows on TV?"

"Mummy calls it a condo. And Nanny Maureen comes in the morning to take me to school, then she brings me home and makes me a snack and helps me with my homework. She's nice."

"What about your dad?" Ethan asked. "Do you get two birthday parties and two Christmases? Wesley said it's the best part of a divorce, but my daddy hasn't started yet."

Matt's heart skipped a beat. He had no idea his nephew had been waiting for his father to start fulfilling his parenting job. Knowing Abby's ex, Ethan would be waiting a long time. One more heartbreak for the boy to deal with.

Toby shrugged. "No. I don't see my dad. You're lucky you have Uncle Matt. I only have my grumpy grandad."

Anna was a single mom in the truest sense. Did the deadbeat pay child support? Part of him said he should feel vindicated Anna's relationship had failed, but he couldn't find it in himself to feel any happiness. Not when a child was caught in the middle.

Toby started telling Ethan about his school—that he'd been going there since he was three and he wore uniforms. Ethan listened like Toby was telling him some crazy tale, but Matt wondered more about Toby's father. The man Anna had chosen to have a child with.

"Do you see your other grandparents?" Matt asked before he could stop himself.

Toby's gaze moved to Matt's. The color of his blue eyes—a bright cornflower—were just like his mother's. Even the set of his mouth when he concentrated on something reminded him of Anna. He was very much his mother's son. "No."

No father or grandparents part of Toby's life... was Anna home for good? And why did his heart trip at the thought? Matt began to wonder about things he had no business wondering.

# Chapter Seven

Anna decided to take advantage of her three hours of alone time. She'd told her father she was running errands—which was basically true—but the errand just happened to be checking out his potential new home.

"As you can see, the colors are soothing and go well with most color schemes," the woman said as she showed Anna an apartment at the Sunny Days Assisted Living Center. The name alone would send her father running, and the bland taupe walls and vinyl floor were an added incentive.

"There's no carpet," Anna said.

"It's hard to push a wheelchair on carpet."

"But my father's not in a wheelchair."

"Not yet."

Anna's chest tightened and she felt dangerously close to tears.

What the hell was she doing?

She moved to the window and stared out into the parking lot and the hospital across the street. Just a reminder to her father that he was a short ambulance drive away from the place his wife had died.

The woman moved next to her. "Many residents appreciate the proximity of the medical center."

Anna's mouth lifted in a wry grin as she stared out the window. "My father's not like most people." She turned toward the woman. "Is there another room with a different view?"

"The rooms in the back overlook the highway."

Well, that was no better. She wandered into the small bedroom.

"This room is furnished, but if you wish to move some furniture in with him, we'll need to see photos as soon as possible to make sure they meet with our approval."

Anna spun around to face her. "You have to approve his furniture?"

"Some furniture is unsafe."

Anna laughed at that. "Unsafe furniture? Is this place like a Stephen King novel?"

"What?"

"Never mind." Shaking her head, Anna moved into the universally designed bathroom while the woman gave her an explanation of why they denied some pieces of furniture, but Anna tuned her out. It was all very clean, but sterile. Very clinical. It was like a holding pen to send her father while he waited to die.

He would *hate* it here. She could barely stomach the idea of putting him here herself.

What if he couldn't bring his favorite recliner?

Suddenly a memory of Matt popped into her head. Only a few months into their relationship, they'd gone to the lake with some friends and Matt had sat in a camping chair that collapsed underneath him. She'd teased him that he'd drunk too many beers, but he'd grabbed her wrist and pulled her down with him and said he was dangerous to furniture. She remembered staring into his eyes and thinking it was funny he'd declared himself dangerous since he'd always made her feel so safe.

The memory only added to her melancholy.

Being so close to Matt was dangerous to her psyche.

*Matt isn't part of your life.* It didn't matter if she'd spent the past four sleepless nights remembering every moment of their year together. She knew she'd thrown away something precious, yet she wasn't so sure she'd made the wrong decision. She hadn't been ready and she would have resented him for ending up just like her mother...a slave to her husband's wishes and demands for their lives. Anna argued with herself that Matt wasn't even close to being like her father, but if she'd given up her dreams and followed Matt along as a passenger to the plans he had for his life, she was just one step away from being the woman her mother had become. Domineered. Controlled. Unhappy.

No thank you. She'd rather spend her life alone.

"Are you ready to look at the paperwork?" the woman asked.

"I guess...I mean, yes, thank you." She agreed with Dr. Martin that her father shouldn't live alone, which meant she didn't have many options. Though this place was seeming less and less like an option at all, she should still get all the information in hand.

A half hour later, Anna stood next to her car, staring up at the residential care center feeling more depressed than ever. What was she going to do?

It would be easier if she could move back home, but that would never work for multiple reasons. First, her job was in London. Sure, she was working here now, but her boss's impatience made it obvious this arrangement wouldn't last much longer. Two, other than her father, there was nothing for her here. Before his accident, she barely spoke to him a few times a year. She'd been home for over a month and had yet to see her best friend, Ashley. Matt's face appeared in her head, but he was more of a reason to leave than stay, no matter how tempted she was by him. But third, and most important, a British asshole was the deciding factor.

Phillip.

She'd wanted to leave England with Toby after their divorce, but he'd fought her. Phillip made sure the decree stated that Anna couldn't move their son out of the country without his written permission. To Phillip, Toby was a possession. He didn't necessarily want his son, yet he wasn't willing to let him go either. The fact that Phillip hadn't seen Toby in three years and hadn't paid child support didn't matter. He'd fight her tooth and nail just because he could.

But the simple fact was that their life was in London. Her job. Their home. Toby's schools and friends. No. She was good and stuck in London. At least for ten more years. But that didn't help her father now.

Her phone rang and she was surprised to see Ashley's name flash on her screen.

"Ashley," she said with a forced cheeriness. "I was just thinking about you."

"Was it racy?"

Anna laughed, which felt good after so much angst. "No."

"That's a pity."

"I thought you were out of town for another week."

"The damned red-shafted flickers decided to cooperate so I wrapped up early and rushed back home to see you before you jet off to *Merry Old England*." She added the last part with a badly executed English accent. "Gotta make hay while the sun shines."

"Do I want to ask about the red-shafted guy?"

"If only it was a guy…Sadly, I photograph wildlife and not porn, although I suspect the pay's a lot better with porn. So what do you say? Ready to hit the town, bestie?"

"Do people still say 'bestie'?" she teased.

"Who gives a rat's ass what other people say?"

God, Anna had missed her. She needed more of Ashley's attitude in her life. "I can't leave Toby with my father."

"So bring him with. I haven't seen the little guy in ages."

"You know he's five years old, right? We can't go drinking."

"You're sure we can't pass him off as a little person? Send me a recent photo and I can have a fake ID by nine tonight."

Anna laughed. "His bedtime is at eight thirty."

"Damn. Old-school mum all the way, huh? Who would have thunk it?"

"Guilty as charged."

"OK, so we tone things down a bit. We'll take him to Ruby Tuesday's or Chili's or whatever chain place kids like, but Auntie Ashley draws the line at Chuck E. Cheese."

"Deal."

Ashley paused then turned serious. "I've missed you, Anna."

They'd been best friends all through high school and college, but had barely seen each other since Anna moved to England. At the time it had felt like a natural progression of things, but now she wasn't so sure. "I've missed you, too."

"So pick the restaurant and the time, then text me the deets and I'll meet you there."

"Deets?"

"You get your English terms like 'bugger off'; let me have my 'bestie' and my 'deets.'"

"I've never once told someone to bugger off."

"Opportunity lost there, mate," she said with her fake accent. "I'd take advantage of the lingo down under."

Anna smiled. "Now you're channeling Australia. I'll see you later."

She hung up, feeling better. She and Ashley hadn't see each other since Toby was a toddler, when Ashley had scored some job in the English countryside to photograph badgers. Sure, they talked on the phone every month or so, but it wasn't the same. She was eager to finally see her best friend face-to-face.

She still had an hour before she picked up Toby, so she went by Starbucks and pulled out her laptop to catch up on some work. The Internet tab with the list of assisted living centers in the area reminded her that she needed to set up more tours, but she didn't have the heart to look through more of them now.

She opened a spreadsheet and tried to focus on her work, but her mind kept drifting to Matt. How was he not married? Had he ever been? How many girlfriends had he had after her? Had he changed his mind about getting married and having kids? Or had he not found the right person? She had no right to the relief that washed through her, yet it filled her nevertheless.

Why was she obsessing over him? She couldn't ignore the fact that she still had feelings for him. But did she still love him or the idea of him? She'd realized years ago that he'd ruined her for all other men, but twelve years had passed. She was a different person, and it stood to reason he'd changed, too. She reminded herself that she loved the man he'd been before; she didn't know the man he'd become. But the kindness he'd shown her son after all the pain she'd put him through told her all she needed to know.

Matt Osborn was a good man.

Sighing, she realized she wasn't getting any work done and packed up her laptop. She would get to Matt's about ten minutes early, but maybe she could use the time to convince Matt to meet her later in the week so she could apologize.

She pulled into his driveway and turned off the engine, taking in the yard and the exterior of the house. The houses in the neighborhood were older, but they were well kept, Matt's included. This was a family neighborhood. Maybe he had gotten married and then divorced.

Her heart hammered in her chest as she stood on his front porch and rang the doorbell. The door opened and he filled the space, his face expressionless.

She gave him a sheepish smile. "I know I'm a few minutes early…"

"It's okay. The boys are playing Legos in the dining room. I can get Toby."

"Actually," she said, trying not to sound breathless, "can we talk for a minute?"

He glanced over his shoulder then stepped out onto the porch, partially closing the door behind him. "The boys practiced soccer for about an hour, I gave them a snack of apples and peanut butter. They've been playing Legos ever since." He paused and his expression softened. "Toby's a good boy."

He thought she was checking up on him. "That's not what I wanted to talk about, but thank you," she said softly. "So they got along well?"

"Very well. Ethan's wanting Toby to spend the night, but I told him we needed to take it slow."

"Good idea," she said. "Toby's never spent the night with a friend."

"You've never left him before?" he asked in surprise.

"Only with his...sitter." Lord only knew what he'd think of her if she'd called Maureen the nanny.

A ringtone began to play inside the house, and she heard Ethan shout, "Uncle Matt, Grandma's calling on your phone."

He glanced over his shoulder. "Go ahead and answer it. Tell her I'll call her back in a few minutes."

"Okay!" his little voice called out.

"Listen, Matt," Anna said. "I was wondering if you and I could get together for coffee this week...and chat."

His face was blank again. "Chat?"

"I hated leaving things the way I did. I'd like to make it right." Even as she said the words, she knew how ridiculous they sounded—and how bad she appeared. She was trying to make herself feel better for leaving him the way she had. How had she not seen that before? "This can be your chance to tell me off like you probably wanted to after you proposed."

His face paled. "Anna..."

"Uncle Matt," Ethan said, his voice sounding closer. "Grandma says it's important."

"Okay. Tell her I'll be right there."

Ethan appeared next to Matt's legs, his eyes wide as he held the phone to his ear. "She says it's an emergency."

"This can wait," Anna said. "Take the call. I'll go in and get Toby." Then she realized she'd just invited herself into his house. "If that's okay."

"Yeah," he said absently, reaching for the phone.

He stepped back inside, letting Anna brush past him. She found Toby sitting at the dining room table, concentrating on attaching a Lego piece to an airplane.

"Look, Mummy," Toby said with a huge grin. "Coach Matt helped me make a Lego airplane."

"That's terrific, Toby. You had a fun afternoon?"

"Yeah! Coach Matt is awesome."

Anna heard Matt's voice behind her. "Mom, stay outside and wait for me. I'll call Kevin and Holly and see if they can watch Ethan."

Ethan watched his uncle with worried eyes.

"Hey, Ethan," Anna said as she pointed toward a Lego helicopter. "Can you show me what you've been working on?"

Matt shot her a look of gratitude before he stepped out the front door.

Ethan watched him walk out the door then took a cautious step toward the table.

"Is that Batman?" Anna asked, picking up the booklet next to the helicopter. "Where does the Robin figure go?"

"Robins! That's our last name, Mummy!" Toby said.

"Yes, it is, except we have an *s* on the end," Anna said. "*This* Robin is Batman's sidekick."

"Who's Batman?" Toby asked.

"Who's *Batman*?" Ethan asked in disbelief. "Haven't you seen *The Lego Movie*?"

Anna added that to the growing list of movies to watch with Toby. For some reason, Nanny Maureen had put it on the *banned* list, and Anna had never questioned it.

Ethan launched into an enthusiastic explanation about Batman, and Anna was thankful he seemed to have forgotten his uncle. But Matt came back inside a minute later, wearing a look of frustration.

Anna moved toward him. "Is everything okay?"

Matt hesitated and motioned her into the living room, then lowered his voice. "My mom's security alarm went off, but it's gone off so many times with false alarms, the security system people want her to check before they call the police. Mom's asked me to come over to check it out, but I don't want to take Ethan in case someone really broke in and my friends aren't available."

"I can watch Ethan," she said.

His gaze frosted over. "That's not necessary."

"Matt, let me help. You just watched my son for three hours, I can watch your nephew while you check on your mother."

"I'm sure it's fine. She can get excited over absolutely nothing."

She smiled. "I remember." She'd loved his parents, and while his mother *had* been prone to overreaction, she'd been harmless and entertaining.

His face softened. "This probably won't take long."

"Is it okay if we stay here? I'm living at my dad's…"

"Yeah, of course." But he didn't look totally convinced it was a good idea.

"I promise not to snoop through your things," she stage-whispered.

His eyes widened.

"I was teasing." She couldn't blame him for hesitating. She would have hesitated, too, if the situation were reversed. But then her conversation with Ashley gave her an idea. "How about I take them to Chuck E. Cheese and they can play some games? Toby's never been before so I'm sure he'll love it, especially if Ethan's with him. Then when you're done, you can meet us there. Or I can drop Ethan off somewhere. Whatever's convenient for you."

He studied her, the tension in his jaw easing. "It's Saturday. You probably have plans."

"Not until later."

His eyes darkened. She could only imagine what he was thinking, but she saw no need to explain herself.

"The boys will love it."

A war waged in his eyes, but he cast a glance toward his nephew, who was waving his half-finished helicopter around as he explained a scene from *The Lego Movie*. Matt's shoulders dropped in defeat. "I'll get Ethan's booster and put it in your car."

She tugged her keys out of her jeans pocket and handed them to him. He headed out the front door without a word, but she counted this as a victory.

That caught her off guard. A victory in what war? He was obviously unhappy with the concession. What was her endgame? Offering to watch Ethan was more than a step toward closure. Was she just doing a good deed, or was she hoping for more? The way she'd obsessed over him during the last four days hadn't helped. Nor did seeing so many hints of the man she'd loved. But hope was dangerous and foolish. Besides she was leaving in a little over a month. She wouldn't hurt him again.

Still, she couldn't deny that if she really wanted to do the right thing, she needed to leave Matt alone. But that was next to impossible with the two boys in the next room becoming even better friends, and she couldn't very well change her mind now.

"Good news!" she said to the boys. "Ethan's coming with us, and we're going to Chuck E. Cheese."

The two boys squealed with delight as Anna herded them out the door and toward her car. Matt was already in her backseat, installing Ethan's booster seat. His rear stuck out the open door, his jeans hugging his butt. She stopped short, sucking in her breath.

His gaze met hers as he climbed out of the car.

Great. He'd caught her checking him out.

Her face flushed, but he ignored her and squatted in front of Ethan.

"You listen to Ms. Fischer…uh, I mean Mrs. Robins, okay?"

"Fischer?" Ethan asked with a giggle. "Why'd you call her Ms. *Fischer*?"

"Hey!" Toby said in excitement. "My grandad's name is Fischer. Albert Cranky-Pants Fischer."

"Cranky-Pants?" Ethan asked as he continued to giggle.

Toby giggled, too. "That's what Mummy calls him sometimes. Even to his tummy."

Ethan scrunched up his nose in confusion. "Why would she call his tummy cranky pants? It's the wrong side. Or is it one of those England things?"

"His face," Anna said with a sigh. "I call him cranky pants to his *face*."

Ethan's eyes widened in wonder. "Because his face looks like a butt?"

"No, Ethan," Matt said, trying to sound serious even though the corners of his mouth kept tilting up. "Saying something to someone's face is an idiom. It means she meant for him to hear her call him 'cranky pants.'"

Ethan seemed to consider Matt's explanation before he repeated, "Because his face looks like a butt?"

Matt couldn't hide a small chuckle. "No, Mr. Fischer's face doesn't look like a butt. Or at least it didn't used to."

"You've seen my grandad's face?" Toby asked.

Matt's smile fell as though he realized what he'd just admitted. "I have to go check on Grandma. Mind Toby's mother and be a good boy."

"I will, Uncle Matt."

"I'll come as soon as I'm done with Grandma."

"Don't come too fast, okay? I haven't been to Chuck E. Cheese since I was a little kid."

"A little kid?" Matt asked as he stood. "You were there just a few months ago for Wesley's birthday party."

"I was five and a half then. Now I'm almost six. But you have to promise not to come too soon. I want to win a *lot* of tickets."

"I'll see what I can do." He helped the boy into the back of the car and fastened the seat belt around him, then gave him a kiss on the cheek before he shut the door.

"You have my number?" he asked, keeping his gaze on the driveway as he offered Anna a twenty-dollar bill.

She refused to take it and crossed her arms. "I have your number, but I don't want your money. I'm thrilled that Ethan's coming to play with Toby and that's enough. I'll call you if there's a problem, but I'm sure we'll be fine. Go take care of your mother."

"Thanks," Matt said as he reluctantly put the money in his pocket. He looked like he wanted to say something then closed his mouth and went back into his house.

Toby had already gotten into the car and strapped himself in, beaming with happiness.

As long as her son was happy, she could endure anything. At least, that's what she told herself.

# Chapter Eight

Matt found his mother standing at the edge of her driveway wearing black yoga pants, a white fitted T-shirt, and a black athletic jacket. He would have thought she'd raided his sister's closet if she didn't have a yoga matt rolled up under her arm.

He parked his truck in the street and walked toward her. "When did you start taking yoga?"

"A month ago. There's this wonderful elderly woman who just started giving classes at the Blue Springs Fitness Center. She really knows how to help us old women open up our pelvic floors."

Matt's mouth dropped open, then he shook his head in an attempt to lose the mental image. "I really don't want to hear about your pelvic floor, Mom."

"Roger appreciates it."

"And I *really* don't want to hear about Roger."

"You don't want to hear about my boyfriend? Or that he appreciates my open pelvic floor?"

"I'm going to have to sign up for therapy as soon as I leave here. You know that, right? I'm going to send you the bill."

His mother laughed.

"Maybe you should have called Roger to come check your house."

"I would have, but he's at the lake fishing with his grandsons."

Matt stared at her as the new shock set in. "You were seriously going to call him?" It was bad enough his mother had started dating less than two years after his father died, but now she was letting the guy take over Matt's job of taking care of things around the house?

She glanced over at his truck. "Where's Ethan? Did you get ahold of Kevin?"

"No. Ethan's with a friend." He wasn't about to tell her who. Especially after his mother had taken Anna's side during the break up. "I'm going inside to check it out, but after I give you the all clear, we need to talk about Abby."

His mother's smile faded. "Okay."

"Which section was triggered?" he asked.

"The back of the house. By the kitchen door."

"Okay, wait here and I'll be right back."

He walked around the side of the house and let himself through the gate into the backyard. He moved to the back door, not expecting to find anything amiss, so he stopped in his tracks when he saw the broken windowpane. Pulling out his cell phone, he called 911 and reported a break-in, then headed toward the front.

His mother was still waiting at the end of the driveway, and the moment she saw him, she knew something was wrong.

"It looks like someone broke the window over the doorknob. I've already called 911, so all we need to do is wait."

She cast a worried glance toward the house. "Are we safe?"

"There are no strange cars on the street so I doubt anyone is still inside."

She didn't look convinced.

Matt sent Anna a text saying he'd be longer than he planned, which would make Ethan happy. She sent a text back moments later telling him Ethan was having fun with Toby and to take as long as he needed.

"Who are you texting?" his mother asked.

"No one."

"No one?"

"The person watching Ethan. I want to let her know I'll be longer than I planned."

*"Her?"*

"Mom," he sighed her name in exasperation, but he knew she would press on until he gave her something. "She's the mother of one of Ethan's teammates."

*"Oh?"*

"Stop with the matchmaking, Mom."

"Who said I was matchmaking? I simply want to know who is watching my grandson."

He gave her a smirk. "Like I said, she's the mother of one of Ethan's teammates. Ethan's new best friend."

"Toby?" she asked in surprise.

"You know about Toby?"

"Ethan's mentioned him a time or two when I've picked him up after school. I also know Toby doesn't have a father in the picture."

"Mom." She knew more about Toby than he liked but not enough to make the connection...yet. Obviously, the best course of action was to change the subject. "Abby canceled another call with Ethan."

"She's so busy with school." When he didn't answer, she continued, "This is why he's with *us* and not with her. Not because she doesn't want him, but because she's trying to make a better life for the both of them."

"I know. I know," he said in frustration. "And I fully supported her going to med school—still do—but I'm dealing with a very disappointed little boy. I thought things were getting better, but now I'm not so sure. I'm worried I'm screwing it all up."

She gave him a soft grin. "Welcome to parenthood. We spend ninety-nine point nine percent of the time worried we're screwing it up. The fact you're worried about it means you're probably doing it right."

He wasn't so sure about that, but he was still stuck on her welcoming him to parenthood. He was playing at parenthood with Ethan, making him want it even more than he'd expected.

His mother was silent for several moments. "I've been thinking about something else that's a bit…difficult to broach."

"What?"

"Ethan's stayed with you since Roger and I went on our cruise. Are you happy with the arrangement? He seems happier with you."

Matt's gut tightened. "Are you saying you want him back?"

"No. Not unless *you're* unhappy."

He pushed out a sigh of relief. "I'm not. I love having him."

She smiled again. "Good. I think you're both good for each other. I'm asking because I have a friend who is raising her grandkids and her daughter is giving her temporary guardianship. We don't have anything formal with Abby,

and if Ethan got hurt and had to go to the hospital...I just
think we should have something legal set up. And if he's living with you, that would mean *you* would get guardianship."

*Holy shit.*

"It's a lot to think about," she said. "A lot of responsibility. Take some time to think about it."

"No," Matt said with a shake of his head. "I don't need
time to think about it. I love Ethan and love having him in
my life. I'll do it."

She pulled him into a hug. "You're a good man, Matt. I'm
proud of you."

Matt felt guilty that his reasons for accepting Ethan's
guardianship weren't entirely altruistic.

His mother leaned back with an ornery grin. "Now that
that's settled, tell me more about Toby's mother."

\* \* \*

The policeman determined that whoever had broken into
Matt's mother's back window hadn't taken anything. Nothing in the house was missing, but he had a crew come out
and dust for prints in an effort to figure out who'd broken in.

Matt stayed until after the policeman drove away an hour
later, then he cleaned up the glass and placed it in his
mother's trash can.

"Thanks for helping, Matt. I don't know what I'd do without you."

He kissed his mother on the cheek. "Good thing you'll
never have to find out. I'm not going anywhere and neither
are you." He headed for the front door. "I'm going to go
pick up Ethan, but I think you should come stay with me
tonight."

She waved him off with a chuckle as she followed him

out to his truck. "I'll be fine. It was probably some kids causing mischief."

That didn't make him feel any better. What if someone tried to break in at night while she was here all alone? "Mom. I think you should reconsider."

"I'm fine. I have an alarm and I think I'm going to install some cameras like that nice officer suggested." She grinned. "For the record, I'm letting you off the hook with details about Toby's mother," she said. "But I'll expect a report the next time I see you."

At least he had some warning.

"Call me if you need me, Mom," he said, resting his hands on her shoulders and looking down into her face. "I mean it."

"You worry too much." She reached up on her tip-toes and kissed his cheek. "I love you, Matt. Don't shut out good things."

"What does *that* mean?"

She'd already headed back into the house, but lifted her hand and waved as she walked through the door.

Chuck E. Cheese was a fifteen-minute drive away, which unfortunately gave him time to think. What had his mother meant about shutting out good things? He embraced the good things in his life. Look at Ethan. He could have grumbled and complained when he'd started watching the boy, but he loved having him around. He'd taken over his father's construction business, convinced his best friend, Kevin, to come be his CFO—and when Kevin promptly discovered the previous bookkeeper had embezzled, had Matt complained? No. He'd rolled up his sleeves and figured out a way to keep the company afloat. And now with Kevin's help, his company had turned a corner and they were close to making a profit again.

He turned off the highway and headed toward Chuck E. Cheese, going over his interaction with Anna when she'd come back to pick up Toby. What had she wanted to talk about? He'd seen her checking him out when he put Ethan's booster seat in the car. Did she want to get back together? Like he was crazy enough to jump back on that train.

Matt, Kevin, and Tyler had been right back in June when they'd all decided they'd spent their entire dating life with crazy women. Matt had had his share of them, and Anna was right there in the middle of them. What woman tells her boyfriend during his proposal that she doesn't want to get married and have kids ever, after she's spent the last six months mentioning getting married and starting a family?

*Crazy.*

Which meant he'd be absolutely insane to consider starting something up with her again. And yet he had to admit, she didn't seem all that crazy.

When he walked into the restaurant, he told the girl manning the roped entrance that he was picking up his nephew. After he pointed him out, she stamped his hand and let him in.

Anna was standing next to both boys by a skee ball machine. Ethan was rolling a ball up the ramp as she coached him, wearing a warm smile so bright it stunned him.

She was gorgeous.

Motherhood had made her curvier, and that just added to her beauty. She moved behind Ethan and grabbed his arm, swinging it back and moving it forward, giving Matt a nice view of her ass, proving that her added curves made her look even better in jeans.

No. He could *not* go there.

He stopped about six feet behind them and asked, "How's it going?"

"I'm playing skeeter ball, Uncle Matt!" Ethan exclaimed as he turned around to face him. He held a wooden ball in his hand, and Matt struggled to keep his gaze on Ethan's face and away from Anna's ass.

*Focus.*

"I see that," Matt said with a grin. "And getting lessons, too."

"Anna says I have a hook when I swing my arm, but I told her I'm not fishing."

Matt laughed. "No, you're not, but she's right. I saw you roll the last ball as I was getting my hand stamped. Your ball rolled to the left."

"You know how to play skeeter ball, Uncle Matt?" Ethan asked in awe. "You know how to do *everything*."

He grinned. "Not quite, but Mrs. Robins seems to be doing a good job teaching you. I'll just watch." He crossed his arms over his chest and finally lifted his gaze to hers.

Holy Mother of God.

The way she was looking at him—a mixture of warmth and fire, friendliness and longing—he was ready to say fuck it all and walk over and kiss her.

*What was he thinking?* No! This was crazy.

He broke his gaze and confusion set in. What was he doing? This woman had crushed his heart. Was he really going to consider letting her off the hook?

"Anna, Uncle Matt," Ethan said insistently.

He blinked. "What?"

"She says to call her Anna. Or Miss Anna, but she says not to call her Mrs. Robins."

"Why not?" he asked, sounding crankier than he'd intended.

"Because she says she's not a dragon."

"What?" He lifted his gaze to Anna's.

She gave him a soft smile. "Mrs. Robins is my ex-husband's mother's name. A truly horrifying woman that reminds me of a fire-breathing dragon." She leaned over and tickled Ethan's stomach.

The boy broke into giggles then she spun and tickled Toby next, who joined in.

Anna was bent over and laughing with them, but Matt's gut seized. This was how he'd pictured her with their own kids. Instead, she'd broken up with him and married some other man. Matt had offered her something wonderful and she'd thrown it away to marry a jerk who couldn't be bothered to raise his kid. It felt like a slap in the face.

He glanced down at Ethan, trying not to turn too serious and ruin his nephew's fun. "You can call a grown-up by their first name if they give you permission, but otherwise you have to call them by their last name."

"So does Toby have to call you Mr. Osborn?" Ethan asked, sounding confused.

"No. Toby can keep calling me Coach Matt. Or just Matt." He ruffled the boy's hair. "Go ahead with your lesson," Matt said although he couldn't look Anna in the face.

"Come play with us, Uncle Matt!" Ethan said, grabbing his hand.

Toby's face lit up with excitement. "Yeah, come play!"

Matt shot a glance to Anna, much too tempted to join them. "No, thanks. I'll just watch."

"Please?" Ethan asked.

"I don't have any tokens."

Anna gave him a hesitant smile and shook her red cup, setting off a loud jangling sound. "We've got plenty."

His gaze held hers, his irritation seeping through. "I said no."

Anna's previously buoyant attitude deflated and Ethan's smile fell.

"If you'd like to leave..." she said softly and that pissed him off, too.

*Dammit.* Why'd he have to go and ruin Ethan's fun with his surliness? "No. Ethan's enjoying himself. I'm going to get a beer." Without waiting for an answer, he turned on his heels and headed toward the counter. It was only after he was walking back toward them with his beer in hand that he realized he'd just prolonged his agony. He should have accepted Anna's offer to leave, yet when he saw how much fun the boys were having, he wasn't sorry he let Ethan stay. And they *were* having fun again. His departure had lightened the mood.

Anna was showing them how to roll the ball but she was putting her own spin on it—literally—spinning around in a circle then rolling the ball and accidentally rolling it into the machine next to the one they were playing on. Both boys started giggling and Anna laughed, too, her cheeks turning pink with her merriment. Ethan turned and caught Matt's dark gaze, and the boy's smile fell.

*Jesus.* When had he become a fun sucker?

Matt forced a big smile and waved, feeling better when Ethan grinned and waved back.

His phone rang and he pulled it out of his pocket, surprised to see Tyler's name on the screen. "I thought you and Lanie were in Atlanta this weekend."

"Lanie came down with the stomach flu."

"Yikes. So you're looking for a place to stay?"

"What?" Tyler asked in surprise. "Why would I do that? Who would take care of Lanie?"

"*You're* cleaning up vomit?"

"Lanie happens to be a grown ass woman who can make

it to the toilet. Sounds like you've been hanging out with a certain five-year-old. Which means you need a night out. Why don't you come hang out with me in Westport? I'm calling Kevin next."

"I thought you said you were taking care of Lanie."

"She said I'm hovering too much and is kicking me out tonight."

"Can't make it. Mom's got plans with her *boyfriend* tonight and can't watch Ethan. In fact, there's something I'd like to talk to you about."

"Yeah, sure," Tyler said in surprise.

"Since Ethan's been staying with me, Mom thinks I should get temporary guardianship of him."

"Do you think Abby will go for it?"

That was the glitch in all of this. She'd confessed that she felt like a failure as a mother for leaving her son to pursue her dream. She might not agree for that reason alone. "If it's presented the right way—as in this is a temporary situation."

"*Is* it a temporary situation? She's in her first year of med school. She has three more years, then a residency with lots of on-call hours…"

"I'll be here for Ethan as long as he needs me."

"Are you ready for that? Raising a kid is a huge responsibility. Hell, I'm not ready for that, and I'm married."

Matt's defensiveness rose. "News flash: I *have* been raising him. I've been taking care of him for the past three months. Hell, he's been with me every night of the last month with the exception of a few nights. We're just making it legal." His voice lowered as he glanced over at his nephew. "Besides, we both know this was what I always wanted—a family with kids of my own."

"But he's not your kid. He's Abby's."

"But Abby can't raise him right now, and I'm more than

willing to. I don't care if he's mine or not. Besides"—he took a breath—"I think it's time to accept that I'm not getting a family the traditional way. Maybe this is how it's supposed to be. And I'm okay with that."

Tyler was silent for several seconds. "Okay. I support you one hundred percent, but I suspect you need to talk to a family attorney."

"You can't help me?"

"No, but I know the perfect person, well, couple actually. Kevin knows them, too. Remember Blair Hansen? Kevin's sister's best friend? She's an attorney now and in a practice with her new husband, Garrett. I'm sure she'll talk to you."

Matt felt like he was trying to pull a fast one on his sister, but his mother had assured him that she'd talk to Abby. "Okay."

"Good. Now that's out of the way, how about we do something with the kid? I can see if my brother Eric wants to come."

"Isn't Eric seventeen? He's not going to want to hang out with a five-year-old."

"He won't care. He likes kids. And as long as we don't go to Chuck E. Cheese, we're both good."

"No worries there," Matt said as he took a long drag of his beer. "I'm already in the rat's hell."

"You're at Chuck E. Cheese? Is Ethan at a birthday party?"

Matt hesitated. He hadn't told anyone that Anna was back and he wasn't sure how Tyler would react, but he was tired of keeping it a secret. "No, he's here with a friend. *Why* he's here is a long story which involves my mother and her home security system, but the bottom line is that he's here with his new best friend, Toby, and his mother."

"Is she single?" Tyler teased.

"As a matter of fact, yes."

"Is she hot?"

"You have no idea."

"So ask her out. What are you waiting for?"

"Her son is British."

"Since when did you start discriminating against British people? Wait. He's British, but she's not?"

"No. Actually, she's from Blue Springs and you know her...or knew her. Before she moved to London right after our college graduation."

"*No.*" Tyler sounded horrified.

"Yes."

"How the fuck did *this* happen?"

"It's a long story I'm not getting into over the phone."

"But you're seeing her?"

"If you call noticing her on the sidelines at soccer practice seeing her. Or barely talking to her when she dropped her son off at my house this afternoon for a playdate seeing her."

"What?"

Matt groaned then decided to give him the condensed version. "I told you—her son, Toby, and Ethan are best friends, and he happens to be on my soccer team. I had no idea he was Anna's son. But Toby's shy and was scared about playing in a game, and Ethan promised Toby I'd help him. So I set up the playdate." He paused. "Look, Toby... he's a good kid. And Ethan really likes him. Why should they suffer because Toby's mother was a bitch twelve years ago?"

"You're a better man than me."

"I'm not so sure about that. But I really love Ethan. We're here now because Mom had her security issue and I didn't have anyone to watch him. Anna had come to pick up Toby so she offered to watch Ethan and brought them to Chuck E. Cheese."

"And you're there with them." He paused. "Nope. I don't see a frozen winter land outside my window. I don't think hell's frozen over."

"Very funny."

"So what's the plan? Are you going to ask her out?"

"And let her destroy me again? I don't think so."

"How is it? Is she nice? Hateful?"

"She's bending over backwards to make this easy for me. It's almost worse than if she were a bitch."

"At least if she was a bitch, you wouldn't want to start something with her again."

"Exactly. And I'd like to add that you're usually the more emotionally obtuse one of the three of us."

"What can I say?" he said in a sly tone. "Lanie's changed me."

She had. Just like Holly had changed Kevin. And Matt would be lying if he said he wasn't jealous of what they had. "So if you want to hang out, how about we grill at my house again? I'll grab some steaks on the way home. Let's say six thirty?"

"Sounds good. I'll call Eric and Kevin."

Matt hung up and looked at the time on his phone, surprised it was almost five thirty. He hated to be the killjoy any more than he had been, but he hoped Ethan would be more willing to leave if he found out that Kevin and Tyler were coming over.

He tossed his half-finished lukewarm beer in the trash and headed toward the kids, who had since moved on to the whack-a-mole game.

"Ethan, we need to leave in a few minutes. Uncle Kevin and Uncle Tyler are coming over to cook out." When the boy didn't look as excited as Matt had hoped, he added, "And Uncle Tyler's probably bringing his little brother, Eric."

He narrowed his eyes. "Does he play soccer or Legos?"

Toby watched his friend and wrapped his arm around his mother's leg.

Great. Now he was upsetting Toby. "Eric's in high school so he's a big kid, but Uncle Tyler says he likes little kids."

Anna put a hand on her son's shoulder. "We have to go, too. I forgot to tell you. We're going to eat dinner with my friend Ashley."

Toby looked confused then his eyes widened. "The one who hangs out with animals?"

"Yep."

"What kind of animals?" Ethan asked.

"All kinds," Toby said, getting excited. "Frogs. And rabbits. And even lions."

"No way." Ethan looked up at Matt. "I'd rather go with Toby."

"Sorry, big guy, that's not possible. But we'll see Toby at practice tomorrow afternoon." Oh, crap. He hadn't asked Anna if they were coming. "Well, if he comes."

"We'll be there," Anna said, keeping her eyes on Ethan.

Ethan looked down at the floor. "Okay…"

Anna dug into her pockets and pulled out a wad of tickets. "But right now you get to pick a prize. Look at all the tickets you won!"

His face lit up and Matt was amazed at how easily he was distracted. But hadn't Matt been doing the same thing with him over the last few months? Distracting him from his mother's absence?

"Do I get a prize, too?" Toby asked, looking excited.

She smiled at him. "Of course you do. It's one of the best

parts of going to Chuck E. Cheese." Then she handed him another wad. "Let's go count them up."

Matt went to a ticket machine and let Ethan feed the ribbons into the slot while he gave surreptitious glances toward Anna. She was patient with Toby, far more patient than he'd seen a lot of mothers here at the handful of birthday parties Ethan had attended. There was no doubt that she and her son were close and that he adored her.

Neither boy had accumulated many tickets, but it still took them several minutes to decide what to get. Standing so close to Anna was torture. His mind remembered how she'd broken his heart, but his body insisted that was firmly in the past. The sooner he got away from her, the better.

Ethan picked a couple of pieces of candy and a plastic spider ring and Matt turned to Anna. "Thanks again for watching him. We'll see you tomorrow," he said in a cold tone that made him sound like a dick. So be it.

He turned to leave without waiting for a good-bye, when he heard her say. "You're forgetting something."

He turned to face her.

"Ethan's booster."

*Dammit.*

He scrubbed a hand over his head, looking obviously frustrated. He dropped his hand when he realized Ethan was watching him with a frown.

He glanced back up at Anna and the sadness in her eyes sent a stab of pain to his chest. *Why?* Why did he care how she felt? She hadn't cared about how he'd felt twelve years ago, but something deep down told him that was a lie. Believing the lie had just made the rejection easier to deal with.

"Toby's almost done."

Toby looked up at his mother. "I have to go to the toilet."

"Can you wait?"

He crossed his legs and cupped the front of his jeans. "No, Mummy."

Anna gave Matt a worried look then dug her keys out of her pocket. "Why don't you get the booster seat, and we'll hurry and meet you outside."

"Okay, but don't rush him." Then he grabbed Ethan's hand and led him to the exit.

"I don't want to go, Uncle Matt," Ethan whined, tugging on his hand. "I want to stay with Toby."

"We'll play with Toby another day. We need to go get ready for our cookout."

"Why can't Toby come?"

"You heard his mom. Toby has plans."

Ethan didn't seem convinced, and Matt had to drag him the last ten feet to the door, stopping in front of the roped-off exit.

Matt started to unhook the chain, but a teenage boy rushed over. "I have to check your stamps."

"What?" Matt asked.

"The stamps you got when you came in."

Ethan tried to pull loose and Matt tightened his grip as he lifted his free left arm.

The teen shined a black light flashlight on the back of his hand then said. "Now your son's."

"He's not my dad!" Ethan shouted, still trying to pull loose.

The teen looked alarmed.

Matt clenched his jaw. "Ethan, show the boy your hand."

"You can't make me!" he shouted. "You can't make me go with you!"

Matt looked down at him in shock. Ethan had had a few uncharacteristic outbursts over the last month or two, but never like this.

"I'm sorry," Matt said as he tugged Ethan's hand closer to the worker. "I think he's overtired."

"I'm not going with you! I want my mom!" Ethan shouted, digging in his feet and leaning backward.

The teen's eyes widened, and as he shined the light on the back of Ethan's hand, he shouted. "Code Teddy Bear! Code Teddy Bear! This is not a drill!"

*Oh, shit.*

Lights began to flash from the ceiling and a siren sounded.

Ethan had fallen to his butt, and Matt was bent over trying to get him to his feet.

"Sir. I need you to let go of the child," a man said behind him.

*Fuck.* Matt let go of Ethan's hand and stood, turning to face the middle-aged man behind him.

Matt lifted his hands in surrender. "I know this looks bad."

"Their stamps don't match," the teen boy said in a rush. "And the boy says he's not his dad."

"I can explain," Matt said. "I'm his uncle."

The middle-aged man looked even more on edge. "Sir, I need you to move away from the exit while we wait for the police."

"Police?" Matt asked in dismay. "That's really not necessary. I'll show you my I.D." He dug into his pocket to pull out his wallet, but his pocket knife fell out on the floor.

The teen boy let out a shriek Matt challenged any teen girl to top, then stumbled backward, tripping on a child behind him. "He has a weapon! Repeat! *He has a weapon!*"

"No!" Matt shouted, lifting his hands again. "It's not a weapon!"

Ethan got to his feet then took off running past the middle-aged man.

"Ethan!" He started to run after him but the manager's eyes widened even more as he blocked his path.

"Sir, you can't go back there."

"That's my nephew! I'm not letting him go back there all alone!"

What if Ethan ran out the back door?

*Dammit.*

He wasn't waiting. He tried to dart around the manager, but the man tried to block his path again. Adrenaline raced through Matt's blood, and he bumped into the man's shoulder harder than he'd intended.

As the manager stumbled, his foot slipped and he fell to the floor.

The teen and the children who had gathered around him began to scream, but Matt's sole focus was on Ethan.

*Please, God, don't let him run out the back door.*

"Stranger danger!" a girl shouted, pointing to him as he ran past. "Stranger danger!"

"I'm not a stranger. I promise," Matt said as he ran past her, bolting for the back of the restaurant. "Ethan!"

"I don't want to go with you!" Ethan shouted and Matt spotted him in the party room area.

Thank God. "Ethan! Just come here, and we can talk about it."

The boy stopped and stared at him then began to scream.

What the hell?

Something big and hard slammed into Matt's back and he fell forward, face planting onto the carpet. The heavy object remained on top of him, and something bony pressed into his shoulder blade.

"I caught him!" a muffled voice shouted. "I get the reward!"

Matt turned to his side with a jerk, throwing the guy off

balance. His captor fell forward, and Matt found himself staring into a giant plastic mouse face.

Ethan had run over, but continued screaming at the top of his lungs, "Chuck E. Cheese is killing my Uncle Matt!" Then he started to kick the mascot's side repeatedly. "Leave my Uncle Matt alone!"

The mascot fell off Matt and rolled into a ball, shouting, "Help! Somebody save me!"

Matt pushed himself into a sitting position and grabbed Ethan around the waist and pulled him onto his lap, burying the sobbing boy's face into his chest.

He took a moment to let the last twenty seconds seep in and found himself staring up into Anna's stunned face. Toby clung to her legs with tears in his eyes.

Then Anna's shock faded, and she gave him a hesitant grin. "I guess you never made it out to the car."

# Chapter Nine

D<sub>o</sub> I want to ask?" Anna asked. She'd laugh if Ethan hadn't been so upset. The sirens and lights had started blaring and flashing while she was in the restroom with Toby, so she knew something had happened, but she'd never imagined that Matt could be in the thick of it.

"I'm not sure."

A balding man in a uniform walked up behind her. He grabbed her arm and tried to pull her back while jabbing a pair of silver salad tongs at Matt. "Ma'am, you need to get away from the dangerous criminal."

"Dangerous criminal?" she asked, tugging free then squatting in front of Matt. "What did you do?"

Matt opened his mouth to answer then shook his head.

"I'm sorry, Uncle Matt," Ethan sobbed. "I'm sorry."

Matt held him tighter. "It's okay, big guy. It's going to be okay."

A giant mouse lay on the floor rocking back and forth, saying, "Please, don't hurt me. I want to live. I haven't even been to Comic Con."

"You can get up now," a teenage girl said in a disgusted tone, standing behind the manager. "The toddler stopped kicking you."

"Ethan kicked Chuck E. Cheese?" Toby asked, sounding distressed.

Ethan stopped sobbing and shot him a defensive look. "He was going to kill Uncle Matt. Wesley said Chuck E. Cheese is a murderer."

Matt rolled his eyes and helped Ethan to his feet. "Wesley is wrong. Chuck E. Cheese isn't capable of murdering anyone."

"That's not true," the mouse said, holding up his arms and trying to flex. "I've been working out. I knocked you flat on your ass, and if you'd just held still, I could have wrapped my legs around your neck and snapped you in two."

Several children watching them began to scream.

"Chuck E. Cheese said a bad word!"

"Chuck E. Cheese is a killer!"

"Wesley's right!" Ethan shouted then pointed to the mouse. "He *is* a murderer."

"He's *not* a murderer." Matt got to his feet and shot the mascot a look of disgust. "He got in a lucky potshot." He picked the still crying Ethan up and set him on his hip. The boy wrapped his legs around Matt's waist and buried his face into the curve of his neck.

The man behind Anna leaped forward and jabbed toward Matt with the salad tongs. "Get back on the floor. The police are on their way."

"Police?" Anna gasped.

"He was kidnapping that boy."

"His nephew?" she asked in disbelief.

The balding man blinked. "What?"

"That's his nephew."

"But their numbers didn't match." He turned to a teenage boy wearing a uniform. "You said the numbers didn't match."

"They *didn't* match," he said defensively.

"See?" the manager said with attitude. "They didn't match."

"Of course they didn't match. Ethan came with Toby and me and his uncle came later. I was watching Ethan until Matt came to pick him up."

"But the boy said he wasn't his dad!" the teen boy shouted.

Anna put her hands on her hips. "Because Matt is *his uncle*."

"But," the boy said, sounding less sure of himself. "He said he didn't want to go with him."

Anna dropped her hands to her sides. "Because Ethan was having fun and didn't want to leave. I assure you nothing underhanded was going on. You'll see that his stamp matches mine."

"But he ran past me," the manager said. "Why'd he do that if he wasn't guilty?"

Matt sighed. "Ethan was scared and mad and no one was watching him when he took off. I was terrified he'd run out the back door."

"See?" Anna said. "It's just a huge misunderstanding. So cancel the police and let the man take his traumatized nephew home."

The manager's face waffled between determination and concession until he finally said, "If the boy's numbers match yours, he can take him home, but"—his voice turned stern—"tell your nephew we take safety seriously around here so he can't make us think he's being kidnapped."

Anna offered him a warm smile. "And we very much appreciate that you do, don't we, Matt?"

Matt didn't look totally convinced, probably because of the giant knot that was growing on his forehead, but he said, "Yes. Thank for your diligence."

Anna pried her terrified son from her legs and took his hand. "Let's go, Toby."

His feet remained in place. "Is the giant rat going to tackle me, too?"

"No," she said, trying not to laugh. "And if he did, I think Matt would take him out for you."

Matt met Toby's gaze. "I'd do it in a heartbeat."

While he might be doing it to protect Toby, Anna was sure there was a bit of vindictiveness in his declaration.

"Let's go," Anna said. Matt nodded and she lowered her voice. "There are a couple of ways we can take this walk of shame. We can hang our heads and walk out with our tails between our legs, or we can go out with style." She grinned. "Personally, I prefer the second, but it takes a lot of attitude. Which do you prefer?"

"This isn't a walk of shame, so the attitude for sure."

She bent at the knees and picked up Toby, setting him on her hip. "Good. Then let's do it."

Something in Matt's eyes shifted, and they started walking to the exit while Toby clung to Anna and Ethan remained firmly attached to Matt's side. She leaned closer to Matt and whispered, "Are you ready to make a run for it when my number doesn't match Ethan's?"

Matt stopped in is tracks, terror filling his eyes.

She grinned. "I'm teasing. Too soon?"

He started to protest then amusement filled his eyes. "You always knew how to make a terrible experience better."

"I'm not sure about that," she said, lifting a hand and giving a parade wave to the crowd. "But I'll be sure to let you know when I figure it out."

He grinned and his eyes lit up like they had back when they were together, and she realized how much she missed him.

They reached the rope blocking their escape, the lights still flashing and the sirens still screeching. Anna lifted her hand, waiting for one of the employees to catch up. The manager reluctantly picked up the black light and shined it on Anna's hand and then on Ethan's and Toby's. He unhooked the rope and said, "It might be best if you don't come back for a while."

"That won't be a problem," Matt said gruffly as he headed for the exit. Anna followed then gave one last wave before she walked out the open door.

Anna tried to put Toby down when they reached the parking lot, but he locked his ankles around her waist and refused to budge.

"My car's over there," she said, pointing to it.

"I know. My truck's next to it. It seemed easier that way." He grinned. "In theory."

"Best-laid plans…" she said. "Life never works out as you planned."

He stopped next to her car and looked down at her, his nephew wrapped tight around him. "No. It doesn't."

She regretted saying it, reminding him of what she'd done, but his anger seemed to have faded, and melancholy had taken its place. Could he sense her sadness, too?

"Matt, when I showed up early to your house…"

He glanced down at Toby as if to remind her they had an audience.

"I'd still like to meet with you next week. I'd like to explain some things."

His body tensed and Ethan shifted. "You don't owe me anything."

"Actually, I do, but it's not out of obligation." She looked up into his guarded brown eyes. "You have every right to tell me no, and I won't press you on it. But I hope you say yes." She paused. "I'm not looking for anything from you. Your only job is to listen to my reasoning back then and ask questions. I just want to try to make this whole situation with the kids easier."

"Ask questions?"

She nodded. "I'll answer anything."

His chest expanded as he sucked in a breath, and she remembered what it was like to snuggle into him and have him hold her, but she reminded herself that wasn't what this was about. She wanted to help him see that he hadn't misunderstood her. That she'd given him mixed signals.

"Okay," he said quietly. "My mom takes Ethan to church on Wednesday nights. Can you get away then?"

She'd have to figure out what do to with Toby, but that was her problem. "I can make it work."

Matt handed her the car keys, and she unlocked the passenger door. "Old school," he said, pulling Ethan free and setting him on the pavement in front of Anna.

"It's my dad's car."

"What happened to your old PT Cruiser?" he asked as he opened the back door and climbed in to grab the booster.

"My dad sold it."

"You loved that car."

She shrugged and gave him a pained smile. "We both know it was a piece of crap. It was always breaking down." She'd been upset because at that point she'd still planned on coming back. She'd paid for the used car herself with money she'd earned working at McDonald's during high school. She'd scraped together every penny she could until she could pay cash, and then the stupid thing had broken down more times than she could count. But if she were honest, she knew part of her was upset because it was where she and Matt had their first kiss.

Matt set the booster on top of the car and lifted Toby out of her arms. "Let me help you get buckled, okay, Tob?"

He nodded and released his hold on Anna and let Matt take him. Once he was settled on his booster seat, Matt grabbed the seat belt and pulled it over Toby's chest.

"What you saw in there was pretty scary, huh?" Matt asked, keeping his gaze on his task.

"Yes," Toby said quietly.

Anna heard the click of the buckle before Matt lifted up his face. "It's important that you know that your safety and Ethan's safety are the most important thing. When you are with me, I will always make sure you are safe. Okay?"

"Okay, Matt."

Tears filled Anna's eyes. Within seconds, Matt had driven home how badly she'd screwed up everything. Phillip had never been the man that Matt was, and it was obvious he would never be. Why had she been stupid enough to fall for Phillip's charm? How could she have been so careless that she got pregnant? Now her son was stuck with an irresponsible father who didn't give a crap about him when he could have had someone as wonderful as Matt. But she reminded herself that Matt wouldn't have been Toby's father, and she couldn't imagine her life without her son. She may have made countless errors getting to him, but she would never regret *him*.

Matt watched Toby's face for a moment longer, then got out of the car and shut the door.

"Thank you," Anna said in a whisper when he stopped in front of her.

"You're lucky to have him, Anna."

She tried to swallow the lump in her throat. "I know."

# Chapter Ten

Ashley was already seated when Anna and Toby arrived at the restaurant. She hopped out of her booth seat, letting out a happy shriek as she ran to them and pulled Anna into a hug.

"Oh, my God!" Ashley said, squeezing her tight. "It's really you!"

Anna laughed. "Yeah, it's really me."

Ashley leaned back and looked at Anna's face then batted her hair. "Look at you! You cut off all your hair! You look so hot and *sexy*."

Toby, who'd been standing behind Anna, leaned to the side to look at Ashley. He tugged on the bottom of Anna's shirt, looking up at her with wide eyes. "She said a bad word."

Ashley bent over at the waist until she was eye level with Toby. "Yes, I did." Then she looked up at Anna and stage-whispered, "What did I say?"

Anna laughed. "The S-word, but never mind." Then she hugged her friend again. "I've missed you."

"I've missed you, too." Ashley made a big production of looking on either side of Anna. "Where's Toby? I thought you were bringing Toby."

Toby poked his head around Anna's leg. "I'm Toby."

"Nah," Ashley said, still looking. "You can't be Toby. The last time I saw Toby, he was a little baby and you're a big boy."

Toby giggled. "I grew up."

"*What?* No way."

"Yes way."

"Well, come on, big boy," Ashley said, waving wildly toward the table. "Let's get you something to eat so you can grow even more."

Toby giggled and climbed into the booth, staring at Ashley.

"His accent is adorable," Ashley said, then turned to Toby, leaning closer. "Keep the accent and you'll have the *lay-dees* lining up to date you."

Toby scrunched up his nose. "Eww…girls."

Ashley pointed at him. "One day you'll say 'yay girls' and I'm gonna remind you of that."

He giggled again.

Ashley looked over at Anna, turning serious. "I can't believe you're back."

A lump filled Anna's throat. Being with Ashley only brought home how few friends she had in London. "I'm not *back* back, Ash."

"But you're here right now. That's what matters."

The waiter came over to take their drink order, then before he walked away, he looked at Toby. "Have you seen the giant fish tank?"

Toby looked at him wide-eyed. "No."

"Want me to show you?" the waiter asked, turning to Anna. "If that's okay with your mom, of course."

"Can I?"

Anna smiled. "Sure." She slid out of the booth and Toby followed the waiter.

"I can't believe the overprotective mother I know let her son walk off with a stranger," Ashley said in disbelief.

Anna pointed toward the back corner. "I can see the fish tank from right here. He's not out of my sight."

Ashley grinned then turned serious. "Then let's not waste the few minutes we have talking about fish tanks. How's your job?"

"Good."

Ashley narrowed her eyes. "Try again. I know your boss is an asshole."

Anna twisted her mouth as she kept her gaze on her son. Ashley was right. Her boss would be back in the London office on Monday, and she wouldn't be surprised if she got an e-mail telling her that her services were no longer needed. With everything else going on, she'd tried to put it out of her mind, but she couldn't ignore the fact that she was likely to be jobless in a few days.

Anna considered changing the subject, but she hadn't voiced her fears to anyone. Who better to share them with than her best friend?

She cringed. "I might lose my job."

"What?" Ashley's mouth dropped open. "What happened?"

Anna pushed out a huge sigh, trying to hold back her tears. "My boss hates me being here, and our bank has faced some bad publicity lately, which has caused some of our clients to transfer their accounts. I have a higher retention rate than some of my coworkers, but I'm the lone woman and...I'm here. I can't carry my full load right now so I'm the easy pick."

"Oh, Anna. I'm sorry."

Anna forced a smile and swiped a stray tear.

Ashley leaned closer and said with a teasing glint in her eyes, "I'm not sure if you've heard this yet, but we have actual jobs here in the US."

Anna laughed and rolled her eyes. "Ash."

"Sure, your job paid well, but you've also told me it costs a fortune to live there."

"I can't move."

"Why not?"

"One word. Or to be more specific, one person. My ex-husband."

Ashley's brow lowered in confusion. "Phillip? I thought he disappeared from your life years ago."

"Maybe so, but our divorce decree says I can't move Toby out of the country."

"Why didn't you tell me this before?"

"I don't know... Maybe because I was embarrassed over being stupid enough for marrying him in the first place."

"You divorced him five years ago. When was the last time he saw Toby?"

"Three years ago. When Toby was two."

"And how long has it been since he paid child support, because the last time I asked, it had been years. He obviously has no interest in his son at all. Just move here. Toby will be enrolling in high school before Phillip figures it out."

"I can't do that..." Anna said. "It's a legal decree, Ashley. I'm not sure I can get away with it. What if I move here and Phillip raises a stink? I have no idea what the ramifications would be."

"Then find out."

"*Ashley.*"

"Do you have an attorney?"

She couldn't believe she was having this conversation. Sure, it would be great to live close to Ashley, but the truth was that Ashley wasn't here all the time. She could move anywhere in the United States and probably see her friend as much. But they weren't talking about Anna moving to the United States. They were talking about her moving back here, to Blue Springs, and damn if her heart didn't trip a little at the thought.

Matt.

No. Matt didn't fit into any of this. If she wanted to do the right thing, she would go back to London and forget him. Or at least go back to the regret she'd lived with for the last twelve years.

But even so, she couldn't help thinking it would be good to be free of the hold Phillip had on her son.

"I had an attorney, but he retired and died soon after. I tried to call him about the child support issue and then I decided receiving no child support was worth not having Phillip in our lives."

Ashley pulled out her phone and started typing. "I have the perfect attorney for you. She's like a barracuda."

Anna made a face. "A barracuda? I don't know."

Ashley's face jerked up. "Uh, Anna, you want a barracuda. Blair Hansen is the best. Her specialty is helping women whose husbands are trying to screw them over. My sister says most of the divorce attorneys around town are scared to face her in court and almost always settle."

"But Phillip's attorney is in London."

She resumed her typing. "Just talk to Blair, and if she thinks you need a British attorney, she'll let you know. She can probably help you find one."

Anna's phone dinged and she reached for it in her purse.

"That's from me," Ashley said. "It's Blair's contact

information. Listen, she's hard to get into so be sure to tell her that you know Maddie Ternary's sister. They went to high school together."

"Thanks. I'll think about it."

Toby came running back to the table, his eyes glittering with excitement. "Mummy! Mummy! They have a shark!"

"A shark?" Anna said. "No way! That tank doesn't look big enough."

"It's a tiny shark, but Steve says it will get bigger."

"That's so cool."

"Can I get a shark?"

Anna laughed. "No, you can *not* get a shark."

"Can I get a puppy? Coach Matt is getting a puppy for Ethan. Ethan showed me where he's going to put his food and water."

"Well, that's wonderful for Ethan and Matt, but how would we have a puppy in our condo back in London?"

Toby's brow furrowed. "Will I get to see Ethan when we move back?"

Anna's body tensed. "When we come back for a visit."

"Not every day?"

"No, baby. Just every so often."

Crossing his arms across his chest, Toby scowled. "I don't want to go back."

Anna put an arm around his back. "Let's talk about it later, okay?"

"Okay," he said, but he didn't look happy about it.

"I want to hear more about Coach Matt," Ashley said.

And Anna wanted to tell her, but little ears were listening. "I'll tell you, but I don't want to send Toby off to look at the shark again."

Toby's gaze jerked up. "I get to go see the shark again?"

"No. Steve will be back soon to take our order so I want

you to stick around." She looked over at Ashley. "I think we can talk as long as we don't get *too excited*, okay?"

Ashley's eyes bugged out. "I'm going to get excited?"

"I don't know if 'excited' is the right word, but I expect *some* reaction out of you."

Ashley rubbed her hands together. "Okay. Go on."

"Coach Matt is Matt Osborn."

She narrowed her eyes in concentration. "Matt Osborn... oh!" She covered her mouth with her hand. "Oh, my God!"

Toby was bent over the table, coloring his kid's meal menu. Anna darted her eyes down to him and grimaced. "*Someone* doesn't know anything about any of that."

"What's with the face?" Ashley asked. "Are you constipated?"

"Oh, my God. Didn't you get what I meant?"

"I think a dead man could get what you meant."

Anna rolled her eyes. "The less he knows, the better."

"I get that, but how did this happen?"

"Toby is best friends at school with Matt's nephew and Matt is their soccer coach."

"And this was all just serendipity?"

Anna hadn't looked at it that way, and she wasn't sure she should be feeling flutters in her stomach at the thought. "Yeah."

Toby glanced up at the mention of his name. "Coach Matt is awesome. He helped me kick the ball at his house today."

Ashley gave him an exaggerated look of surprise. "You guys went to his house?"

Anna caught her gaze. "Toby had a playdate with Ethan."

Ashley watched her for a moment. "So all is forgiven?"

"Not exactly..."

Ashley continued to pin Anna with her eyes.

Anna sighed. "It's been strained, and we haven't had a

chance to talk except for social pleasantries, but I asked him to meet me for coffee on Wednesday night to discuss it."

Toby's mouth dropped open. "You're going to see Coach Matt? Can I come, too?"

Anna plastered on a smile. "No, because Ethan will be with his grandmother. I was going to see if Auntie Ashley could hang out with you."

Toby frowned. "But why do you need to talk to him?"

Why indeed? "So we can talk about soccer drills."

"Oh."

Anna glanced up at her friend. "What do you say, Auntie Ashley?"

Ashley's previous merriment had faded. "Do you think this is a good idea?"

"None of this is ideal," Anna said, choosing her words carefully. "But our current living conditions aren't the best. My dad is even crankier than when we were kids, and all three of us are living in a very small house. Ethan is the one bright spot Toby has and now he has soccer, too."

"You broke Matt's heart, Anna. Are you sure you want to open up old wounds?"

Toby's face jerked up. "You made Coach Matt have a heart attack?"

Anna inwardly groaned. "No, silly. Coach Matt didn't have a heart attack." Then she added to throw him off track, "He was worried about Ethan's grandmother. He thought someone broke into her house."

"Did someone?"

"I don't know." How did she not ask? She'd been too busy getting flustered at having him so close.

Ashley pulled out her phone and swiped a couple of times. "Hey, Toby. I have a game on here you might like, wanna try?"

Toby's eyes widened as he glanced up at his mother. "May I?"

She smiled. "Sure."

After Ashley set up the game, and Toby was engrossed within seconds, she leaned closer and lowered her voice. "Tread lightly, Anna. He wasn't the only one who ended up with a broken heart."

Anna sighed then whispered, "I know, and I'd planned to put Toby on another team, but he's just so happy. Besides, when I suggested moving Toby to *you-know-who*, he said he could handle it."

Ashley snorted. "Well, of course he's going to say that. He's a big, badass man. He's not going to admit to weakness."

Well, crap. Ashley was right.

"Look, sweetie," Ashley said, covering Anna's hand with her own. "I know this has eaten you up since the day you turned down his proposal, but some things are just better left in the past."

"But what about closure?"

Ashley snorted. "That only works in books and movies."

"What if I want to do it anyway? Will you watch Toby?"

"Of course, I'd love to hang out with the little guy. I'm not telling you not to do it. Just be careful."

"I will. I don't want to hurt him any more than I already have."

"It's not him I'm worried about."

\* \* \*

"Let me get this straight," Kevin said while leaning back in his patio chair, balancing a beer bottle on his knee. "You sent your nephew off with the bitch who turned you down? I know you tried to call me while I was helping Holly with a wedding, but you could have called Tyler."

Kevin calling Anna a bitch sent a jolt through Matt. "Don't call her that," he said in a low growl, despite the fact he'd called her that to himself more times than he could count.

Tyler's eyebrows shot up. "*Jesus.* You want her back."

Matt's back straightened. "No. I didn't say that."

"You didn't have to."

Matt pushed out a breath of frustration. Why hadn't he foreseen their reaction? "Look, her son is on my team. It's good to clear the air."

"I don't get it," Kevin said. "Why would you let him on your team? When did you become a fucking martyr?"

Tyler snorted. "You're seriously asking him that? It's Matt. 'Martyr' is practically his middle name."

Tyler's statement pissed Matt off, but it wasn't the first time he'd been called that. He cast a nervous glance at his nephew, making sure he was out of earshot. He was close enough to hear, but seemed too engrossed in passing his soccer ball back and forth with Tyler's seventeen-year-old brother, Eric, to notice.

"Look," Matt said, leaning over his legs. "I had no idea who he was at first. I only knew he was Ethan's new best friend. Besides, I'm a fucking grown-up here. I have to think of Ethan."

"Would it really be the end of the world if her son changed teams?" Tyler asked.

"Ethan hasn't been taking Abby's absence very well. He's been acting out lately, so if I can include his best friend on his soccer team, why not?" He took a sip of his beer and looked Kevin in the eye. "Mom's going to ask Abby to legally give me temporary guardianship of him."

"Wow." Kevin took a long pull from his bottle. "Are you sure you want to do that?"

"I love him. You know I've always wanted kids. This is my shot."

Kevin leaned forward. "You're only thirty-four, man. There's still lots of time."

"I'm sick of waiting. I'm done putting my life on hold. I love Ethan, and I'm lucky to have him in my life."

"But what happens when Abby finishes school and takes him back?" Kevin asked. "What will you do then?"

Matt had considered it more times than he could count. He'd told himself not to get too attached for when that very thing happened, but it was impossible. Ethan needed him to be there for him, and that meant opening his heart even if he risked getting it broken. "I'll deal with it when the time comes."

"I just hate to see you get hurt any more than you already have."

Tyler's younger brother had walked up toward the end of the conversation and listened as he drank from his water bottle. "It's a lot like me and Tyler."

Tyler's head jerked up in surprise. "How so?"

"We started hanging out, then Lanie was moving to Atlanta, and I told you to go even though you didn't want to leave me."

"It's not the same," Tyler said quietly.

"But it kind of is. I got really used to you being there for me. I felt like you were leaving me behind."

Tyler stood and moved in front of his brother. "Why didn't you tell me the truth? You gave me your blessing to go."

Eric looked his brother in the eye. "Because Lanie's awesome and you need her. I loved you enough to let you go."

He turned to Matt. "And you'll love Ethan enough to let him go, too."

All three men were silent for several seconds before Kevin blew out a breath. "Well, damn. He's right."

Tyler gave Matt a sad smile. "I told you the kid gave good advice."

"No shit," Kevin muttered then took another drink.

The men were silent again before Tyler said, "But none of that changes the fact that you have to deal with Anna. So you keep her kid on your team, but that doesn't mean you have to fraternize with her. Tell her you've changed your mind, and you don't want to meet her."

That was the smart thing to do, Matt knew it, and while he also knew he should listen to his friends' advice, he decided to go with his gut on this one. "No. I want to hear what she has to say. The boys won't be there, and it'll be in public. If it gets too weird, I'll just leave and be done with it. Besides, Toby says they're going back to England when his grandfather is better. It's not like there could be anything between us anyway."

"If you're going to do this," Kevin said with a frown, "don't let her take your heart again when she leaves."

It was too late for that. She'd taken it twelve years ago, and he'd never gotten it back.

# Chapter Eleven

Late Sunday afternoon, Anna stood on the sidelines of the makeshift soccer field in the grassy area next to the church, amazed at the progress her son had made in only a few practices. While she was shocked that he wasn't the worst player on the field, it was the fact that he was having so much fun that got to her. His face beamed with happiness as he listened with rapt attention to Matt's instructions.

"Looks like someone's got a bit of hero worship," a woman said next to her.

Anna's back stiffened, prepared to deal with some soccer mom's hostility, but she was greeted with Phyllis's smiling face. "Yeah."

"I hear Matt's been working with him."

What did Phyllis know? Anna wasn't sure how to answer. Some of the other mothers were a little territorial when it came to *Coach Matt*, especially the ones whose kids had been on his team the previous season—territorial and cliquey. But Phyllis seemed above all the nonsense so Anna decided to confide in her. "Ethan is best friends with Toby. They had a playdate on Saturday."

Phyllis leaned closer and lowered her voice. "Ethan told me, but don't be spreading that around. Lisa over there would flip her shit." They both glanced over at the pony-tailed woman who was intently watching what was happening on the field. "On second thought," Phyllis teased. "Maybe we should."

"No way," Anna said, tugging her sweater closed tighter and bracing herself from a sudden cool gust. "I'm trying to fly under the radar."

Phyllis laughed. "Honey, it's too late for that."

Anna wasn't happy to hear that piece of information, although she wasn't surprised. She knew she'd made an entrance at the first practice, but she'd hoped things would die down.

"So…" Phyllis said. "I don't see a ring on your finger. Are you divorced or are you one of those liberated women who have a baby on their own?"

Anna usually hated sharing personal information with people she hardly knew, but she was beginning to like Phyllis. "If only I'd done it on my own—it would have been a lot easier."

"Messy divorce?"

"Just complicated," she said in a tone that suggested she didn't want to talk about it.

"Okay," Phyllis said, nodding her head. "You don't want to give details. I can appreciate that. Were you divorced recently?"

Anna shot her a mock glare then grinned. "When Toby was a baby."

"Any significant others in your life?"

Anna laughed. "Why does it feel like you're signing me up for a dating site?"

"No worries there," Phyllis said with a grin. "Besides, you don't need a dating site."

Anna twisted around to face her. Something about Phyllis's tone of voice sent off alarm bells. "Why not?"

"It's so obvious there's a man right here at this practice who's interested in you."

Anna shot a glance back to the father who had been at Tuesday night's practice. "Um...I'm not looking for a man right now."

"Honey," Phyllis said, waving her hand. "That's what they all say."

Phyllis fell silent, but a few minutes later Matt looked over at the parents. "I need a volunteer to help me with a drill."

Several mothers lifted their hands, saying, "Me! I'll help!"

But Phyllis gave Anna a shove, making her stumble forward. "Anna should help. Isn't the UK the land of soccer?"

Anna gave Matt an apologetic look. "I don't have to—"

"Hurray!" Toby shouted. "Mummy's going to help!"

Ethan shared his friend's enthusiasm. "Yay!"

Both boys ran toward her and simultaneously held her hands as they dragged her onto the field until she stood in the middle of the group of kids.

Matt looked less than thrilled, but being Matt, he rolled with it. He grabbed a laundry basket full of pool noodles and said with a grin, "I bet you guys have been wondering what these are for. Do you think we're going swimming?"

The kids laughed and shouted, "No!"

Remy, the kid who'd given one of the mothers a bloody nose, started to rip off his shirt.

"Remy!" his mother shouted. "What are you doing?"

He gave her an exasperated look. "Coach Matt said we were swimming."

"And where do you plan to swim?" she asked, shaking her head.

He glanced around before understanding dawned. "Oh."

"Keep your shirt on," Matt said with a laugh. "You're about to fly a spaceship."

"Cool!" the boy said with wide eyes.

"I want to fly a spaceship!" several of the other children protested.

Matt held up his hands. "Everyone who wants to fly a spaceship gets to. That's why Toby's mom, Mrs. . . . Robins," he said, sounding like he choked on the name, "is going to help me. We're aliens and we're going to be kicking space rocks."

"Real space rocks?" Toby asked in a whisper as he looked up at Anna.

She smiled down at him. He'd been obsessed with the stars as long as she could remember. "No. I'm pretty sure they're pretend."

Disappointment filled his eyes. "Oh."

"Mrs. Robins is right," Matt said. "They're pretend."

"Uncle Matt!" Ethan shouted, waving his hand wildly. "Her name's Miss Anna. She's not a dragon."

Matt looked like he considered that debatable.

"Ethan is right," Anna said as she smiled at the kids. "I'm Miss Anna." Then since Matt didn't look like he appreciated the side bar, she said, "I'm excited to hear about your spaceships."

Matt ignored her and said, "Everyone gets a noodle and

that's your spaceship. You're going to hold it out in front of you." He pulled out a noodle and demonstrated. "Anna...and I are aliens with space rocks that we're going to be kicking at you. If we hit you, your spaceship gets damaged and you crash to the ground." He turned to his nephew. "Ethan, kick a ball at me."

Ethan shook his head with a serious expression. "No, Uncle Matt. I'm not an alien. Miss Anna has to do it."

Matt looked like his patience was wearing thin. Obviously, he wouldn't have picked her but he was stuck with her now. She intended to make the most of it. "Ethan, pass me a ball."

Wearing a huge grin, Ethan hurried over to a ball on the ground and kicked the ball to her.

"Good job," she said, stopping the ball with her foot on top. She glanced up at Matt to see if he was ready.

"So Miss Anna is going to kick the ball to me," Matt said. "But I can put up my force field and kick it away and not have any damage." He shot her a look. "Go ahead and kick it to me."

She kicked the ball and he easily deflected back to her. She stopped the ball with her foot again.

"See?" he said. "I saved my spaceship. Now I'm going to let her hit me with it and you can see what happens then." He glanced her way again. "See if you can get it higher this time."

She kicked the ball with the side of her foot and with more effort than before. The ball flew up and hit Matt in the side.

He started staggering around, waving his pool noodle wildly. "I've been hit." Then he started making alarm sounds mixed with sputtering as he careened to the right then fell to the ground with a loud crash sound.

The kids watched him with excitement, and when he sat up, he asked, "Who wants to be a spaceship?"

They all started yelling at the same time, and Matt got up and handed out pool noodles, but Toby stayed next to Anna's side and looked up at her with a worried expression. "Mummy, are you a scary alien?"

"No, baby," she said with a soft smile, smoothing his bangs away from his forehead. "I'm a nice alien."

Matt came over and swooped Toby off the ground and flew him like an airplane toward the laundry basket. "Captain Robins, we need you to man your spaceship."

He set Toby down while making noises like he was landing an aircraft then handed him the last noodle. "Do you accept your assignment, Captain?"

Toby giggled. "Yes, sir."

Matt grinned then jogged over to the pile of soccer balls, and dribbled one to the middle of the field for himself since Anna already had one. "Now if your spaceship crashes, you stay on the ground until only one spaceship is left. Everyone spread out, and Anna, why don't you come into the middle of the field."

The kids and Anna did as instructed, and when everyone was in place, Matt asked, "Ready?"

"Ready!" they called out.

"Go!" He gave a light kick to a girl next to him and she stopped the ball before kicking it back to him.

"Kick it to me, Miss Anna!" Ethan shouted from the back of the group, waving his pool noodle around.

Anna took her cue from Matt, and her first attempt was a gently placed kick to a boy to her side. He easily stopped it and kicked it back.

For the next five minutes, they played, Matt and Anna getting more aggressive as the game went on until there was only one kid left—Remy, who stopped the ball and kicked it right into Matt's gut.

He doubled over and Anna moved closer. "Are you okay?"

He glanced up at her with big eyes, and she started to freak out, worried he'd really gotten hurt until he mouthed with a thin, raspy voice. "Air knocked out..."

"That boy's dangerous," Anna said, only half teasing as she told the kids they could get up.

Matt seemed to recover moments later, and the kids jumped up and down, "Can we play again?"

For the next half hour, they played multiple rounds of the spaceship drill until Anna was sore and out of breath.

"Okay!" Matt said. "That was a great practice! Put your noodles away, and I'll see you on Tuesday night!"

"I had no idea I'd be getting such a workout," Anna said, leaning over and sucking in lungfuls of air.

"Thanks for your help," Matt said as he watched the kids put their noodles into the laundry basket.

"Cute game," she said, standing more erect. "Toby definitely got better by the end."

"Several of the kids did."

"Matt!" the woman with the ponytail called out.

Probably to reestablish her territory.

Anna knew the woman didn't stand a chance with Matt, but she couldn't stick around and watch other women trying to hit on him either. She needed to get out of there as soon as possible. "Let's go, Toby."

His face scrunched up into a pout. "But I'm helping Ethan put the balls in a bag."

Her options were to force him to leave and go home to her father, who had actually been nicer since her talk with him several days before, or she could suck it up and deal with her jealousy while her son was being helpful.

After the boys picked up everything several minutes later, Anna told Toby it was time to go.

He clenched his fists at his sides and glared up at her. "No."

Her eyes flew open in shock. She could count on one hand the number of times he'd been so obstinately disobedient. "Toby," she said, moving closer to him and keeping her voice down. "You picked up all the balls and now it's time to go."

"Ethan said I could go with him to Coach Matt's house."

She frowned. "Coach Matt didn't say anything about it to me, and even if he did—which I sincerely doubt—it's too late to go for a playdate on a school night."

He scrunched up his face. "You're so mean! You don't want me to have any friends!"

*Where had this come from?* She squatted in front of him, trying to keep her patience. Part of her wanted to just reprimand him and order him to the car, but the mother in her knew that this was so uncharacteristic that something had incited it. "Why are you so upset?"

Tears flooded his eyes. "I want to play with Ethan."

"And you just did during practice and a long time yesterday. Plus you'll see him tomorrow at school." She gave him a hopeful smile.

"Can I have a playdate with Ethan tomorrow at Grandpa's?"

She grimaced, already knowing this was not going to end well. "No, baby."

His back became rigid. "Why not?"

"A number of reasons. One, it's a school night. Two, I don't think Grandpa would like"—two rough and tumble boys underfoot—"a playdate. He doesn't like changes to his schedule."

A tear slipped down his cheek. "That's not fair."

"I know," she said, overwhelmed with guilt. "I'm sorry. Maybe we can figure out another option, but right now we have to go. Besides," she added, "six days isn't *that* long." But she knew six days was an eternity to a five-year-old.

To her dismay, Toby started to sob.

"Toby," she said, taking his hand in hers, but he jerked his hand free. She picked him up and started up the hill to her car, fully aware that half the mothers were in the parking lot watching in horrified fascination. She reminded herself that in less than two months, she'd never see any of them again, but instead of making her feel better, it only made her feel worse. One more drastic change for her sensitive son.

As soon as she reached the car, which was parked next to Matt's truck, she opened the car door to get him into the backseat, but he thrashed back and forth, trying to break free. It took her a half minute to get him into his booster and strapped in. She hurried into the driver's seat and turned the key, trying to stay calm when the car refused to start.

*Don't panic. Don't panic.*

Toby continued his meltdown in the back, only now he was shouting, "You hate me! Why do you hate me?"

It was all too much. Finding a home to put her father into. Dragging her son across the globe and back. Her confusing feelings about Matt. After she'd watched him with those kids and seen how kind he'd been to Toby... she knew she still loved him.

What in the hell did she do with *that*? It only made her feel hopeless.

And to top it all off, now she had to deal with the stupid car.

To her irritation, she started to cry.

A knock on the window made her startle and she jumped in the seat, even more horrified when she saw Matt bent over and peering in the window. She turned to face out the windshield. Maybe if she ignored him, he would go away. A quick glance in the rearview mirror confirmed that the other mothers were standing next to their cars, watching her.

"Anna," he said, his voice muffled through the glass. "Open the door."

"No. I'm fine."

"Anna."

She covered her face with her hands. Could she be any more embarrassed? She was used to dealing with cutthroat businessmen and associates and holding her own with an aloofness that had earned her respect, but now she'd been reduced to tears by a raging five-year-old and a fifteen-year-old car.

The passenger door opened and Matt climbed into the seat next to her. "What happened?"

Toby started to shout, "I hate you!"

Matt leaned closer and lowered his voice. "What set him off?"

Feeling like a fool, Anne swiped at a tear rolling down her cheek. "He wanted to go to your house. I told him you hadn't invited him, and even if you had, he couldn't go because it was a school night, but he insisted that Ethan had invited him."

Matt frowned. "I suspect Ethan did. He asked before practice, and I'd said no for the very same reasons."

"He's not usually like this," she said. "I know every mother probably says that, but in Toby's case, it's true."

"After spending time with him yesterday, I believe

you." He opened the door and got out, and she was sure he'd satisfied his curiosity and was leaving, but to her surprise, he opened the rear door and got into the backseat.

"Toby," he said, his voice low and calm. "Look at me."

The boy continued to cry.

"Toby," he said, more direct this time. "Can you stop crying so I can talk to you about Ethan?"

That seemed to stop his hysteria, but his chest still heaved as he struggled to catch his breath.

"I want you to take a deep breath," Matt said in a soothing tone. "Can you do that for me?"

Toby sucked in a breath and pushed it out immediately.

"That was good, but slower this time." Matt took his hand and held it tight and maintained eye contact with Toby until his breath was more even. "That a boy," Matt said with a soft smile. "You were upset with your mother, huh?"

He nodded, his chest still heaving.

"Your mom loves you. I bet she loves you more than anything but sometimes things get big and scary, huh?"

Toby nodded with surprise in his eyes.

"The next time things get too scary, tell your mom, or if I'm around, you can tell me, too. Okay? We'll help you before things get scarier."

"Okay," Toby hiccupped.

"We'll arrange a playdate for you and Ethan, but not on a school night. Ethan's not going anywhere. He's not going to make a new friend and forget about you. He wants to play with you, too."

"Okay," Toby said, sounding calmer.

Matt got out of the car and Anna flung open the driver's door, climbing out to intercept him. "How'd you do that? How'd you know what to say?"

He moved closer and lowered his voice. "Ethan. When he first started staying with me, he raged quite a bit." A sad smile lifted his lips. "The wife of one of my contractors is a child psychologist, and I asked for her advice. She said he felt like his life was out of control and he had no idea how to process those scary feelings, so they manifested into rage. You saw it yesterday at Chuck E. Cheese. That was his worst one yet. His mother…" His voiced faded and he made a face suggesting he regretted saying so much. He gave her a reluctant smile. "You're a great mother, Anna. This isn't your fault."

*Oh, but it was.*

She swiped at her cheeks again, sure she'd reached her quota on embarrassment for the next two years in less than ten minutes. Plus, she still had to deal with the stupid car. "Can you recommend a tow truck service?"

"Is something wrong with your car?"

"It won't start."

He hesitated, then said, "Let me take a look."

"No," she said emphatically. "That was not my subtle way of trying to get you to look at my car. It was a straightforward question."

He put his hand on her upper arm, and surprise filled his eyes then they darkened. "I know." His fingers dug in slightly and he moved a step closer. "You never played games when we were together, and I always appreciated your straightforwardness, which was why I was so shocked when…"

*When she turned down his proposal.* She shook her head. "Never mind. I'll just check inside the glove box and see if Dad has had it towed before."

His grip on her arm tightened. "Anna."

She paused, if for no other reason than his hand was on

her arm, and as pathetic as it was, she'd missed his touch. But she could swear he'd been affected by touching her, too.

Glancing around him to check on Toby, she saw that a few mothers were still in the parking lot, watching their exchange with open curiosity. "You're going to be the source of gossip at the next practice."

"You know I never cared about that shit. I still don't." He gave her a sad smile. "Believe it or not, a year ago I was the topic of much bigger gossip than this. I can handle it." He paused. "I guess the real question is if *you* want to deal with it."

"Can I handle women jealous over a nonexistent relationship?" She gave him a wry grin. "Please, in my world, I deal with misogynistic assholes without batting an eye. These women are nothing."

"Then there's no reason I can't check out your car before you call a tow truck, now, is there?"

But it was too close...too much like the times he'd helped her with her car before, making the pain of losing him even more agonizing.

When she didn't answer, he walked around her and got behind the wheel of the car. A few seconds later she heard the hood pop open, and Matt got out and walked around to the front of the car.

He lifted the hood and looked around, then closed her hood again. "Sadly, I haven't learned any mechanic skills since we were together. My knowledge is limited to rudimentary skills like jump-starting a car. Are the cables attached? Are the oil and gas in the proper tanks?" He grinned. "It seems all the above are in order."

"Thanks for looking," she said sincerely. "Now if you have a recommendation..."

"Actually, Tyler's dad has a mechanic's shop. An old car

like this…Tyler's dad's pretty old school, not to mention he's good and reasonable."

"Okay. Just tell me the name of the tow service and the garage, and I'll call them right away."

But Matt already had his phone out and was tapping on the screen.

"I can call a tow truck, Matt." She didn't mean for it to sound so defensive.

But he just smiled and lifted the phone to his ear. "I know you can." His expression changed. "Hello? Yes, I need a car towed to Norris Garage on Highway 40." He gave them the directions then hung up. "He said he'd be here in about fifteen minutes."

"Thanks."

"We should get Toby out. Maybe he'll be happy that he gets to ride with Ethan."

She squirmed. "Matt. You've done more than enough to help."

"Do you have someone to come pick you up?"

Ashley came to mind, but she'd mentioned she was doing something with her parents and sister tonight. "We'll be fine." She could call a taxi or an Uber.

Without saying a word, Matt opened the back door and poked his head in. "Guess what? Ethan and I get to take you home."

"Really?" she heard her son ask in excitement.

"Yep. So we have to get you out before the tow truck comes."

He climbed farther into the car, then emerged seconds later with Toby and his booster seat.

"You don't have to do this, Matt."

He glanced at her with a nearly expressionless face. "I know."

By the time the tow truck arrived, Matt had both boys buckled next to each other in the backseat of his truck. A light rain began to fall.

"You can wait in the truck, Anna," he said. "I'll make sure he's got everything he needs."

"*Matt*. I'm not some helpless female."

"You are the farthest thing from a helpless female I know. Yesterday I had a bad day and you stepped up and helped me. I'm only repaying the debt."

She suspected there was more to it, that this had far more to do with the fact he was a genuinely nice guy. She'd always appreciated and respected that about him before. Twelve years and a whole lot of life experience later, she appreciated it even more. "Thank you."

She got into the cab of the truck, relieved that Toby was more like himself and talking to Ethan about the spaceship drill. But if Matt was right, she wondered if she should take him to see a child psychologist. What if his absent father and moving here then back to England screwed him up for life? His acting out was a sure sign that he was in turmoil.

The rain began to fall in earnest. The driver's door opened, and Matt climbed in, rain droplets clinging to his hair and rolling off his jacket. "All set," he said as he started the truck.

Anna resisted the urge to reach up and brush the water from his hair.

"Uncle Matt," Ethan said, leaning forward and straining against his seat belt. "Can Toby eat dinner with us tonight?"

Anna worried she would set off Toby again when she told Ethan they had to go home, but Matt beat her to it.

"Not tonight, big guy. School night."

"Mummy?" Toby asked.

Anna tensed, prepared to deal with the fallout. "You heard Coach Matt. Maybe next weekend. Okay?"

"Plus you'll see each other at school tomorrow," Matt said, "and practice Tuesday night."

All this forced togetherness was killing her.

The boys talked about their teacher while Matt drove them to her father's house without asking for directions.

"You remembered where my father lives," she said in surprise.

"Of course," he said without further explanation.

By the time he pulled into the driveway, the rain had begun to pour down.

"I don't have an umbrella in the truck," he said with regret as he stared at the front door.

"Real men don't need umbrellas," she teased.

He grinned, that lazy, confidant smile that had always sent flutters through her stomach. Time hadn't changed that. She was playing a dangerous game.

His grin faded as he said, "Let me know when the car's fixed, and I'll help you pick it up."

"Thanks," she said, but she didn't plan to call him. She needed to cut this off, and the sooner the better. In fact, she was regretting asking him to meet her on Wednesday. Talk about self-torture.

He leaned into the back and helped Toby unbuckle his seat belt then pulled the booster seat into the front. "You and Toby can make a run for the front door, and I'll carry the booster seat for you."

Anna took it from him and looked away so he couldn't see how hard this was for her. "There's no sense in you getting any wetter than you already are. Besides, Toby's about to take a bath, so he'll be wet anyway. We'll be fine." She paused and looked into his face, hoping her words conveyed her sincerity. "Thank you for everything you've done...you've been so generous...I don't know how—"

"Anna." His warm eyes held hers. "Let's pick this up Wednesday night."

His words could have sounded ominous. Instead they sounded promising.

# Chapter Twelve

⁓

Matt was a good five minutes early, only making himself look even more like a desperate loser.

Anna hadn't asked him to help get her car and Tuesday's practice had been rained out. Matt hadn't seen or talked to her since Sunday night when he'd dropped her and Ethan off at her father's other than the mass text he sent about canceling practice (to which she didn't respond) and his text early today asking if they were still meeting tonight and, if so, they could meet at Starbucks at seven.

Her response: Thank you.

*Thank you.* What the hell did that mean? She was the one who'd asked him to meet her, but after the way they'd parted on Sunday night, he wasn't sure she still wanted to go through with it. What if it had been one of those spur-of-the-moment requests? The one you regret after a good night's sleep.

He sat at a table, slipping off his jacket in the too warm room and contemplating sending her a text to cancel when he saw her walk through the door. All reasonable thought fled his brain, and sitting back in his chair, he knew he wasn't going anywhere. The truth was he was at Anna's mercy. He always had been, and apparently, he still was.

*What an idiot.*

She saw him sitting at the table for two and headed toward him. She was wearing jeans that clung to her shapely legs and a pale blue shirt that did amazing things to her complexion. Her blond hair hung in loose waves to her shoulder, and she nervously tucked a strand behind her ear. "Hi."

"Hi."

She gestured to the counter. "I'm going to get a drink. I see you already got one. I was going to pay for yours, but you already got one." She paused and grimaced. "I already said that. I'm nervous. I guess I shouldn't have admitted that either."

Seeing her like this—betraying a rare moment of uncertainty when she was usually confident—reminded him of the woman he'd fallen in love with. He'd been drawn to her confidence back then and humbled when she felt comfortable enough to let down her guard and show him her rare moments of self-doubt. But he'd also been drawn to her utter goodness. She was a package of sexy and sweet, and he found her just as irresistible now as he'd found her back then.

He stood and reached for her hand before he realized what he was doing and dropped his hand in an awkward move.

She was leaving. She was flying across a damn ocean, and who knew when she'd ever be back, yet all he could think about was unfastening the buttons on her shirt so he could see more of her.

He fisted his hands to keep from acting on his thought.

"It's okay, Anna. I'm not going to bite." *Damn.* Wrong choice of words, because he was dying to lower his mouth to her full lips and rake his teeth across them.

She looked up into his eyes, and her lips parted, then she seemed to remember why she was here and took a step back. "I'm going to get a drink."

He almost offered to walk her to the counter, but he needed to let her set the boundaries here, and he needed to let her give her explanation. There was no doubt she had destroyed him when she'd turned down his proposal, but seeing her now and getting to know her again over the last few days, he knew she hadn't changed. He had no idea why she'd really turned him down, but she hadn't turned into the cold-hearted bitch he'd made her out to be.

She was back a few minutes later with a tea bag label sticking out from under the lid on her cup.

"You've learned to like tea?" he asked in surprise. "You used to hate it."

She eyed him as though looking for some hint of accusation, and he purposely kept his posture casual and nonconfrontational.

Shrugging, she lifted the lid off her cup and checked inside before putting the lid back on. "Couldn't be helped, I guess."

"What's the best part of living in London?"

She sat back and eyed him for several seconds before she said, "You're serious."

"Yes."

She was quiet for a moment then smiled. "That's so hard to answer. There's no one big thing, more like lots of little things."

"Such as?"

Her smile spread. "High tea, for one. They have the best

scones." She pointed in the direction of the bakery case. "Those things are sad imposters. And they serve them with clotted cream, which is like butter but twenty times more delicious and a fat content so high it should be illegal. And then there's the architecture and the history."

"You loved European history," he said with a genuine smile.

Sadness filled her eyes. "We talked about touring Europe after we graduated."

Instead he'd proposed. For the first time he wondered if they would still be together if he'd taken it slower. Or if he'd tried to understand why she'd said no.

"Have you traveled much of Europe?" he asked.

Again, she studied him as though trying to determine if he'd set a trap. "Not as much as I would have liked. In the beginning, I was working insane hours trying to prove myself. Once I was established...I don't know...it seemed like a lot of work. I wanted to relax. Then Toby came along, and I didn't want to travel alone with a toddler." She glanced down at her cup then back up into his eyes. "Matt, I owe you an apology of epic proportions."

"Actually," he said softly, "I think maybe I owe you one instead."

Her mouth parted in surprise. He was pretty sure that was the last thing she'd expected him to say.

It was the last thing *he'd* expected to say. He'd been stubborn and stupid. Why had he presumed the worst of her? The woman he'd grown to love would never callously hurt someone, and there was every indication that, at her core, she was still that woman.

"I'm serious," he said. "I was so busy consoling and coddling myself over how I'd been wronged, I never once stopped to think about how badly you had to be hurting, too."

"I . . . I don't know what to say." Her eyes shimmered with unshed tears. "I never wanted to hurt you, Matt."

"I know." And he did. Why did it take him so long to see it?

"Those fourteen months with you were the happiest of my life. But I was offered that job in London and I wanted it, *really* wanted it."

"Why didn't you tell me?" he asked quietly. "Why didn't you tell me you were considering it?"

"It's like I told you when you proposed. I knew you wanted to come back home and work with your dad. And I knew if I came back that I was never leaving, you know? I knew that if I was going to see the world, that was the time to do it." She gave him a sad smile. "The irony is I've seen a lot of the inside of my office, which admittedly has a great view of the London Eye and Parliament, but I've given my life to my job."

"Did you mean it when you said you weren't sure about getting married and having kids?" he asked. "We'd talked about it, Anna—getting married, having kids. I never once got the impression you didn't want those things. You have to know that hit me out of nowhere."

She leaned back and cupped her tea with both hands even though the shop was too warm. "I know. I'm sorry." She took a sip of her tea then set down the cup. "I knew about the job several days before you proposed. I was confused about whether to take it or not, so I called my mother." She frowned, her brow creasing as she glanced down at the cup. "I should have known better. She told me I was foolish to even consider it, that I was throwing something good away. You." She glanced up at him with glassy eyes. "The thing is, I knew she was right. I knew it deep in my soul, but she kept pushing marriage and kids and telling me that I'd screwed up my priorities. So I rebelled and told her I didn't want to get married and have kids. And while I was saying it to her, it sounded right. It sounded *true*. I didn't want to be tied down like she had been. But when I said it to you, I wasn't so sure anymore. Even so, I knew I needed to go to London. I couldn't marry you because I was afraid of living a larger life than my mother dared to have. I needed to marry you for the right reasons."

"For the right reasons? You didn't love me?" he asked, feeling pathetic for asking.

She gasped then looked at him in earnest. "I loved you more than I've loved any other man. Any other *person* with the exception of Toby, but that's not even a fair comparison because they are two completely different kinds of love."

He felt like a fool when his heart skipped a beat at her declaration. "I understand. I know from Ethan. I love that little guy more than I ever thought possible."

She nodded.

"But what about Toby's father?" he asked, needing to know even if it hurt. "You must have fallen in love with *him*."

She shook her head with a sad smile. "I won't deny I was drawn to him. He was charismatic and cocky and a bit of a bad boy." She made a face. "He was totally unlike you. I didn't realize the comparison until a few years later, but it's true." She sighed. "It was a disaster. I had no idea he was sleeping around while we were dating until I found out I was pregnant and went to his flat to tell him. He was in bed with another woman." A sardonic smile spread across her face. "Score one for karma."

"No," he said emphatically. "I never would have wished that on you."

She shrugged. "Nevertheless, the universe is a fickle bitch."

He couldn't deny it.

"We weren't married. We'd only been dating six months, and I thought the last three months were exclusive. Then...somehow, I ended up pregnant. My mother had just died. My father had a chip on his shoulder the size of the world. While I was home for the funeral, I began to suspect I might be pregnant, but I waited until I got back to London and made an appointment at the clinic to confirm it. I refused to take a home test, even though I knew. I just couldn't accept it."

He'd expected to feel some sort of vindication, but all he could think about was how terrible it must have been for her. She'd just lost her mother, found out she was pregnant, then discovered the father of her child had betrayed her.

Tears filled her eyes and her chin quivered. She took a breath then continued. "After I found him with his girlfriend, I'd changed my mind about telling him about the baby, but it slipped out in the heat of an argument." A tear rolled down her cheek. "You have no idea how badly I wished I hadn't told him. He's made my life hell ever since."

The protective side of him roared to life. "What has he done?"

She smiled and swiped absently at a tear. "I can see by the look in your eyes that you think it might have been physical. Trust me, psychological hell is just as bad."

He wasn't sure how to answer that.

"Phillip is five years older and his family had been pressuring him to settle down. He said he wanted to try to make us work. And even though we might be living in the twenty-first century, I was worried how my bosses and clients would have taken a single woman having a baby. The banking world is conservative. So...I married him." Another tear leaked from her eye. "The third biggest mistake of my life."

"Third?"

"The second biggest was telling him about Toby." She paused. "It was a rushed wedding. I was four months pregnant and his family did *not* approve. Neither did my father. He refused to come to the wedding. I felt so alone after my mother died, and you know I was never close to Dad. I thought I could make my own family. I was determined to make my marriage work and Phillip was so convincing. And at first, he was determined. But the closer I got to the delivery, the more freaked out Phillip became and the more he was ... gone." Defeat and embarrassment filled her eyes. "He missed Toby's birth."

"Please tell me he was out of town."

She shook her head. "He was at a pub getting drunk and going home with a woman he'd just picked up. And the only reason I found *that* out was because I called him to let him know he'd missed seeing the birth of his son. She answered, telling me he was sleeping it off."

"Anna, I'm sorry."

Anger filled her teary eyes. "No. Don't you dare feel sorry for me. I got what I deserved."

He stared at her in disbelief. "You really believe you deserved that?"

"After what I did to you? Yes. And more."

He shook his head, but her gaze was focused on the table.

"That was it for me. I realized that he'd never given up the other women, and he never would. I was done. I had the locks of my apartment changed, even while I was still in the hospital ward. I had Toby at three in the morning and Phillip came by the next day—not the same day, the *next* day, thirty-six hours later, walking in with a giant teddy bear and a cigar."

"He *what*?"

"I filed for divorce soon after I brought Toby home from the hospital, before I even went back to work early to compete for a big client when he was four months old. And even though his family didn't like me, Toby was their flesh and blood, and they refused to let me bring him back to the States." She grimaced. "That was mistake number four—not coming to the States to give birth. He has a dual citizenship, but I would have more rights if I'd had him here." She ran her finger around the lid of her cup. "My divorce papers say I'm not allowed to take him out of the country for more than four weeks."

"Then how did you bring him here now for this long?"

"Phillip doesn't know we're here and I'm fairly certain he won't find out. The last time I talked to him was three years ago."

"He doesn't see his son?"

"No."

"Does he pay child support?"

She didn't answer and Matt's mind went into overdrive trying to figure out how to help her.

A warm smile lit up her face even though her eyes still shimmered with tears. "Stop."

"Stop what?"

"I know you, Matt Osborn. You're sitting there trying to figure out how to fix this for me. And while I'm touched, it's not your problem."

He gave her a dubious look.

"Matt," she said with more force. She looked like she was about to say something, then closed her mouth before she said, "I didn't expect this to go so well."

He gave her a sheepish grin. "Honestly, neither did I. I was pretty angry when I saw you last week."

"But you're not anymore?"

"No. It's a lot easier to wallow in your self-righteous anger when you don't have to see the pain the other person has gone through."

Her eyes pleaded with his. "I'm truly sorry, Matt."

"Me, too."

They sat in silence, as though both were unsure how to handle this truce. He'd spent so many years trying to hate her, he was grappling with the feelings flooding in to replace it.

"So what about you?" she asked. "Did you ever marry?"

"No." He shifted in his seat, feeling even more foolish about letting her go a decade ago. "I dated several women, but none seemed right." No, Anna Fischer had ruined him for other women. They had all seemed like a pale imitation of what he'd always wanted: her. "I lived with a woman for several months last year, but she turned out to be a bank robber."

Her eyebrows shot up. "*What?*" She sat up straighter.

"Yeah..." He drew out the word, trying to determine how much to tell her. "She'd assumed an alias and was living a quiet life with me in Blue Springs. Imagine my surprise when the police busted in my front door to storm the place and arrest us both."

Her mouth dropped open.

"I was later released, but it still made the news. Business suffered for a bit."

"And your girlfriend..."

"Pled guilty to robbing banks in five states." He shook his head with a wry grin. "She told me she was broke. You think she could have shared some of the money with me. Or taken me on a trip to Fiji."

She gave him a wry grin. "She was probably afraid to leave the country."

He laughed. "True."

"Anyone else?" she asked, sounding hopeful.

"No." No one worth mentioning. He realized how pathetic he sounded and sat up with a smile. "But I bought my house soon after the incident and decided I didn't need someone to make my life complete. Dad died a couple of years ago, and I took over the business. Kevin moved back last summer, so now I have both him and Tyler close, and we see each other often. I have Ethan, and I love every minute I get with him. And soon I'll have a dog." He took a sip of his drink, embarrassed about sharing that last one. "For Ethan."

Sadness filled her eyes. "You always talked about getting a dog."

"The timing never seemed right until now." This was becoming far too introspective and melodramatic.

"Maybe losing your father spurred things," she said. "I'm sorry to hear about his passing. He was a great guy. What happened?"

"Heart attack."

"I'm sure he'd be proud of the way you're taking care of Ethan."

That filled him with more pride than he'd expected. "I'd like to think so. Mom had a hard time at first, but now she's dating." He made a look of disgust.

Anna laughed. "Spoken like a son."

Still cringing, he rubbed the back of his neck. "Yeah. I guess..."

"I always liked your mom," she said wistfully.

"She liked you, too. She took your side after the breakup."

"What?"

He smiled. "She said we were twenty-two and too young to tie ourselves down. I think she would have friended you on Facebook if she thought I wouldn't have been offended."

An uncomfortable silence loomed over them.

There was so much Matt wanted to know about her life, but he knew better than to push his luck. "Toby said you're here because your father's ill?"

She spent the next several minutes telling him about her father's broken leg and his doctor's concern about him being alone. Tears filled her eyes when she told him how she'd spent the previous Saturday touring an assisted living facility to move him to. "I have an appointment on Friday to visit another place in Lee's Summit, but even if it's better, he's still going to hate it." She shook her head. "I don't know how I'm going to tell him. He'll hate me all over again."

"All over again?"

"He was angry when I moved to London, then pissed when I came home for Mom's funeral and left again." She paused. "He's too frail to leave unattended, but there's no way he'd come to London. Even if he did, he'd be miserable...*we'd* be miserable."

"What about hiring someone to help him at the house?"

She shook her head. "He needs to be watched full time, or at least left alone for no more than a few hours. He broke his leg when he fell outside and his neighbor found him. If he'd fallen in his house, I have no idea how long it would have been before he was found." She paused and worry filled her eyes. "I'm not sure what I'm going to do."

"How long before you go?" he asked. "To London?"

And that was the question he'd been dying to ask since the moment she'd walked in the door. How long until she walked out of his life again.

"Five weeks."

"That's not much time."

She sighed and sank into her chair. "I know."

"If you need any help, let me know," he said.

She gave him a tiny smile. "You're doing it again. Trying to fix this for me."

"Ever heard of networking?" he asked with a wry grin. "I'm a business owner. I know a lot of people in the community." He dug his phone out of his pocket. "In fact, I know the director of nursing at a brand-new residential care facility that's set to open in another month. I can send her an e-mail and introduce you two then let you take it from there."

"I don't know what to say," she said, shaking her head. "You've been far nicer to me than I deserve."

Matt had a feeling she'd spent more than enough time beating herself up over the last twelve years. He reached across the table and grabbed her hand then squeezed. "Let's make a deal. Let's agree to let the past go and just move forward. Okay?"

Tears filled her eyes again, but she smiled as she nodded. "Deal."

He glanced down at his phone and resisted the urge to groan. "I'm going to have to leave so I'll be home when Mom drops Ethan off."

Her eyes flew open. "Oh. Of, course." She stood and picked up her purse. "Sorry to keep you."

"Anna." Matt stood and put his hand on her upper arm and felt a jolt of awareness shoot through him. He'd felt it when he'd touched her on Sunday night and he knew this was a bad idea, yet he was drawn to her regardless. "Don't be sorry. I wish I could stay longer." He dropped his hand before he did something stupid like try to kiss her. "Let me walk you to your car."

He expected her to protest, but instead she smiled softly and turned toward the door. They walked in silence until they reached her father's car. He almost commented on her not calling him to pick up the car from the shop, but stopped. The evening had cooled off, the air was crisp, and the sky was cloudless, revealing the stars. She looked up at him with her keys in her hand, and he didn't want to spoil this moment, didn't want to mar it with polite lies and half truths. They both knew why she didn't call.

He studied her, in awe that she was standing in front of him. How many nights had he conjured up her image in his head? How many times had he wished he could hold her again? Kiss her full lips and hold her body next to his as they made love. He couldn't have any of those things—she was leaving and they had no future—but he could look at her now, her face glowing in moonlight. He could commit this to his memory. A newer, happier memory to replace that night twelve years ago when his world fell apart.

"Matt..." she breathed out in a small sigh. He heard the sorrow in her voice, the regret in his name.

"I know." He took the keys from her hand and unlocked the door, then opened it and waited for her to get in. When she was seated behind the steering wheel, he handed her the keys. "Anna...thank you."

He didn't wait for her to respond, just turned and headed for his truck, wondering how he'd survive the next five weeks.

# Chapter Thirteen

Time to wake up, sleepy head!" Anna said, lying next to Toby on the bed.

He was burrowed under the covers and had an arm slung over his face.

"Toooobyyyy," she sing-songed as she put her cold hand under the back of his pajama shirt. "It's time to get ready for school."

He rolled to his side and made a groaning noise.

She lay still next to him, closing her eyes for a few seconds. Then she jolted upright when she realized she'd dozed off and searched frantically for the digital clock on the nightstand. How long had she been asleep? She exhaled in relief when she saw she'd been out for only a couple of minutes.

Sitting up, she rubbed her sleeping son's arm. "Time to get up. It's PE day."

That got his attention. He pushed back the sheet to look up at her. "We're doing fitness tests in PE today. I'm going to do *twenty* push-ups, Mummy."

She smiled. "Your arms must be getting so strong if you can do *twenty*!" She scooted to the edge of the bed and forced herself to get up. Starting her day at three thirty in the morning was beginning to wear her down. At least she didn't have to commute to work—the kitchen table and the bedroom she shared with Toby served as her office, but since her father could be left alone more frequently, she'd started working at Starbucks after she dropped Toby off at school, if for no other reason than the endless caffeine supply.

She'd made it to Thursday and still had a job, which helped relieve the tight band of anxiety squeezing her insides. Did that mean her boss had decided to keep her after all? One less thing to worry about.

Now that Toby was up, he bounded off the bed with energy that made her envious. "Mummy, it's soccer practice day!"

The thought of seeing Matt did weird things to her insides. What the hell was wrong with her? She wasn't in middle school. Not to mention, Matt was off limits. She needed to stay away from him.

Toby grabbed a pair of jeans and a T-shirt, then ripped his pajama shirt over his head and tossed it on the floor.

"Do you want pancakes this morning?" Anna asked, grinning at how quickly he went from sound asleep to bouncing around. "So you'll have strength for all your push-ups?"

"Uh-huh."

"Don't leave your clothes on the floor," she said over her shoulder as she walked out of the room.

She headed into the kitchen and made the batter while the skillet heated up. Toby came in moments later and sat at the small kitchen table.

"I see you're making flapjacks," her father said from the kitchen doorway.

Toby's eyes grew wide as his gaze lifted to his grandfather.

"Yeah," Anna said absently as her father sat next to her son.

"Have you got flapjacks in England?" her father asked Toby.

Toby's mouth dropped open and he glanced back at his mother. She smiled and nodded. Her father had made several efforts to reach out to Toby after her talk with him last week, and while Toby was still shy, he didn't act so terrified of him.

"What are flapjacks?" Toby asked in a whisper.

"What are flapjacks?" her father asked in disbelief. "Only the best breakfast food in the whole daggum world." He leaned forward and lowered his voice. "Some people call them pancakes."

Toby laughed and declared flapjacks to be the funniest name ever for a pancake.

Her father leaned back in his chair. "Once when I was your age, my mother made me tiny flapjacks and I tucked them into my pocket." Her father mimicked hiding tiny pancakes in his pants pocket. "And then I used them to play checkers."

"What's checkers?" Toby asked.

"What's checkers? Only the best game in the whole daggum world."

Toby frowned. "Oh."

"We have it here someplace," her father said, waving his hand absently. "Your mother used to play."

Toby's mouth dropped. "She did?"

"She was good, too. Sometimes she even beat me."

Anna set a plate of pancakes on the table along with a plate for her father. "And he didn't let me win either."

Her father put a pancake on Toby's plate then took one for himself. "I can teach you to play if you like."

"Really?" Toby asked.

"Yep. I'll have your mother find the set."

Toby grabbed the syrup bottle. "Can we play with flapjacks?"

"We'll save the flapjacks for our bellies."

Toby giggled and Anna stared at her father in disbelief. He glanced over at her and she mouthed, *Thank you.*

He gave a slight nod then plopped a dollop of butter on his grandson's pancake. "Let me show you the right way to eat a flapjack, grandson."

Anna turned her back to the pair to hide her teary eyes. Strangely enough, her father had never claimed Toby as his grandson so openly. Trying to forge a relationship with her son was one of the greatest gifts her father could have given her.

She cleaned up the kitchen, then glanced at the clock. "Toby. Time to go to school." She turned to her father. "I'm headed to Starbucks to get a few hours of work in before your physical therapy appointment. Do you need me to do anything before I go?"

The hard shell snapped back into place. "I'm a grown man. I don't need babysitting."

"I know, Dad, I..." Her voice trailed off. Some things just weren't worth the fight. "If you think of something in the next five minutes, let me know."

He refused to talk to her again before she left, but she made sure he had everything he needed next to his recliner—the TV remote, a fresh cup of coffee, the newspaper, and a sharpened pencil to do the crossword puzzle.

When she and Toby started to walk out the door, Toby stopped in the opening and turned back with a beaming face. "Bye, Grandad! Have a good day!"

Anna's back muscles tightened and she prepared herself

for the brush-off her father was sure to give her son, but instead, her father's tight jaw loosened and the hint of a smile tickled the corners of his mouth. "You, too, grandson."

Toby's smile spread and he bounded out the door, giddy over his newfound superpower—making his grandfather nice.

Memories of her childhood rushed back, when her father had been softer. Her mother had always had a way of taking off his edge, until she'd gone back to work when Anna had been in middle school. That was when she'd become more acquainted with the crabby man he was today.

Anna stopped and studied her father, trying to analyze his change in attitude with Toby, but any hint of his smile vanished and he glared at her. "What?"

Taking a lesson from her son, she gave him a soft smile. "Have a good morning, Dad."

He seemed surprised and said, almost without thinking, "You, too."

Anna remained lost in thought as she drove the short distance to Toby's school. She missed her mother so much. She was supposed to be there helping Anna navigate motherhood. She was supposed to be there, helping navigate her father.

She could hear her mother's voice in her head, encouraging her to continue to try to knock down her father's walls. Cracks like she'd seen this morning gave her hope. Maybe Toby was the key.

# Chapter Fourteen

*I'm a moron.*

Maybe it was a moment of weakness. Or maybe it was because this gave him the opportunity to see Anna, but he'd let Ethan convince him to invite Toby to spend the night on Friday. The next thing he knew, he'd pulled Anna to the side at Thursday night's soccer practice and extended the invitation.

She'd searched his face as though trying to figure out if there was an ulterior motive. "I don't know."

"I know Toby's never spent the night away from you before. And I warned Ethan it might not work out, so don't feel like you have to say yes. I understand it's difficult to trust people in this day and age."

Her eyes flew open and she gasped. "What? No! There's no one I trust more. It's just I don't know how he'll do. He might want to come home, and I'd hate to disappoint Ethan."

"How about we try it, and if he misses you too much, I'll bring him home?"

She frowned. "I couldn't ask you to do that. I'll come get him."

"We can work that part out later. Do you want to give it a try?"

"I'm game if Toby is."

And of course he was. And now it was five fifty-five, and Ethan was in the living room with his nose pressed to the window, waiting for his best friend.

"Did you order the pizza, Uncle Matt?"

Matt grinned. "Yeah, big guy. I ordered an extra cheese and a pepperoni."

Ethan swung his head around to face him. "Toby doesn't like pepperoni."

But his mother does. He gave himself an involuntary shake. *Stop.* "That's why we got one with extra cheese."

"He's here!" Ethan shouted, pushing away from the window and running to the door.

The boy opened the door and stood in the opening, hanging on to the doorknob. "Toby! Uncle Matt ordered pizza!"

About ten seconds later Toby appeared in the doorway, holding a small duffle bag in his hand. He stopped when he reached the threshold, twisting his mouth into a frown as he stared at Ethan then past him to Matt.

Anna appeared behind him and put a hand on top of his head. "Toby, you ready to go in?"

But Toby hesitated, looking unsure.

Matt walked over, suspecting Toby was having second thoughts. "Hey, Toby," he said. "The pizza should be here soon. Maybe your mom could stay and eat with us."

Wide-eyed, Toby glanced up at Matt then at Anna. "Mummy?"

Anna gave Toby a smile so beautiful it stole his breath.

"As long as Coach Matt doesn't mind." Her gaze rose up to Matt's face, but he couldn't read her expression.

"I ordered more than enough," he said. "And if you're here, I won't feel so bad about drinking a beer. After the week I've had, I could really use one." Then he realized he was putting her in an awkward position. "Unless you have plans. Or have to get back to your father." Oh shit, why hadn't he thought about her father?

A grin tugged at the corners of her lips. "Dad has a friend bringing him dinner tonight and they're watching some old war movie. I was going to go see a movie myself." She graced her son with that dazzling smile again. "But I think I'd rather stay and eat pizza with a few of my favorite guys."

The tension drained from Toby's body and a smile lit up his face. But Matt shrugged off the tension rolling up his back. She did *not* mean him with that phrase.

Ethan grabbed his arm and dragged him into the house. "Uncle Matt got an extra cheese just for you."

Anna still stood on the front porch and her eyes widened. "I hope you didn't order a cheese pizza just because of Toby."

"Cheese is the universal kids' pizza topping, right?" he asked, slightly unnerved that she still stood on the front porch. "Besides I got a pepperoni, too."

Hesitation flickered in her eyes. "My favorite."

"Is it?" he asked, feigning ignorance. "I thought it was the second most popular kids' topping."

Relief filled her eyes. "True."

He moved closer and lowered his voice as he said with an ornery grin, "You can come in, Anna."

A tiny smile ghosted her lips, and she took a step inside the house. "You really don't have to do this."

"Do what?" he asked as he closed the door.

"Invite me for dinner." She waved her hand as she lowered her voice. "I get why you invited me in, and I thank you for that. Toby wants to stay so badly, but he's also scared. My staying for a little bit will help ease him into it, but I'm sure we can get him transitioned before your pizza arrives."

"I think it's good if the boys see us getting along, don't you think?" he asked.

Her brow furrowed. "I hadn't realized we'd made them think we weren't." But then she shrugged. "But then again, they probably picked up the uneasy undercurrent. Kids are perceptive."

"Yeah," he said, watching her and taking in the jeans that clung to her ass like a second skin and the dark gray Beatles T-shirt that hugged the curve of her breasts. He wasn't sure what he'd agreed to but the view was distracting.

Glancing around his living room, she smiled. "Your house is lovely."

He was proud of his house. Kevin had flipped a house last summer and fall and had inspired Matt to buy his own. It had been one more step on the path to the new Matt, the one that accepted that life might not work out as he'd planned, so he'd find a new way. He was proud of the person he'd become.

But Anna was staring at the painted brick fireplace, the new hardwood floors, and the leather sofa.

And Matt was staring at *her*.

*Get your shit together, Osborn.*

Shifting her purse strap on her shoulder, she turned to look at him, and he realized she was expecting an answer. Had she asked a question? The last thing he remembered was her compliment about his house. "I bought it last year and spent my free time updating. The kitchen needs an overhaul, and so does the master bath. Most of what I've done has been cosmetic."

"It's very... warm and homey," she said with a wistfulness that filled him with questions.

She glanced into the kitchen and out the back door. "Ethan must love playing in that huge backyard."

"It comes in handy when he needs to burn some energy." He paused, wondering if he should bring up her personal life, but now would be a good time to find out if her spirit of openness had been limited to Wednesday night. "Toby said you live in a condo. That must be hard with a small child."

She grinned. "Toby's not like most boys. He's more quiet, more introspective." She paused and then seemed to consider her next words. "It makes me grateful Phillip has chosen to stay out of our lives. He wouldn't understand his son. He'd try to make him into... something else."

That caught Matt off guard, and his back straightened. "Into what?"

Her lips twisted and she shrugged, looking like she regretted bringing it up. "More of a guy's guy." Embarrassment washed over her face. "But he leaves us alone and we're happy."

*Was* she happy?

\* \* \*

Five minutes later, they were sitting on Matt's covered patio, eating pizza, while the two boys talked about a rowdy four-square game at recess that afternoon.

Anna tried to stop herself from stealing glances at Matt, but now that he'd let his guard down, she was more drawn to him than ever.

She should get up and go. That rom com movie started in ten minutes and she could be in her seat before the end of the previews. Toby was comfortable now and obviously happy. He'd be fine if she left. There was absolutely no reason for her to stay, yet she couldn't make herself go.

Leaning over to pick up her beer bottle, she noticed Matt glancing at her, and the look in his eyes told her that he was facing the same struggle.

How awkward would it be if she just got up now and left her half-eaten pizza slice and a half-drunk beer? That's what she should do. *Just go! Save yourself!*

"Tell us about your school, Toby," Matt said, jerking his gaze to her son.

He scrunched up his face in confusion. "It has an awesome playground, and sometimes a guy walks around in a tiger suit."

Ethan nodded. "I love that guy in the tiger suit. He roars really loud, but he's not scary."

Matt laughed. "That's the school you go to with Ethan. Your mascot is the Tigers. I meant your old school in London."

Toby made a face and half shrugged. "It was okay, but this one's better." He flashed a grin to Ethan. "I've got the bestest best friend in the world."

A knot of worry lodged in Anna's gut. A quick glance from Matt suggested he was concerned, too.

"You know we're only going to be here for another month," Anna said. "Then you'll go back to your old school."

Toby's mouth dropped open as he shot her a look of disbelief. "Why?"

"Because Grandpa will be better by then." She hoped. "Because I have to get back to my job." Before her boss fired her.

Tears welled in his eyes. "I hate your job! All you do is work at your job! I want to stay here where I can see you all the time and have sleepovers with my best friend."

She gasped, and shame and regret wove through her like a sharp-edged ribbon. She couldn't deny anything he'd said. But she didn't know what to do about it either.

"Hey," Matt said enthusiastically. "I thought we could watch a movie. If you guys are done eating, why don't you take your plates into the kitchen and go pick one out?"

Ethan glanced over at his friend then his uncle. "I don't want Toby to go away."

"He's not going anywhere tonight, big guy. You can have fun tonight, and we'll worry about the rest tomorrow."

The boys picked up their plates and went inside the house. As soon as the door closed behind them, Matt turned to her. "Anna, I'm—"

"Did you mean it?" she asked quietly. "Did you mean what you said?"

His voice turned husky as he kept his gaze on her. "About making the most of their time while they can? Yeah."

She pushed out a breath and stood, scared she was about to do something stupid if she stayed, scared she'd regret it for the rest of her life if she left.

Matt rose from his seat and moved toward her, approaching her slowly like she was a skittish animal, but then again, she was and so was he. Two wounded people with hearts that had never really mended. She'd tried to date other men, but they had all been a pale substitute for the man she wanted. The man she'd said no to.

Tears filled her eyes as she looked up at him, and a grin tugged at his lips.

"I've missed you, Anna."

"I've missed you, too." A tear rolled down her cheek.

He lifted his hand and brushed it away with the pad of his thumb. "Five weeks," he said softly. "Give me five weeks to get to know you again."

"Five weeks to break your heart," she said.

"Five weeks that will last forever."

Her chin quivered. "I can't stay."

He gave her a lopsided grin, his eyes glassy. "I never asked you to."

She laughed then leaned her forehead against his chest, the same solid chest she'd taken for granted all those years ago. She'd been young and stupid back then...what was her excuse now?

"I know you're leaving in five weeks. I know you can't stay. We'll worry about that tomorrow," he whispered. "I want you, Anna. I want every part of you that you'll share with me before you go. But what do *you* want?"

The longing in his eyes sucked her breath away. But could she survive walking away from him? "I want—"

"I got the movie, Uncle Matt!" Ethan shouted as he ran out the back door with Toby in tow. "We want to watch *The Lego Movie*."

Matt dropped his hand to his side and smiled at his excited nephew. "*The Lego Movie*! Haven't you see that about twenty times?"

"But Toby's never seen it. His nanny wouldn't let him."

Anna cringed. How would Matt react to the fact that Toby had a nanny? But he seemed to take it in stride.

"Then I guess we should ask his mother if he can watch it."

"Please, Mummy?" Toby begged, tugging on her shirt. "Can we?"

She put her hand on top of his head. "Well, after seeing Ethan's Lego Batman helicopter last week, I think you *should* see it, don't you?"

He nodded vigorously. "You're going to watch it, too, aren't you, Mummy?"

Her eyes widened. "Oh... This is *your* sleepover, Toby."

His smile fell.

Matt turned to her. "I'm not sure what movie you planned to see, but you're welcome to watch *The Lego Movie* with us. You should stay. It's a classic in the making."

"Please?" Toby asked. Ethan joined in, and they sang a chorus of *please*'s.

She wasn't sure she *should* stay. She hadn't answered Matt's question, and she didn't really have an answer. Leaving him before had been the hardest thing she'd ever done, but to start something knowing it would end? That seemed like emotional suicide.

So why was she considering it anyway?

She looked up at Matt, searching his face.

"Stay," he said softly.

Her other choice was to see another movie or find something else to do for the next couple of hours so her father could hang out with his friend. But the bottom line was that she didn't want to go. "Okay."

The boys broke out into excited shouts, then ran inside with the DVD case. "I'll get it set up, Uncle Matt," Ethan shouted over his shoulder.

Matt grinned. "You won't regret your decision. It should have won movie of the year."

She laughed. "Now I'm scared."

"As far as kid movies go, I'd give it a nine point five."

"So you're saying this won't be so bad after all."

"I promise you won't regret staying." Then he gestured to the door.

What did that mean? That she'd enjoy the movie or, after their discussion, that he'd make it worth her while?

But Toby was in the doorway, motioning for her to come inside.

Ethan had put the disc in the player when Anna entered the living room, Toby tugging on her hand. "Where should I sit?" she asked, taking in the sofa, love seat, and chair.

"Anywhere you like," Matt said from the kitchen.

She heard the microwave turn on and soon the sound of popping popcorn. Toby made the decision for her, leading her toward the love seat and sitting next to her.

Matt joined them within a minute or so, carrying a large bowl of popcorn and several glasses of water on a tray.

"Popcorn!" Ethan said excitedly. "Come on, Toby!"

Toby jumped up and reached for a handful of popcorn.

"Sit with me, Toby," Ethan said, plopping on the sofa.

Toby sat with him then gave his mother a guilty look, but she smiled. She wanted him to learn to separate himself from her, even if it stung a little.

Matt started the movie then sat beside her, his thigh brushing hers.

*He's playing dirty.* Yet she didn't object. His warmth spread into her leg, traveling to other parts of her body that had no business getting heated from the mere touch of his jeans-covered leg.

The movie started and the boys quieted. She'd been up since three, and she'd been stressing over what to do about her father when she went back to England. The soft cushions and the rhythmic crunching coming from the boys soon made her drowsy, and Matt's warm body next to her just made her even more relaxed. Laying her head back against the seat cushion, she closed her eyes just for a moment, then drifted off to sleep.

# Chapter Fifteen

D id you see Batman, Mummy?" Toby asked. When she didn't answer, he leaned forward to look at her. "Mummy?"

Matt glanced down at Anna, confirming that she was still asleep. Her head was leaning against his upper arm, and it had taken everything in him not to wrap his arm around her. "Shhh," he said quietly as he lifted his finger to his lips. "Your mommy's asleep."

"She fell asleep during the best part," Ethan said in disbelief.

Toby shrugged. "She does that a lot."

"Falls asleep *in movies*?"

"We snuggle together in bed and watch TV before I go to sleep," Toby said. "She falls asleep before I do, but she gets up before the rooster crows."

"You have roosters?" Ethan asked.

Toby started to giggle.

"Is that an English saying?" Ethan asked. "What does it mean?"

"I don't know. My grandpa says it," Toby said, "but her clock says three-zero-zero when the alarm goes off."

Anna got up at three every morning? But then Matt remembered she said she was working while she was here, and with the time difference, it made sense.

When the movie ended, Anna was still asleep and the two boys had droopy eyes. He considered waking her, but decided to put the boys to bed first. He slid out from next to her, relieved when she shifted and leaned her head against the back of the love seat.

He convinced them to quietly brush their teeth then go into Ethan's bedroom. After they were tucked into Ethan's full-size bed, Toby's grin fell.

"Mummy didn't tell me good night."

Matt was torn. Anna obviously needed her sleep, but he doubted she wanted to spend the night sleeping semi-upright on his love seat. Should he wake her now and let her tell her son good night, or see if Toby could go to sleep without her? Which would Anna prefer?

"*I* can tell you good night," Matt said as he sat on the edge of the bed. "I have lots of practice with Ethan."

Toby shot a questioning glance to his friend.

Ethan nodded. "It's true. He was bad at first, but he knows what to do now."

"Okay." Toby sank back into the pillows and looked up at Matt with trusting eyes.

This was Anna's son. While he could choose to see Toby as an example of what he'd lost with her, he decided to look for the good. Toby was proof that Anna was a remarkable mother. Just like he'd known she would be.

"When she falls asleep with me at Grandad's, she snuggles me close," Toby said. "But back in our condo, she tells me a bedtime story."

"Oh!" Ethan said. "Uncle Matt reads me part of a story every night. We're reading Percy Jackson."

"What's that?"

"What's *that*?" Ethan asked. Then he launched into an excited explanation about the middle-school-aged demi-god.

Matt almost picked up the Percy book, but instead grabbed another book off the shelf. "Let's read this one tonight... *The Miraculous Journey of Edward Tulane*."

"Why can't we read Percy Jackson?"

"Because it's not fair to Toby to start in the middle of the story."

Ethan seemed to accept his decision and lay back on his pillows.

Sitting on the edge of the bed, Matt began to read about the china rabbit, Edward, and his ten-year-old owner, and how she loved Edward but he was too selfish to love. He stopped after the third chapter and set the book on top of the nightstand. "Time to go to sleep."

"Why didn't the rabbit know how to love?" Ethan asked.

"I guess he was too selfish."

"Will he stop being selfish and love Abilene?"

"I guess we'll find out."

Matt glanced down at Toby, worried at the way his mouth tilted into a frown.

"Does your mom do anything else when she puts you to bed?" he asked.

He nodded then shot a worried look to Ethan before looking back at Matt. "My bunny," he whispered, and his eyes darted to his small bag on the floor.

Matt squatted next to it and pulled out a small light blue bunny. "This guy?"

He nodded, casting another concerned look at his friend.

Matt handed the stuffed rabbit to Toby and tucked the covers around him.

"Is his name Edward?" Ethan asked.

"No," Toby said, burying his face into the animal. "His name is Mr. Whiskers."

"Ethan," Matt said, "aren't you missing someone, too?"

Ethan nodded then reached behind his pillow and pulled out a worn-looking stuffed bear. "This is Douglas."

A look of relief spread across Toby's face.

"Okay, time for sleep," Matt said as he leaned over the bed and kissed Ethan on the cheek.

He started to rise, but Ethan pulled him back down. "What about Toby?"

"Toby might not want me to kiss him good night."

"I do," the little boy whispered.

Matt pressed a kiss to his forehead.

He rose and walked out of the room and heard the boys' voices.

"I wish I had a dad," Toby said wistfully.

Ethan's voice quickly followed. "I have a dad and Uncle Matt, and Uncle Matt is better. You should wish for Uncle Matt."

Overwhelmed with emotion, Matt headed back to the living room. He needed to wake Anna up so she could go home to her father, but he was surprised to find her sitting upright on the love seat.

"I just put the boys to bed. Toby seems to be doing okay, but if you want to check on him..."

She gave him a soft smile. "I heard."

"You did?"

Embarrassment tinged her cheeks. "Not everything. You finished reading and then got Mr. Whiskers. Thank you."

He sat down next to her. "He's a good boy, Anna. You're lucky to have him."

"I know." She glanced down. "I should go."

"Can you stay for a little while longer?"

Her blue eyes looked into his. "I'm not sure that's a good idea."

"How long was your dad's friend going to stay?"

"Until ten or so."

"It's barely past nine. Which means you have more time." He scrambled to find a reason for her to stay. "I can build a fire in the pit on the patio and we can roast marshmallows."

She laughed softly. "Are you trying to tempt me with s'mores?"

He grinned. "Maybe…"

Still chuckling, she got to her feet. She gave him a reluctant look, and he was sure she was going to tell him good night, but then she stared into his eyes. Her reluctance faded and a small smile replaced it. "You know that's my weakness. Lead the way, oh tempter…"

Was it wrong that he hoped to tempt her into so much more?

*   *   *

They went outside and he gestured for her to sit while he started the fire. "I'll get the stuff to make the s'mores," he said once he'd gotten the fire going.

He left her alone with the roaring fire and her thoughts. She was tempted, so tempted, to take him up on his offer to make the most of her five weeks, but this didn't affect only her. It affected Toby, too. If she started something with Matt, wouldn't it be selfish to give her son a taste of a wonderful father figure, only to take him away?

He returned a few minutes later, juggling a box of graham

crackers, a bag of marshmallows, a couple of chocolate bars, and two metal sticks. "I checked on the boys, and surprisingly, they're already asleep."

"Then you're magic." She was about to tell him that she'd decided to leave, but what harm could there be in a few more minutes? She took the roasting stick he offered.

He laughed then tossed her the bag of marshmallows as he put the box of crackers and chocolate on the small table between them.

"Can I ask you a personal question?" she asked softly.

He glanced up in surprise. "Yeah."

"How did you get custody of Ethan?" When he didn't answer after several seconds, she said, "If it's too personal or painful or...just forget I asked."

He shifted in his seat as he opened the box of graham crackers. "No. It's no secret. I was just thinking about the difference between you and Abby."

"Where *is* Abby?"

"In Oregon. In medical school."

"Really?" Anna asked in surprise.

"Yeah." He shoved a marshmallow on the stick, and considering the amount of force he used, she wondered who he was imagining skewering. "When she graduated from college with a premed degree, she was only a few months from delivering Ethan. Her shotgun marriage lasted three years, and now she's back to pursuing her dream since a premed degree won't get her a decent job." He paused. "The plan had been for her to go to a med school close to home, but the only school she was accepted to was in Oregon. Med school and rooming with another med student meant bringing Ethan would be difficult. So...he stayed here. He was with Mom at first then she went on a trip and he stayed with me. He's been here ever since."

"That's a big commitment." Not that she was surprised. Matt had always been loyal to his family and friends.

"Maybe," he conceded. "But I don't mind. I love having Ethan."

She stabbed her own marshmallow and put it in the fire. "But he's had some trouble adjusting?" Then before he could misconstrue her comment, she added, "Toby's had trouble adjusting to our move. He's finally feeling like he's found his place here and..."

"You're about to move him again."

"Yeah." And it always came back to the fact that she was leaving.

He put his marshmallow into the flames, keeping his gaze on the fire. "Do you ever think about fighting your ex on your divorce decree?" he asked, then he shook his head. "I'm sorry. You don't have to answer that."

She didn't answer, mostly because her brain was flooded with questions. She hated her son being tied to a man who didn't care about him, yet she wasn't sure she should risk upsetting the apple cart. "I can't stay, Matt."

"I know. That's not why I mentioned it." He glanced over at her. "You and Toby deserve better, Anna."

She wasn't so sure *she* did. Matt may have forgiven her, but she wasn't sure she'd forgiven herself.

Her marshmallow caught fire, and she jerked it out of the fire, blowing on the flames to put them out. The marshmallow drooped from the metal stick and fell on the concrete.

"Oh, crap," she said with a grin, hoping to lighten the mood. "I'll clean that up."

He laughed. "One more reason to get a dog."

"Are you really going to get one?" Anna asked. "Toby won't stop talking about it."

"Yeah," he said while he grabbed the marshmallow bag and fished one out. "I'm thinking about going to the animal shelter tomorrow." He handed her a marshmallow and asked, "Want to come?"

"Matt..."

"Anna, I know I'm pushing—"

*"Matt."*

"But it could be fun and—"

*"Matt!* Your marshmallow's on fire."

"What?" He turned and saw the fiery blob, then jerked it out of the fire. It flew through the air and landed on the cushion of the chair next to Anna. The cushion began to smolder.

"Oh, shit!" he exclaimed then ran into the house.

While the cushion hadn't burst into flames, the smoke was increasing and the smell of burnt plastic filled her nose.

Anna tugged off her canvas loafer and started beating the cushion, but the melted marshmallow stuck to the bottom, producing long strings of burnt sugar.

Matt emerged with a pot in one hand and a lid in the other, and before Anna could ask what on earth he thought that would accomplish, he tossed the pot filled with water on the smoke.

The water splashed off the water-resistant cushion and onto Anna's jeans.

"Oh, shit," Matt said, tossing the pot into the grass then covering the smoke with the glass lid.

Anna gasped as the cold water hit her legs, then she started to laugh.

Matt looked up at her like she'd lost her mind, then he grinned.

"What's so funny?" she asked, tilting her head to the side.

"I was about to ask you the same thing."

She gestured toward the pot lid. "It's obvious you were never a Boy Scout."

"Hey," he protested with a laugh. "In my defense, I seriously doubt there's a badge for putting out marshmallow fires."

She grinned. "I'll give you that, but I'm pretty sure there's a badge for dealing with fires in general."

"If I remember correctly," he said in a low voice, "I was convincing you to come to the animal shelter with us."

"You're not going to let this go, are you?"

"No," he said, shadows from the flames dancing on the side of his face. "I'm definitely not letting go."

Was he talking about the trip or her? She took a step back, suddenly flustered. She wanted him to be talking about her, and that was a very bad idea. She had to think of Toby. "Don't you want to make it a special trip for just you and Ethan?"

"No, Ethan seems happier when Toby's around, and right now, I'm looking for anything to make him happy." He took a step closer and his voice took on a sultry edge. "What would make *you* happy, Anna?"

What would make her happy was standing right in front of her, and she was struggling to remember why this was a bad idea. "I have an appointment at one," she said. "Another assisted living center tour. With the friend you recommended."

"We can work around it."

She should turn him down. She knew she should, so why was she saying, "Okay."

He smiled, looking more like good-natured Coach Matt and not Alpha Male Matt, the man she'd gotten to know well in her bed twelve years ago.

Damned if she didn't want Alpha Matt.

He was less than two feet from her, watching her with an intensity that suggested he knew he was making her squirm and loving every minute of it.

"Great," Matt said, as though he hadn't made the air temperature rise twenty degrees just from the timbre of his voice. "If you want, Toby can stay with us when you go to your appointment, and then we'll all go after you're done."

"Yeah." It was a great plan, but standing this close to him made her nervous. She didn't trust herself to walk out the door without doing something foolish, like kiss him, because right now that seemed like a real possibility. "I should go." She took a step back and lost her footing.

Matt reached for her, snaking an arm around her back and pulling her upright against him.

Anna sucked in a breath at the contact. Her hands rested on his chest, and she realized it was just as solid as she'd remembered. Shivers ran up her arms and she found herself molding her body to his.

His hand stayed in place on her back, pulling her even closer.

She knew she should back away, but she wanted this, wanted him, and that was dangerous. She was a mother now. Her son had to come first.

"I can't stay, Matt," she said again, feeling like a broken record, but she had to make sure he didn't feel deceived by her again. He deserved full honesty. "I have to think about Toby. I can't hurt him."

He looked surprised. "Anna, I would never willingly hurt Toby."

"But this…us…if we do this…" Did she confess her son's deepest desire for a father to love him and her worry that this would only confuse him? Was it her secret to tell? "I have to think about Toby. And Ethan."

"We're not going to hurt them, Anna."

"We might. If we get too close." *I might get hurt if we get too close.*

*Too late for that . . .*

He kept his hand on her back, and lifted the other to the side of her neck. He didn't answer, at least not with words. He lowered his face, his lips gently brushing hers.

Her breath caught. His touch was like a jolt of electricity to her heart, bringing her back to life.

"Then just tonight," he whispered. "They're sound asleep. They'll never know."

They wouldn't know, but *she* would. Could she sleep with him and walk away?

She should leave right now and forget he kissed her, forget feeling his arms around her, forget the longing stirring deep inside. Only she couldn't forget. Now that she'd had a taste of him, she couldn't walk away.

She looked up into his eyes. "Just tonight?"

"Your rules, Anna. I'll take whatever you give me." His words could have come across as resentful, but he looked far from it. His eyes were hungry. "Just tonight."

*What harm could come from just tonight?*

She lifted her hands to his face, holding him close as she pressed her lips to his.

As though released from his restraint, he took over and his tongue tangled with hers.

Anna clung to him. She'd forgotten how he could kiss her so thoroughly and leave her breathless and begging for more. And she wanted more. *Now.*

Blindly reaching down, she grabbed the hem of his T-shirt and lifted it over his head, momentarily breaking contact with his lips, before finding him again. Her hands slid over his bare shoulders, then down his upper back as she reveled in the muscles beneath her touch.

Matt's hands were at her waist, tugging on her own shirt and lifting. She laughed when he pulled it free, leaving her in her boring ivory bra. She expected him to kiss her again, but he kept his hand on her lower back, pressing her firmly against his growing erection. He lifted his free hand to her shoulder, his fingertips tracing a slow trail down the rise of her breast, then dipping under the edge of her bra until he found her nipple.

Her back arched as she sucked in a breath. He kissed her, less frantic but just as demanding.

She placed her hands on his chest again, needing to hold on to some part of him. Her world was turning, and he was her anchor, holding her in place.

Reaching behind her, he unhooked her bra and tugged it free, then unfastened the button and zipper on her jeans. He pushed them over her hips and to the patio floor and she realized she was standing in Matt's backyard wearing nothing but her panties.

She pulled back and looked around the yard behind her. "Matt."

"No one can see us," he said as though reading her mind. "The trees out back block the view from the neighbor behind me, and the privacy fence blocks out the neighbors on the side."

"You're sure the boys are asleep?"

"Sound asleep." He unfastened his own jeans and pushed them down, taking his underwear with them so that he stood in front of her completely naked, his erection jutting out in front of him.

She felt a thrill rush through her. She'd spent the last five years being Toby's mother; it felt good to do something so wanton.

His hand firmly grabbed her hip and pulled her to him. "Birth control?" he asked with a grunt.

"The pill."

"I can get a condom…"

"God. No."

His mouth lowered to hers again and his hand slid from her hip, over her butt cheek. He backed up and sat on the wicker love seat, tugging her down to straddle his thighs. Then he kissed her with over a decade of missed passion.

She kissed him back, running her hands over his chest and his arms, wanting to touch him. She needed to make sure this was real and not one of her countless dreams of him.

His hands cupped her breasts and a jolt shot to her core when he brushed both nipples with his thumbs. He slipped one arm around her lower back as his mouth left hers, sliding down her neck with a mixture of nips and licks, down her collarbone. He continued his downward trek until he reached her breast.

Anna arched her back as his mouth covered her nipple, driving her crazy with his tongue and his teeth. His free hand slipped under the edge of her silky panties and into her folds, giving her even more blissful agony. Then he kissed his way to her other breast, resuming his torture.

She ached for him, deep inside, more than just her core, her soul. She needed him. She'd always needed him.

Anna rose up on her knees, reaching to her hips to tug off her panties, but Matt brushed her hands away and ripped the fabric from her body.

She gasped, even more turned on than before, as though that was even possible.

Still on her knees, Anna cupped his cheeks with both

hands. She stared into his lust-filled eyes, and another ripple of want washed through her. He was holding back, she could see it in his eyes, and she smiled as she caressed his cheek with her fingertips, wanting to drive him as wild as he was driving her.

He smiled at her, a combination of the good man she knew him to be and a man desperate to claim her. It only confirmed what she already knew—there would be no other man for her. She needed both sides of *him*.

Anna slid her hand to his chin, running the pad of her thumb over his full bottom lip, and he surprised her when he sucked it into his mouth, his tongue playing with the tip.

She closed her eyes and let out a low moan.

Matt released his own guttural noise as he grabbed her hips and tugged her down, her opening over the tip of his erection.

Anna moved her hands to his shoulders, her eyes locked with his as she slowly lowered herself over him an inch, then rose again until he was just at her entrance, then repeated, sliding down only a fraction of an inch more.

"If the name of this game is Drive Matt Crazy, you're succeeding, Anna," he grunted as his fingers dug into her hips.

Leaning into his ear, she sucked his earlobe into her mouth as she rose, then nipped as she lowered herself a tiny bit more. "You always used to love when I drove you crazy."

He grunted, his firm hands holding on to her to keep her from lowering again. Instead his mouth covered her nipple and mimicked what she'd just done to his ear.

She moaned and he chuckled as he slipped his hand between her legs again and found her sensitive nub. She started to lower onto him, but his arm slid around her waist and held her up where he wanted her.

"Matt..."

His mouth moved to her other breast as his dexterous fingers had her on the brink of climax. But he sensed she was close, and he withdrew his hand as he lifted his head, looking into her eyes with an expression she couldn't read.

She used the opportunity to resume her previous task, but instead of her slow glide, she lowered and fully took him.

His eyes widened as she squeezed her muscles around him and rose again.

Twelve years ago, they'd been like a well-rehearsed orchestra, each piece knowing their parts to crescendo to a mind-blowing climax, and nothing had changed in the time they'd been apart.

They found their rhythm, each thrust sending Anna higher and higher until she was so close she could hardly breathe. She arched her back to take him deeper and felt his hand on the middle of her upper back, giving her support. Her nails dug into his shoulders and he gave another thrust that lifted him off the seat, pushing even deeper, and she cried out, coming apart at her very core.

This man was her undoing. She'd just made the second biggest mistake of her life...the first had been losing him twelve years ago.

# Chapter Sixteen

As Matt came to his senses, he realized the only woman he'd ever really loved was naked and draped across his chest. It felt like a dream, but she was here. He felt the heat of her body on his, her warm breath on his neck.

Anna's head nestled on his shoulder, and he stole a glance at her face. Her eyes were closed and she looked so thoroughly satiated that his masculine pride grew. A short blond wave was pressed to her forehead and he lifted his hand to brush it away.

Anna shivered and Matt wrapped his arms around her back, trying to keep her warm from the chill of the evening air.

He felt like an idiot. So much time wasted. Why had he never tried to see her side of things?

She stirred and looked up at him with a troubled expression, but it quickly faded, and she reached up and kissed him with such tenderness he felt like he'd been kissed by an angel.

And that was when he knew he was in deep shit. He was stupid to think he could sleep with her and just let her go. He was going to be heartbroken all over again.

"I have to go," she said softly against his lips.

He couldn't keep the pain out of his voice when he said, "I know. I knew that going in." But knowing it and *knowing* it were two different things.

Her body stiffened slightly and she sat up. "I meant I have to get back to my dad."

She stood and grabbed her jeans.

"Anna. I'm sorry. I didn't think..." God, he was an utter idiot. And was even more of an idiot as he drove himself crazy, watching her pull her jeans over her bare thighs and her naked ass. Her ripped panties were over by the hammock.

"It's okay. It's true." She sounded resigned as she fastened the button of her jeans then grabbed her bra, turning her back to him as she slipped it on.

He moved over to her and gently pushed her hands away, taking over the task of fastening the hooks. Her hands fell to her sides, her body tense as he quickly clasped the metal hooks and pressed his chest to her back. She leaned back against him and released a soft moan.

She wanted him again. The growing erection pressed to her back proved he wanted her, too.

His mouth lowered to the curve of her neck. He pressed a trail of hot kisses up to her jaw, then impatient, he spun her around, his mouth capturing hers, hungry to taste her again.

Her hands wrapped around his neck, clinging to him as she kissed him back with an urgency of her own.

But then she stepped back and shook her head, a soft smile curving her lips. "I really have to go."

Breaking free of his loose hold, she moved over to her

shirt, which was lying on the edge of the fire pit, only a foot from having ended up in the flames. "Good thing your aim was off or I might have had trouble explaining to my father where my shirt went."

She started to put it on, but Matt gently grabbed her forearm and stopped her, looking down into her face. "Tonight with the boys was fun, wasn't it?" he asked.

She laughed. "I fell asleep."

"You were exhausted." He kissed her again. "But before, with the pizza and the boys. It was good."

"Yeah..."

"So let's have tomorrow. And as many days as we can before you go."

Her eyes turned serious. "I want this more than you know, but the deal was only tonight, Matt. I made that very clear." She shook her head and looked away. "I knew this was a mistake."

He was scaring her off. "No, Anna. Even if this is the only night I get with you, it's not a mistake. No regrets." He wrapped his arms around her and pulled her flush against his chest, kissing her as though this was his last time to do so. For all he knew, it was. "I've been waiting twelve years to touch you again. Kiss you again." He leaned over and kissed her to prove his point. "If you get back on a plane tomorrow, I won't have a single regret over this." Then a new fear hit him. "Do you?"

The emotion in her eyes flickered before she gave him a sad smile. "No."

He smiled back. "But what happened tonight has nothing to do with my invitation for tomorrow."

She narrowed her eyes. "You expect me to believe that?"

"It's a trip to the dog shelter. With two five-year-old boys. Nothing romantic about it." When she didn't disagree with him, he added, "Think how much Toby will love seeing the dogs. And you know he'll have more fun if you go, too."

Amusement washed over her face. "You fight just as dirty as you used to."

*You have no idea.*

He had to find a way to ease her fears over hurting or confusing her son. Toby and Ethan would miss each other when Anna and Toby left, but he wasn't going to use it as an excuse to keep the boys apart. It would send the boys the message that it was okay to turn your back on a friend because his friendship had an expiration date. And he definitely wasn't ready to give up on Anna. He may have agreed to only tonight, but now that he'd held her in his arms again, he wasn't ready to let her go. Not while he still had time with her.

She stepped back and pulled the T-shirt over her head, then bent down and picked up her shoes, the sole of one of them covered in sticky marshmallow. "Now I really have to go." But she hesitated, casting a glance toward the house and reminding Matt that she'd never left Toby overnight before.

He reached out for her arm, stroking lightly. "If he's missing you in the morning, I'll give you a call straightaway."

The tension in her shoulders eased. "I need to take Dad to run a few errands. It might be easier if Toby's not with us."

"See? It works out."

She hesitated. "Okay. Thanks." Opening the back door, she headed into the house.

Matt started to follow her then realized he was stark naked. The boys might be asleep but he would be hard pressed to explain why he was chasing after Anna without any clothes on should one of them wake up.

He jerked on his jeans, leaving the fly and button undone, then scooped up his shirt and walked in the still open back door.

He panicked when he didn't see her in the living room, and was just about to run out to the driveway when he saw her coming down the hall from the bathroom with her shoes in her hand.

"What?" she asked in a whisper when she saw the panic on his face.

He reached for her and pulled her close. "I thought you left."

A hesitant smile cracked her lips, and she ran her fingers through her tousled waves. "I figured I shouldn't go home looking like a teenager slinking through the door after having sex with her boyfriend in the back of his car."

If he freaked out over the thought of her leaving tonight without saying good-bye, how was he going to handle it when she left for good?

He was pretty sure she was thinking the same thing when her smile faded and tears filled her eyes. "Maybe this really was a mistake."

His head was suggesting the same thing, but deep down in his gut, he knew that wasn't true. He needed her and he'd take her for as long as he could get her. "No." He kissed her again. "You and I were never a mistake."

*   *   *

The next morning Anna's father wanted to know when she was going to pick up Toby, and none of her answers had satisfied him.

She was helping him out of the car in the grocery store parking lot when he said, "You hardly let that boy out of your sight, yet you dropped him off yesterday evening and you're not getting him until after lunch?"

She was struggling with missing Toby, but she wasn't about to let her father know. He'd always told her mother that she coddled Anna too much when she was younger, and Anna was much more of a helicopter parent than her laid-back mother had been. She couldn't bear to hear it from her father right now, especially since things had been so much better between them this week. She shrugged. "It's Toby's best friend."

He leaned on the walker and started shuffling toward the store. "And how many kids did he spend the night with when you were living in London?"

"None, but that's beside the point. He's older now."

"He's barely five and you're one of the most high-strung mothers I've ever known."

She tried not to let him see how much his insult hurt her. "He's almost six, and I have to start cutting the apron strings at some point."

"Yeah, but I figured that wasn't going to happen until he was twelve or twenty-one."

She cast a glance at him and saw his grin. "Okay, so I am a bit of a helicopter mother."

"Which makes it even more strange that you left the boy last night, and he's still gone sixteen hours later."

"His best friend's uncle happens to be his soccer coach."

"What does that have to do with anything?"

She resisted the urge to groan. "Ethan lives with his uncle."

"And who's his uncle?"

"Toby's soccer coach," she said, hoping to throw him off.

"And what are you doing this afternoon?"

She sure couldn't tell him about the tour at the residential place, and she wasn't sure confessing the rest of her plans was good either, but she refused to lie to him. "Ethan and his uncle are going to look at dogs at the animal shelter and invited us to come along."

His eyes narrowed as he studied her. "So it's a date."

"No," she said, becoming unnerved when she felt her face get hot. "Matt just thought Toby would like to come and invited me, too."

Now she had her father's full attention. "Matt? Matt who?"

Oh, crap. She hadn't meant to let his name slip. "Dad..."

He shook his head. "You could never pull one over on me when you were a kid and you're still incapable of it." He stopped his forward motion and turned to her. "But I'll let it drop for now."

Had he figured out that Matt was *her* Matt? Surely not or he wouldn't let this go so easily. Her father had never been a huge fan of Matt, but then her father had never been a huge fan of any of her boyfriends. Hell, when she thought about it, he wasn't a huge fan of *anyone*.

The shopping trip lasted an hour, with her father exhausted, and half the grocery list was still unpurchased. She tried to get him to use the motorized cart, but he refused, saying it was for invalids. He'd worn himself out and yet still insisted he didn't need the rest.

Once she got him and the groceries settled in the car, he said, "I changed my mind about the hardware store. I just want to go home."

"If you tell me what you want, I can run in and get it," Anna said. "You can wait in the car."

His head slumped against the passenger window. "No. I just want to go home."

"Dad, you're making great progress. The physical therapist said so on Friday."

"But not fast enough. I'm still using this damn walker instead of a cane. And you're leaving in a month."

He knew the stark reality, too. It might make the conversation about moving into a residential care apartment less of a shock, but she doubted it would be any easier.

Tears welled in her eyes. "We'll figure it out, okay?"

He didn't answer, so she started the car and headed home.

"I miss your boy," he said gruffly. "We were supposed to play checkers this afternoon."

She cringed. How could she have forgotten? She was surprised he actually wanted to play with Toby, but then she wasn't. Toby had wiggled his way into her father's heart. "You can play after I bring him home."

He didn't answer and she considered canceling the trip to the animal shelter, but then he said, "Don't you stop that boy from going to see those dogs. He'll have a lot more fun with them than an old fart like me."

"He likes being with you, Dad. I love seeing you two together." Her voice caught and she took a breath. "Thank you."

He released a grunt. "I don't want him to go back to England and remember me as an old shit."

"I'll do a better job of calling," she said. "How about I get you a smart phone, and I'll teach you how to make video calls?"

"Yeah. Maybe."

When she showed up in Blue Springs a month and a half ago, she thought she'd be chomping at the bit to leave. But leaving was becoming harder by the minute. How was she going to leave her father completely alone?

\* \* \*

Matt wasn't surprised when he saw Toby watching for Anna in the window. Toby had been excited to find out that he was staying with Ethan until the afternoon, and even more excited to find out that he was going to the animal shelter, but by lunchtime it was obvious he was missing his mother.

Matt could relate, not that he could tell Toby. He'd barely slept last night, alternating between replaying his time with Anna on the patio and trying to figure out a way for her to stay. He could hardly wait to see her again, and he had no idea how he was going to keep his hands off her when she walked in the door.

"When's my mummy going to be here?" he asked for the third time in a half hour. "How much longer?"

Matt put the lunch plates in the dishwasher and turned it on. "It's going to be at least another hour. How about we go in the backyard and practice some soccer passes?"

Ethan had tried to cajole Toby out of his sadness, but with each time Toby mentioned missing his mother, Ethan became sadder, too. Ethan walked over to Matt and tugged on his arm.

Matt squatted and looked his nephew in the eyes. "What's wrong, big guy?"

"I miss my mommy, too."

*Well, shit.* He wasn't sure soccer was going to fix this. He considered taking them to the pet store to get supplies, but Anna hadn't left Toby's booster seat.

"Somebody's here!" Toby shouted, then added, sounding less enthusiastic, "But it's not Mummy."

Matt moved to the window and pushed aside the drape. "It's Grandma." *Thank God.* Ethan loved her and hopefully Toby would be intrigued enough to forget about missing his mother for a bit. But he also worried about the reason she was here.

Ethan raced to the front door and out into the yard. Toby followed behind him, but stayed in the doorway.

Matt rested a hand on Toby's shoulder as they watched Ethan greet his grandmother.

"Grandma! Grandma! Guess what? Toby spent the night!"

Matt's mother's eyes widened and a smile spread across her face. "That's *wonderful*." Her gaze shifted to the door as she noticed the boy in front of Matt. "Is that Toby?"

"Yeah!"

"Ethan," Matt called out to him. "How are you supposed to answer a grown-up?"

"I mean, yes, ma'am."

She laughed. "You're becoming quite the gentleman. Will you introduce me to your friend?"

Ethan grabbed her hand and pulled her up the steps. "Grandma, this is my bestest friend in the whole world, Toby. Toby, this is my grandma." Then he looked up at Matt. "Did I do it right?"

He grinned, pride and love filling his chest. "Yeah, big guy. You were perfect."

Matt's mother's eyes twinkled. "Nice to meet you, Toby," she said with a huge smile. "I've heard quite a bit about you."

Toby watched her with wide eyes. "Hi."

Matt backed up, guiding Toby back into the house as Ethan and his grandmother walked inside.

Ethan grabbed his grandmother's hand and pulled her toward the sofa, then sat next to her while Matt and Toby moved to the love seat. "Grandma! We had pizza, and Toby likes cheese pizza so we got one for him."

She beamed at the boy. "Wasn't that thoughtful of you?"

Ethan's mouth twisted. "It was Uncle Matt's idea."

"Well, then both my boys were thoughtful." She shot a glance to Matt and he tried to read her face.

"Toby's mom fell asleep during *The Lego Movie*!" he said in disbelief. "Can you *believe* it?"

"I told you that Mummy gets sleepy at night," Toby said, sounding defensive. "She can't help it."

Matt patted Toby's leg and the boy looked up at him. "It's true."

"I know," Matt said. "Ethan didn't mean anything bad by it."

Matt's mother's gaze shifted to him. "Toby's mother spent the evening with you?"

Ethan laughed. "No, Grandma. *Toby* spent the night, but Miss Anna was gone when we got up this morning."

"Toby's mother went home after the boys went to sleep," Matt added so she didn't read anything more into it.

"She didn't need to get home to her father?" his mother asked.

Matt froze. *Oh shit.* How did she know about Anna's father?

His mother noticed his reaction then said, "I know Toby's here while his mother helps her father convalesce. A broken leg, if I remember correctly."

"Yeah," Matt murmured, realizing he was looking guilty as hell, although when he thought about it, what was there to feel guilty *about*?

Ethan tugged on his grandmother's sleeve. "Toby's grandpa's last name is different than Toby's, just like you and me, Grandma," Ethan said. "Toby's last name is Robins and his grandpa's last name is Fischer."

"Albert Fischer," Toby added.

She looked momentarily startled but quickly recovered. "Oh, well, I sure would love to meet your mother sometime."

"Okay," Toby said. Suddenly overcome with shyness, he hid his face in Matt's arm.

Without giving it a second thought, Matt wrapped a comforting arm around the boy.

"I brought you a present," Matt's mother said as she reached into her handbag and pulled out a small box.

"*Star Wars* Legos!" Ethan shouted as he reached for it.

Matt's mother held it out of his grasp. "I didn't know Toby would be here or I would have brought two. But I know you'll be a good friend and share it with him, won't you?"

"Of course, Grandma. Toby's my *bestest* best friend."

She handed over the box with a smile. "That's my boy. Why don't you and Toby take it to your room so I can talk to Uncle Matt."

"Okay!" Ethan took the box and showed it to Toby. "Look, Uncle Matt!"

Matt glanced down at Toby, who was still plastered to his side. "What do you say, Toby? Want to help Ethan make his Legos spaceship?"

Toby looked up at Matt. "Okay. But if Mummy comes, will you let me know?"

"First thing."

Ethan ran to Toby and held out the box. "Come on, Toby. I'll even let you hold it."

"Okay."

The boys disappeared down the hall, giving Matt several seconds to prepare himself for the impending interrogation.

"You're dating Anna Fischer," she said in a tone he couldn't read.

What should he tell her? What had happened last night didn't exactly qualify as dating. "It's complicated." As soon as the words left his mouth, he regretted them.

"Complicated? Either you're dating her or you're not."

He started to answer then pressed his mouth together. The

answer was a firm *No, we aren't dating*, but he couldn't stomach saying the words.

"You've known Toby's mother was Anna all along and you didn't tell me?" his mother asked, sounding hurt.

"No." He rubbed the back of his neck. "I found out about two weeks ago when Anna brought Toby to the first soccer practice. I didn't tell you because at first I wasn't happy to see her. At. All. But then... I guess I wanted to be more sure about where we stood before I told you."

"And do you know where you stand now?"

"Not a clue," he admitted, trying not to sound dejected.

His mother studied him. "Last Saturday... Anna was the mother who watched Ethan when you came over to my house to check out the alarm."

"Yeah."

Her voice softened. "So you've forgiven her?"

His eyes found hers. "Anna asked me to meet her for coffee this week so she could explain her side of things, but truth be told, I'd forgiven her before she walked in the door."

"That seems like a one-eighty."

He shrugged. "I pulled my head out of my ass and started remembering everything you said when we broke up."

She chuckled. "Not likely. More like you came face-to-face with her and realized she wasn't the ogre you painted her to be at the end."

He was embarrassed over the things he'd said about her in the past, and his mother dredging it up wasn't helping. "I realized we were young, too young to get married. Anna was right to want to go to England before she settled down."

She was quiet for a moment. "It can't be easy seeing Anna with a son. Not after she told you she didn't want children."

He swallowed and shifted in his seat. "I admit it was hard at first, but she's a great mother."

"She's a single mother?"

He frowned. "If that's your way of asking if she's still married, the answer is no. She was divorced when Toby was a baby."

"I know you better than that, Matthew Michael Osborn," she said with a hint of disgust. "I know you would never knowingly have an affair. I was asking if she had him as a single mother."

He cringed, realizing he was handling this badly. "Shit. Sorry."

She was silent for several long seconds before she asked, "Isn't she going back to London?"

"Yeah."

"Do you want to go with her?"

His head jerked up, her question catching him by surprise. "I have a business here."

"Businesses can be bought and sold."

"But I love my business. It was Dad's."

"Do you love it more than Anna?"

He shot out of the seat, becoming frustrated. "That's not fair, Mom. I haven't seen her in twelve years."

"It's perfectly fair. What else is holding you here, business aside?"

"You."

"I've always wanted to visit London," she said in a breezy tone.

He turned to look at her. "Ethan."

Her grin faded and she gave him a slow nod. "He's the biggest reason, isn't he?"

"He might not be a reason at all. He's *Abby's* son. Not mine."

"Abby wants to give you full guardianship. For at least the next three years. Maybe longer."

He blinked, sure he'd heard her wrong. "*What?*"

"I spoke to Abby this morning. She's exhausted and frazzled, and she's torn between what's best for Ethan and whether to continue with school." She paused and tears filled her eyes before she looked down at her lap. "But she knows how good you are with him, and she wants that for him."

He shook his head in disbelief.

She glanced back up at him. "She'll come home this summer to be with Ethan, but she'll go back to school in August and leave him with you. After she graduates...she's thinking about a surgical residency. Her hours will be just as crazy, if not worse." She paused. "You need to give this serious consideration, Matt. He could be with you until he's in high school."

He sat on the love seat, resting his elbows on his knees as he cradled his head. High school? Was it wrong to want that?

"This is a lot to think about. It's a huge commitment. Especially in light of Anna showing back up in your life."

"Yeah..." he mumbled, trying to wrap his head around his sister's decision, let alone what it meant in regard to Anna.

"But, Matt," his mother said, "her one condition is that when she's not in school, she'll come home and live with me, and she'll get Ethan. Breaks included."

He nodded, still in disbelief. "Yeah. Of course. She's his mother."

"That means Christmas. Spring break. Summer breaks until she starts her residency."

"Of course."

His mother looked at him with sorrowful eyes. "But you can't take him to England, Matt. She'll never agree to that."

His eyes widened. "I hadn't planned..."

"I think you should take some time to think about it. When we discussed custody before, I take it that Anna wasn't an issue if you'd only just seen her a few days before?" his mother asked quietly.

"No." It hadn't been a factor, but was it now? He'd never given any thought to moving to England to be with her—he loved his life here. Besides, they'd slept together one time. He had no idea if Anna was even thinking along these lines. But what if she was? "For argument's sake, if I *did* decide to move? What would happen to Ethan?"

"Abby would probably quit school. Or try to figure out a way to bring him out there."

His head jerked up. "What about you?"

"There's something else you should know." She offered him a strained smile. "I've decided to buy a condo in Florida with Roger."

"*What?* What do you mean you've decided to buy a condo in Florida with Roger?" he shouted.

She patted her hands toward him. "Matthew, calm down."

He stood. "You just told me that you're buying a condo in Florida with your boyfriend of a couple of months. *How do you expect me to calm down?*"

She rolled her eyes. "Ten months."

Ethan came running into the room, wide-eyed, and stopped next to his grandmother. "Why is Uncle Matt yelling?"

Matt's mother shook her head and smiled. "Uncle Matt's just a little excited. How's your Lego project coming along?"

Ethan cast a worried glance toward Matt. "I already made it, but we took it apart and now Toby's putting it together."

She tugged him close and kissed his forehead. "You're a very good friend, Ethan. I'm proud of you."

Matt forced himself to calm down. "It's okay, big guy. Grandma and I are just having a lively discussion." He forced a smile. "Why don't you go check on Toby?"

Ethan's eyes scrunched up. "Why do you look like you're pooping?"

"I do *not* look like I'm pooping."

"You do. You get *this* face…" He hunched his shoulders up to his ears, gritted his teeth, then lowered his brow so that his eyes nearly looked closed.

Matt tried to nonchalantly shake the tension from his shoulders. "I'm not pooping. Go check on Toby."

Ethan didn't seem to buy it. "Okay."

As soon as the boy left the room, Matt said, "How did this happen?"

His mother shrugged with a playful look in her eyes. "Ethan must have walked in and seen you pooping."

"Not that," he grunted. "When did you decide to move to Florida?"

"Roger asked me while we were on the cruise, but with Ethan and Abby…it wasn't the right time. Then when I came back, you were doing so well with Ethan, but it still didn't feel like the right time. It was last weekend, after our discussion about Ethan's custody, that I knew you were ready."

"Ready for you to shack up with your boyfriend?" he asked defiantly. "Definitely not."

She chuckled. "Ready to be a parent. That this wasn't just you pretending to be a dad."

A parent? That hit him in the gut. "Mom…"

She held up a hand. "You can do this, and I'll only be gone half the year. We won't move until next fall. But I need you to be sure, Matt. I need you to be sure you're ready to commit to Ethan, so think about it for a few days, or even a week or two. Once you say yes, there's no turning back."

*You mean like Abby turned away?* was on the tip of his tongue, but he wasn't sure that was entirely true. Abby was doing the best she could, and as her brother, he would support her and take care of her son. Besides, having Ethan was a blessing. Matt didn't need a few days or a week to decide if he wanted custody of his nephew, but his mother was right. Anna cast everything in a whole new light.

# Chapter Seventeen

Toby ran out the front door when Anna arrived, nearly tackling her to the ground.

"Did you miss me?" she asked, her heart full of happiness as she pried him loose and squatted in front of him so she could see his smile.

"I missed you bigger than the moon, Mummy." He threw his arms around her neck and squeezed, nearly knocking her to the ground again.

She hugged him back, breathing in his little boy scent.

"That's a very large amount of missing." She grinned and lowered her voice. "I missed you that much, too."

He broke free and looked into her face. "Really?"

"*Really.* I almost came and got you about fifty times. Did you have fun with Ethan?"

"We had the bestest time. And Ethan's grandma showed up and brought him *Star Wars* Legos. Can I see *Star Wars* sometime?"

She gave him a warm smile. "I think that would be fun.

We should see if Grandpa wants to see it, too. The first time I saw it was with him when I was a little girl." How had she forgotten that memory?

"Really? No way."

She caught a glimpse of Ethan and Matt in the doorway and leaned her head closer to Toby's. "Do you still want to look at the dogs? We can go home if you need a break."

His eyes narrowed in a worried look. "You're coming, right?"

"Of course," she said with a huge grin. "I wouldn't miss it. I love dogs. But if you'd rather go home..."

He vigorously shook his head. "No. I want to pet the dogs."

Tapping his nose, she said, "Then let's go see some dogs."

She stood and grabbed Toby's hand then let her gaze land on Matt. She'd felt him watching her before she'd caught a glimpse of him. She'd forgotten that part, the instinctive knowing when he was close.

"Hi," she said softly as she walked to the front porch, unsure how to greet him. She felt like a teenager with a crush—down to the blush on her cheeks. Only this was no crush, but she was too scared to dwell on what it really was.

His gaze swept over her, a combination of warmth and longing. Her own body combusted, remembering the night before.

This was a stupid idea. How would she ever keep her hands off him? If she continued sleeping with him, things would get messy. How did she find the strength to do the right thing? She had to think of Toby and Ethan. Ethan was part of this, too.

Matt walked down the steps toward her. "Hi."

They stared at each other for a moment.

"Uncle Matt," Ethan said, "why are you acting weird?"

That seemed to snap Matt out of his daze. "What are you talking about?"

Fatal mistake.

Ethan scrunched up his face and rolled his eyes. "You look like this."

"I did *not* look like that." He glanced down at Toby. "Did I look like that?"

Toby shook his head.

"See?" Matt asked in a good-natured defensive tone.

"You looked like this," Toby said, letting his mouth drop open and rolling his head to the side.

"I'm going to get two little boys!" Matt exclaimed, reaching toward them.

They squealed and ran into the front yard, running in circles.

"Okay," Matt said. "I call a truce. I'll get my revenge later. Right now you need to go in and go to the bathroom."

"We already did," Ethan protested.

"Well, go again. Who knows if there is a bathroom at the animal shelter? They might make you pee with the dogs."

After Matt convinced the boys that peeing with the dogs was a bad thing, they ran inside and Matt turned his heated gaze on Anna.

Her body temperature instantly rose several degrees.

He moved closer, only a couple of feet away from her. Close enough that he could reach out and touch her, but his hands hung at his sides. "Did you have a good morning?"

"Uh...yeah." Her breath was coming in pants and her fingernails dug into her palms as she fought her overwhelming urge to throw herself at him. "Was Toby okay?"

"Of course." He moved a few inches closer. "He's a great kid, Anna."

Her mother's heart swelled even as her skin flushed at being so close to him. She glanced up into his eyes, not surprised to see his raw hunger.

He lifted his hand, reaching for her. "Anna—"

"We're ready, Uncle Matt!" Ethan shouted as he ran out the door, Toby on his heels.

Anna took several steps away, thankful for the interruption. She was going to need two five-year-old chaperones to get through the rest of the afternoon.

\* \* \*

Matt expected Ethan to be more excited once they got to the animal shelter, but he seemed overwhelmed by the noise.

Toby clung on to his mother's hand as they walked down the aisles.

"Are you looking for a puppy?" Anna asked. "Those Lab mix puppies were cute."

He leaned closer and lowered his voice. "This is going to sound corny as hell, but I was hoping that Ethan and I would just *know* when we saw it. Kind of like I knew the first time I saw you."

She flushed and shook her head. "Matt. You can't say things like that."

"Why not?" he asked, apparently throwing caution to the wind.

What the hell was he doing? His mother came over, told him Ethan was his for practically the next eight years, and he was chasing after a woman he couldn't have. And yet he wanted her anyway. He'd told himself he was going to play it cool this afternoon, but the moment he saw her get out of the car, his plan had flown out the window.

*God, he was an idiot.*

"You know why," she insisted, her eyes wide, and yet he saw her longing.

He moved closer, his mouth close to her ear. "I know you don't want to hurt Toby, and I understand your concern. But he and Ethan don't have to know. We can keep it from them."

Her body froze and her breath became shallow. Was she considering it? He felt himself get hard at the thought of seeing her naked again. Continuing something with her was emotional suicide—Anna was right to be concerned about her son—but damned if he wasn't sprinting right for it anyway.

"What are you whispering about?" Toby asked, watching them with wide eyes.

Anna jerked away from Matt, her face covered in guilt. "Dogs."

"Why were you whispering about *dogs*?" Ethan asked.

Matt grinned. "Tell them, Anna."

She shot him a glare but there was orneriness behind it instead of irritation. "I was telling Matt how cute the Lab puppies were, but I didn't want the other dogs to hear. I didn't want to hurt their feelings."

Ethan narrowed his eyes at his uncle. "Dogs can't understand people talk."

"Sure they can," Matt said. "We'll teach our new dog commands and tricks. But we have to pick him out first."

And so far they were striking out.

"Let's go down that aisle and look at the tags on the cages," Anna suggested, pointing to an aisle they hadn't been down. "We'll keep an eye out for the ones that say they would make a good family pet."

Matt nodded. "Good idea."

"What about this guy?" Anna asked, stopping in front of a cage. "It says he loves kids. Oh…And that he'll do better with other pets in the family." She shot Matt a grin. "I take it you're only getting one today?"

"Definitely only one."

Ethan and Toby had become bolder and ventured off on their own, and Matt stole a glance at her, resisting the urge to reach out and link his hand with hers.

His mother was right. He could walk away from his business...he could hand it over to Kevin to run. Kevin had jumped in as COO last year and learned the business inside and out. He and Anna could see where this took them, and if they worked, he could follow her to London. Twelve years ago, he never would have considered it, but now he knew better. Sometimes love meant sacrifice, willingly given.

But he refused to walk away from Ethan. Matt loved him too much to let him go. Which meant there was only one outcome to this.

*What will you do when she's gone for good?*

"Uncle Matt!" Ethan squealed. "I like this one!"

"Sounds like he might have found one," Anna said, looking over at him.

He was going to lose her again.

"Uncle Matt!"

He paused to take a breath and get control before he walked toward them, painting on a smile. "Which one?"

Ethan pointed in the cage. "There."

The cage contained two dogs. Neither of them were puppies, but they didn't look very old. They were both obviously mutts. One was about two and a half feet tall and had a dull brown short-haired coat. It had small ears and a long tail. The smaller dog had a short tail and short legs and a matted white wiry coat.

"Which one, big guy?" Matt asked as he squatted next to him.

"The brown one," Ethan said.

Anna was reading the tag posted on the cage above his head. "It says they were picked up together by animal control. The bigger one is a boy and is a Lab mix. The little one is a girl and is a terrier mix. It says they are good with children and other pets." She paused then frowned. "It says they hate to be separated."

Matt grimaced. "How about we look at some other dogs?"

"We already looked at the other dogs." Ethan looped his fingers though the wires of the cage and the bigger dog licked his fingers. "He already likes me. Look."

"Okay..." Matt sighed. "I'll tell one of the workers we want to see him." Matt was already feeling guilty as hell over considering separating them, which was ridiculous. They were dogs. They could get over it, right?

Several minutes later a shelter worker introduced herself as Debby and removed the dog they called Cinnamon from his pen, leaving Sugar behind.

As soon as the cage door closed, the howling began.

Debby gave them an apologetic look. "Sorry, she does that whenever Cinnamon is separated from her." But Cinnamon didn't look pleased either, digging in his heels when she dragged him to the play area in the corner, about ten feet away from Cinnamon's cage.

Debby finally got him in and held his leash while Matt, Anna, and the two boys filed in. Anna shut the baby gate–sized door behind them.

"Let Cinnamon smell your hand first," Debby said. "People say hello by showing dogs a closed fist. It's like a handshake only they smell it. But dogs like to smell each other's butts to say hello." The boys released a round of giggles and the woman grinned as she looked up at Matt and Anna. "Do one of you want to try it first?"

"Sniffing his butt?" Matt said with a laugh. "No thanks. I'll pass."

The boys burst into new giggles.

Debby grinned. "I think we can stick with your hand."

Matt leaned forward and let the dog sniff his hand. And while the dog seemed friendly, he kept looking at the door to the play area like he was dying to escape.

Anna and the boys told Cinnamon hello, and the shelter worker let him off his leash. He immediately went to the door and batted at it with his paws.

"He's really a friendly dog," Debby said. "I know he's sad about being separated from Sugar, but he'd eventually get over it. If you want to see his real personality, I suggest we bring Sugar in, too. I understand you're interested in just Cinnamon, but he'll be happier if Sugar is here."

"Yeah. Bring her in," Matt said, then looked at Ethan, who was petting Cinnamon. "But we're only getting one dog, Ethan."

Ethan's head bobbed, and he and Toby continued trying to get Cinnamon to pay attention to them.

Matt glanced over at Anna, who stood to the side. She absently petted the dog while she watched the boys with a wrinkled brow. Was she worried about Toby being around the dog? Cinnamon seemed sweet enough. Or was she worried about separating the dogs? He was about to ask her when Debby returned with Sugar at the end of a leash.

The moment Cinnamon saw Sugar, his tail wagged so hard and fast it wacked the boys, who giggled as they jumped out of the way.

Sugar released a happy yapping noise and ran to the bigger dog and began to lick his face. Cinnamon nuzzled her head with his nose.

"They're bestest friends, too," Toby said. "Just like me and Ethan."

"Yeah," Matt said with a sinking feeling. What kind of monster would he be if he split them apart?

The dogs turned their attention to the boys when they sat on the floor, and after several minutes the boys started throwing balls for the dogs to bring back to them. Cinnamon was all in with the game, but Sugar watched the ball roll away then looked at the boys like they had lost their minds if they expected her to get it.

"What do you think?" Matt asked as he moved next to Anna.

"He's a sweet dog. He's gentle with the boys," she said, but something in her voice sounded off. She moved closer to the dogs and rubbed Cinnamon's head. "Aren't you a sweetie?"

"Is Cinnamon house trained?" Matt asked.

Debby moved closer. "We don't know, but he relieves himself every time we take him outdoors. He's already been neutered so he had owners at some point but that doesn't necessarily mean he's trained. He's very smart, so if he wasn't, I suspect he'll pick up on it right away."

Matt knelt down and rubbed the dog's head. Cinnamon reached up and licked Matt's face and Matt had his mind made up. He'd told Anna he'd know the right dog when he saw it, and Cinnamon felt right.

"What do you think, Ethan?"

The boy's eyes widened with excitement. "We can get him?"

"Yeah. Let's get him." Matt glanced up at Debby. "What do we do now?"

The woman grinned. "Now you get to take care of the paperwork. We can bring him up front with us while you fill out the forms."

She hooked Cinnamon up to a leash and handed the lead to Matt then walked over to Sugar, who was sitting in the corner on Anna's lap. Anna rubbed behind her ears and leaned into the dog's face to whisper something before the shelter worker started to take Sugar out of the pen.

Sugar began to whine until she realized Cinnamon was leaving, too. The two dogs walked side by side until they reached their pen. When Debby opened the door to put Sugar inside, Cinnamon started to follow, but Matt held his leash.

Both dogs started to protest as the shelter worker locked the cage.

"Uncle Matt?" Ethan asked with a worried look. "Why are Cinnamon and Sugar crying?"

What was he going to tell him? The truth. "Because they're friends. They love each other." *Shit.*

Debby leaned closer. "Since they're so bonded, we originally said they had to be adopted together. But their time is running out, and we thought they would have a better chance if we allowed them to be split up."

*Shit. Shit. Shit.*

"When you say their time is almost up...how much longer does Sugar have?"

"A few days."

He glanced over at Anna, who had partially turned away from him. He handed Cinnamon's leash to Ethan and walked over to her. "Anna?"

She quickly wiped her cheeks and turned to him but kept her gaze on the floor. "Yeah?"

"What do you think I should do?" he asked low enough so the boys couldn't hear.

"It's not fair to ask me that, Matt. You're the one who has to take care of them. Two dogs is double the vet bills. Double the food. Double the work."

It wasn't like he couldn't afford it, but he sure hadn't planned on walking out with two dogs. "Why are you upset?"

She shook her head and refused to look at him as fresh tears fell down her cheeks.

"Anna."

She looked up at him with reddened eyes. "It's stupid."

"If it's something bothering you, it can't be stupid."

She bit her lower lip and looked over at the boys. "It's so much like you and me."

"Oh, Anna…"

She gave him a sad smile as her eyes filled with more tears. "I told you it was stupid."

There was so much he couldn't give her, so much he couldn't fix, but he could give her this. He turned around to face the shelter worker. "Get another set of paperwork. Sugar's going with us, too."

The boys erupted into cheers and Ethan threw his arms around Cinnamon's neck. "Did you hear that? Your best friend gets to come home with us!"

Cinnamon licked Ethan's cheek and he giggled. The sound warmed Matt's heart, but Anna's grateful smile nearly bowled him over.

He'd do anything to make her happy. But no matter what he did, it ultimately wouldn't be enough.

# Chapter Eighteen

Anna was wracked with guilt. She knew her tears pushed Matt into getting both dogs, but the two excited boys, each holding puppies in the back seat, helped ease the burden.

Matt glanced into his rearview mirror. "Let's stop at the pet store and get the dogs some food and supplies. We can bring them into the store with their leashes."

The boys released shouts of excitement.

Matt reached over and grabbed Anna's hand, holding it next to the back of the seat so the boys wouldn't see. He snuck a glance toward her and lowered his voice. "I wanted both dogs. You didn't coerce me into anything."

She nearly startled when he touched her, but she couldn't make herself pull away. She liked the feel of his skin on hers—a mixture of comfort and lust. "Are you sure?"

"I promise you that even if I'd made it to the reception area with only one dog, I would have left with two. My own guilt would have eaten me alive." He looked in the back again. "Now we have to decide if we're going to keep their names or change them. What do you think, Ethan?"

The little boy made a face. "How can we change their names? That's weird."

Toby nodded in agreement. "So weird."

"Okay," Matt laughed. "Cinnamon and Sugar it is."

An hour later, they were back at Matt's house, with a crate, food, toys, treats, and dog shampoo and a brush to get the mats out of Sugar's coat.

They took the dogs into the backyard and let them sniff the grass and pee in multiple places. Sugar took the lead and Cinnamon followed her around as though he was afraid to let her out of his sight.

The boys chased them around and soon had Cinnamon running after a ball while Sugar wandered toward Anna and put her front paws on Anna's legs. Anna grabbed the brush and sat down on the patio and began to brush the dog's matted hair.

Matt sat down next to her. "You don't have to do that, Anna."

"I want to." The dog curled up on her lap and seemed to enjoy the metal bristles stroking her back.

"When do you need to go back to your dad?" Matt asked.

"Soon," she said with a sigh. Her father had been alone for four hours now and that was pushing it. He'd said he was doing fine when she'd called, but she suspected he'd tell her that he was fine even if he'd set himself on fire.

"Ethan looks happy," she said, continuing to brush the dog.

"So does Toby."

"He's always wanted a dog," she sighed. She was treading on dangerous ground, and she needed to change the subject quickly.

But Matt beat her to it. "How did your visit to the assisted living center go?"

"Much better than the last place. I asked her to hold an apartment for him, but he's still going to hate it, just less than the previous place." She paused. "He's lived in that house for thirty-six years. His whole life is there."

Matt put a hand at the small of her back. "I'm sure it will be hard, but while your father was always stubborn, the man I knew wasn't a fool. Surely he'll understand."

"I hope." She sighed again as she continued to brush the dog. "There's another problem. His apartment won't be available for another six weeks and I have to return to London in four."

"What are you going to do?"

She remained silent for a moment. "I'll ask for an extension, but I suspect they won't grant it. I may get fired, which means I'll have to look for a new job when I get back."

"Will that be difficult?"

She slowly turned her head to look at him. Her heart warmed when she saw the concern in his eyes. He could easily give her a guilt trip for going back to London with an uncertain future when she knew he wanted her to stay, but that wasn't Matt.

"Maybe. I make a nice salary and the economy isn't the greatest. I'll undoubtedly take a pay cut, and it may take me several months to find something."

"And if you lose your job?" he asked, seeming to choose his words carefully. "How long would you stay before you go back?"

Her muscles tensed, worried about where this was going, hoping she wasn't wrong about her previous assessment of him. "I'd send out my résumé and try to arrange for interviews soon after Dad's settled, but I can't interview across an ocean."

His hand rose to the back of her neck and began to massage her tight muscles. "Then we'll hope for the extension."

Her gaze jerked to his.

A soft smile spread across his face. "I won't lie. I'd love to have you a few extra weeks, but I would never want you to be anxious about your future." He glanced into the yard, and she turned to see what he was looking at.

Cinnamon was lying on his back, and the two boys were huddled over him, rubbing his belly.

"Anna," Matt said, and she turned to face him. "I love you. I always have and I suspect I always will. I was an idiot in the past but I'm not going to let history repeat itself. This isn't what either of us would choose, but we're stuck in it. I need you to know that I would never be selfish enough to find joy in your pain."

"Oh, Matt..." She couldn't believe this was real. Every day since the night he left her at her apartment door after the disastrous proposal, she would have given anything to hear him say he loved her. But she was going back to London and he was staying here. How could something that made her so happy fill her with so much sorrow?

He leaned closer and placed a gentle kiss on her lips. "We'll figure out something, okay?"

She knew they were destined for heartbreak, but she found herself nodding anyway.

"Mummy?" Toby asked from across the yard.

Anna jerked back, worried her son had seen her kiss his best friend's father. "Yes?"

"Can we get a house in London like Ethan has? Then we could get a dog."

She faked a smile. "That would be lovely, wouldn't it? But houses with yards are hard to find and very expensive. We'd have to move out of the city, and that's where my job is and your school. If we found a house, I'd have to take the train, and I'd be gone even longer."

Toby walked over and stood in front of her. "I like spending time with you," he said quietly. "I don't want to go back."

Her throat burned and she took a breath as she tried to figure out what to say. This only drove home that this glimpse into suburban life—complete with the father and the dog—might be hurting her son more than helping. She set the brush on the patio next to her. "You know what? We need to go."

"What?" Toby asked in disbelief. "Why?"

"Grandpa is probably getting hungry. And while it was very kind of Matt and Ethan to let us tag along to the animal shelter, we need to let them get Cinnamon and Sugar settled into their new home."

She gave Sugar one last pat on the head, and put her on the concrete before standing.

Matt stood, too, and she half expected him to protest, but he gave her a sad smile that radiated, *I understand.*

But Toby didn't. "I don't want to go."

Ethan had joined them, and Cinnamon had followed, standing between both boys and looking up at them.

"I know you don't want to go," Anna said quietly, "but Cinnamon and Sugar are Ethan and Matt's dogs. I'm sure Matt will let us come back and see them very soon."

"You can come back tomorrow," Matt said. "Maybe you want to bring your dad."

"What?" she asked in shock. "My *dad*?"

"Why not?" he asked as he seemed to be thinking on

the fly. "I can invite Kevin and Tyler and their wives. And
I can invite my mom. Your dad always liked her. We'll
call it a *welcome to the family party* for Cinnamon and
Sugar."

"Matt."

"Yay!" Ethan shouted. "A party for the dogs!"

"I want to come to a dog party!" Toby said, tugging on
Anna's arm.

"It would probably be good for your dad to be around
other people, right? And the weather's supposed to be perfect tomorrow. We'll have a cookout and sit outside."

*What was he doing?* But she knew. He'd just told her that
he loved her. Any man in love would want to spend as much
time with the woman he loved before she left. But she had to
think about Toby. He was getting too attached. She glanced
down at her son. "I don't know..."

Matt's gaze landed on Toby and he lifted his eyes to hers,
guilt washing over his face. "I'm sorry."

"Why are you sorry, Uncle Matt?" Ethan asked, his face
scrunching in confusion.

"Remember how I told you it was impolite to ask me
if someone could come over while they are standing right
there? That it puts me on the spot and makes them uncomfortable if I say no? Well, this is one of those situations. I
should have asked Anna when Toby wasn't listening so he
wouldn't be upset with his mommy if she says no."

Ethan looked even more confused. "Why would she say
no? Toby *has* to be here for the party. He helped pick them
out."

"But they might have plans," Matt insisted. "It was rude
of me to ask." His gaze shifted to her face. "I'm sorry."

She needed to say no, but Toby was looking up at her,
pleading with his eyes. She felt like she was always letting

him down. Which was worse? Not letting him come and hurting his feelings, or continuing to let him get attached?

But there was another issue to think about.

"What about Tyler and Kevin? How will they feel if they see me here?"

Matt shoved his hands in his front jeans pockets. "They already know you're back in town, and they'll be fine."

That news surprised her, then it didn't. Matt had always been close to his friends. She should say no, she knew it, but sadly, she was lacking self-control. "Okay, we'll come." The boys cheered. "But make it potluck. Let me know what time and what to bring." She needed to be strong after this and in-sist this was the last time they socialized outside of soccer.

Matt blinked, looking as though he was sure he'd heard wrong. "One o'clock and whatever you want."

"But there's one problem," she said. "Ashley and I were going to take Toby to the park. I hate to cancel."

"Ashley Ternary? Your best friend?" he asked in dis-belief. "Ask her to come, too."

"You're sure?"

"The more the merrier." He glanced down at the boys. "Ethan, why don't you and Toby go inside and get his things ready to take home."

"Yes, sir," both boys said as they ran inside.

"Yes, sir?" she parroted. "You've been teaching my son Southern manners?"

He gave her a halfhearted grin. "We can discuss my awe-some parenting skills later." He turned serious. "I really am sorry, Anna, that I put you in a difficult position. I don't want to make things more difficult. Obviously I wasn't thinking."

She slowly shook her head. "Matt . . ."

"Uncle Matt," Ethan shouted from inside the house. "We can't find Toby's toothbrush."

Matt leaned his head back and groaned. "It's in his bag, remember?"

"Ohhhh..."

Matt looked back down at Anna. The love and lust in his eyes sent a wave of hot need through her body. "It's killing me that I ran you off."

"You didn't. I just really need to go."

"I understand."

Common sense told her that she needed to walk out the door and make sure she avoided him until she got on a plane in four weeks. But her heart—oh, her heart—it begged her to stay. She'd spent most of the last twelve years thinking with her head, and now that she'd woken her heart, it refused to go quietly back to sleep. She studied his face. "You'd really invite all those people over as an excuse to see me?"

Matt wrapped an arm around her back and tugged her closer, her chest pressed against his. "I'd invite the whole damn town if that's what it took. Never underestimate a man in love."

There it was again. His declaration of love. She loved him, but she'd never stopped while he'd spent much of the last twelve years resenting her. How had he flipped so quickly? She'd been so protective of bringing men into Toby's life. She couldn't stop now. *Especially* now. "It's been over a decade, Matt. How can you be sure you still love me?"

He lifted a hand to her face, tracing her cheekbone with his thumb. "Because you're still the same woman. Sure, you have more life experience now—we both do—but the woman who couldn't bear to leave a small, sad dog alone...that's the woman I fell in love with thirteen years ago. I've been so stupid, Anna. I wasted so much time. I don't want to waste any more."

Her heart overflowed with emotion and she parted her lips, about to tell him that she loved him, too, when she realized two little boys were standing in the open doorway, their mouths hanging open in shock.

"Uncle Matt?" Ethan asked. "What are you *doing*?"

# Chapter Nineteen

After Matt came up with the weak excuse of looking for something in Anna's eye, she practically bolted from the house with Toby in tow. Ethan moped around the house for a half hour after Toby and Anna left, not that Matt could blame the boy. Matt was doing his best not to show how much he missed Anna. He was facing a countdown and every minute counted, yet he knew and understood her hesitation. But it didn't make it any easier to accept.

He and Ethan jumped on setting up the dogs' crate and putting out their food and water bowls. Matt finished brushing out Sugar's mats—although Anna had gotten most of them out already—then he and Ethan gave the two dogs a bath.

Matt made them a quick dinner, and while he and Ethan sat at the kitchen table with the dogs lying at their feet, he realized he'd never told Anna about his sister giving him legal guardianship of her son. Was it because he was considering following Anna to London? His heart was breaking.

He knew that he would never love another woman like he loved Anna. Seeing her again proved that. How ironic that fate had finally brought back the woman he loved when it had also offered him a child. Was this his punishment for abruptly ending their relationship when it hadn't fit within his parameters?

But it made him understand Anna's dilemma. Once you had a child, they always came first, and Ethan might not be his biological child, but there was no doubt he'd wiggled firmly into his life and his heart. Ethan needed him. In the end, it wasn't even a choice.

\* \* \*

Anna tucked Toby in bed and went into the living room to tell her father about the assisted living center. He was in an unusually good mood after playing several games of checkers with Toby and eating his favorite dinner of fried chicken and mashed potatoes, which Anna had cooked for him.

He sat in his chair, his eyes glued to a history documentary on the television.

She sat on the sofa and crossed her legs.

"You've got a good boy, Anna."

"Thank you, Dad," she said. "He had a good time and wants to play with you again tomorrow. I'm really grateful you've been getting to know him."

He shook his head. "I was an ass. I was pissed at you and taking it out on him." He turned to look at her. "And I've been an ass to you. You had a life in London, yet you dropped it all to come help me, even after I'd said some terrible things to you. I'm sorry for that, too."

She stared at him in shock. "Dad...thank you."

"I wish you could move back, but Blue Springs isn't fancy like London."

"That's not why I can't come back, Dad. I've loved being here and I'd give anything to spend more time with you and Toby like I have since I've been back, but I can't. When I divorced Phillip, his family fought hard to make sure I couldn't move out of the UK. The irony is that they haven't seen him since he was two, Phillip included."

Her father's jaw set. "That Brit isn't taking care of your boy?"

She smiled. "We're better off without him, but the order still stands."

"Well, if the prick isn't gonna see the boy, then sue him and do whatever you want with him."

"I'm not sure it's that easy."

"So you're just gonna let the prick dictate your life?"

"According to the divorce, at least until Toby turns sixteen."

He shook his head. "That's not right. That boy needs to be around people who love him, not some stuffed-shirt London folk."

She laughed. "How do you know they're stuffed shirts?"

"They've got money, don't they? Isn't that how they got that part in your divorce?"

"Yeah."

He gave a sharp nod.

Since he was being so surprisingly supportive, she decided to come clean. "There's another reason I want to come back."

His expression softened. "Matt."

She blinked. "What?"

"I know you're seeing Matt Osborn. I may have trouble getting around because of this damned leg, but I'm not senile."

A laugh erupted before she could stop it. "I never accused you of being senile."

"Damn good thing, too." He grinned and then it faded. "You want to move back for him?"

"If you're asking if Matt is the only reason I want to move back, the answer is no. If he wasn't in the picture, I'd want to move back anyway."

"It's been a lot of years, Anna. People change."

"I know," she said softly, glancing down at her lap. "But like Matt said today, we've both lived through a lot of life experiences, but we're still the same people."

He nodded. "Good. I always liked that boy."

"*Matt Osborn?*" she gasped in shock. Her father had never given her the impression he liked him. In fact, it had been the opposite.

"Yep. Can't stand that Phillip prick."

She shook her head and laughed. "You never met him."

He pointed his finger at her. "Which tells you a lot about his character. Remember when you brought Matt to meet us?"

The memory warmed her heart. "He was so nervous. He knew you were a force to be reckoned with."

"And yet he came anyway. Nice and polite boy. But I understand why you turned him down when he proposed."

"*What?*"

He waved his hand. "I know your momma didn't approve, but she had selfish reasons. She didn't want to lose you. But you'd always felt stifled here. You needed a chance to spread your wings and find out who you are."

"But you were so angry with me when I came back for Mom's funeral."

"I was mad at the world, Annaliese. I was bitter and I hurt you in the process." He pushed out a heavy breath. "Life's too damn short to give in to selfish pricks. I've never seen you happier than when you were with Matt. If he's who you want, you need to fight for him."

She stared at her father in disbelief. What had happened to him?

As though reading her mind, he gave her a soulful look. "Spending six years alone is bad for a person. Turns out a certain five-year-old boy is the antidote."

Anna fought to keep from bursting into tears. How was she going to leave her father, too?

His eyes filled with determination. "Fight for what you want. For the man and the life you want. Don't give up and don't give in."

"But I have to think about Toby. I can't let him get hurt in the process."

"You can't protect him from everything, Annaliese, no matter how much you try."

Still, it seemed irresponsible to knowingly put her son in a situation that would undoubtedly lead to heartbreak. She'd call the attorney Ashley had told her about, but she refused to dangle a life her son so desperately wanted, only to snatch it away. "I know. But some things are still in my control."

In light of this conversation, was the next part right or foolish? "Dad, Matt is having a cookout at his house tomorrow. He's inviting several people, including his mother. He'd like for you to come, too."

He shook his head and waved his hand. "No. You and Toby go. I'll stay here."

"It's going to be a beautiful day, and you won't even have to talk to many people."

He didn't say anything.

"Toby would be excited for you to come." She grinned.

"He could show you the dogs he talked about nonstop all night."

"That boy doesn't care if I go."

"I think you'd be surprised, Dad."

"Fine, if he wants me to go, I will." He paused. "There's a box of things your mother kept for you on the floor in my bedroom. I should have given it to you before but..." He shrugged. "I guess I was waiting for the right time."

Her heart caught in her throat. "Mom left me something?"

"Somethings. It's not much, but... it's on the floor in front of the closet. I would have put it in your room but I couldn't pick it up."

"You shouldn't have gotten it at all," she scolded lightly. "You could have hurt yourself."

He shrugged again.

Anna stood then leaned over and kissed him on the cheek. "I love you, Dad. I don't ever tell you that, but I need you to know it's true."

He glanced up at her with glassy eyes. "I love you, too, Annaliese. I'm proud of the woman you've become."

"Thank you, Dad. That means more than you know."

She found the small box where her father said he'd put it, then carried it into her room. Toby was asleep, but a soft light glowed from the lamp on the bedside table.

Anna sat on the floor and opened the box, excited to see a pile of photos on top. She spent the next ten minutes going through them, and found a photo of her mother, holding a then preschool-age Anna, and her father next to them. Her mother looked up at her father with adoring eyes. How had her soft and loving mother loved the hard-edged father Anna remembered? Maybe she'd seen the softer man her father was just now showing her—and Toby.

Under the photos were programs from Anna's old school plays and concerts, and at the very bottom was a ring box. Had her mother left Anna her wedding rings? She was pretty sure her mother had been buried with them. She reached for the box and opened the lid, gasping when she realized the ring was the engagement ring Matt had given her. After Matt had left it on the table, she'd picked it up and put it in her purse, intending to leave it in his car, but she was so upset she had forgotten. Then she'd brought it back six years ago when she'd rushed home to see her mother, hoping to give it back to Matt and apologize. And if she were honest, she'd wanted to see if he was open to trying again. She'd been seeing Phillip, but she'd begun to suspect he was conning her, and she'd become nostalgic for Matt.

She was looking at the ring, her legs buried in photos and programs and old grade cards, when her phone rang. She reached for it on the nightstand, but the phone was just out of her grasp. She scooped up the photos and put them in the box then shoved the other papers to the floor, standing up to grab the phone. By the time she picked it up, the phone had stopped ringing, but her heart fell to her feet when she saw the name on the screen.

Phillip.

She'd called him before she'd left London, but he hadn't answered. He rarely did. She'd left a message that she needed to talk to him and to call her as soon as he could, and of course she'd never heard back from him.

So why was he calling now?

It was well after midnight in the UK, but it was Saturday night so he was probably out in a pub, drunk dialing her. He'd done it before, more times than she could count, but the majority of them had been during the first few years of Toby's life. Drunk off his ass, he always told her he knew what a terrible father he was and that he wanted them to be a family. She'd halfway believed him in the beginning and invited him to come spend family time with Toby—the three of them together—but he'd shown up only a few times before Toby turned two. He'd called only a few times since— the last well over a year ago. Once she realized he wasn't going to change, she'd stopped answering, instead letting his drunken and often slurred message go to voice mail. She stared at her phone now, but the voice mail message never appeared.

She tried not to freak out over what that could mean.

# Chapter Twenty

Anna wasn't sure what to expect when she showed up to Matt's, but she was prepared to run a gauntlet. Matt had been evasive when she'd tried to pin him down about his two best friends' attitude about her attending the cookout, which she took to mean they weren't too thrilled. The only thing he'd told them was that they were friends again and planned to spend time together before she returned to London, but that was enough to set them on edge. Nevertheless, she would accept whatever they dished out as penance.

In fairness, Ashley had been equally reserved. "Are you sure this is a good idea?"

"We're just friends. We're doing this for the boys."

"You're playing with fire, Anna, but you're a big girl who knows how hot fire is, so I'll give you my warning and let you handle the rest."

Anna had started to tell her about Phillip's weird call, but she couldn't make herself do it. She wanted to think it was a butt dial and nothing purposeful, but if it had been purposeful and he hadn't left a message, she wasn't sure she could deal with what it could mean. Not today. She'd deal with it tomorrow.

Anna was running late, which already had her anxious. She hated being late, but the baked beans had taken forever to heat up and after she'd boiled eggs for the deviled eggs, several of them had ripped apart when she removed the shells, and she'd had to run back to the store to buy more.

Several cars were parked in front of Matt's house when they pulled up to the curb. Ethan stood with his nose pressed to the window, waiting for Toby. Anna grinned when she saw the dogs on either side of him, staring out the window, too. Leaving her father in the car while she took the food inside, she expected Ethan to run out the door as she and Toby approached, but he remained in place until they knocked. Ethan cracked the door and poked a sliver of his face through. "Uncle Matt says I have to be *super careful* and make sure the dogs don't go outside. He says I can't open the door very wide."

"Very smart advice," Anna said as she juggled the two dishes. "We'll make sure we don't let the dogs out."

Ethan opened the door just enough for them to get inside, not that the dogs seemed interested in escaping. They were too excited to see Toby. Cinnamon jumped up and licked Toby's face, eliciting a round of giggles from both boys.

Anna cast a glance out the back windows as she set the two containers on the counter. Her stomach twisted when she saw Tyler and Kevin, along with two women she didn't recognize, and one she did—Matt's mother.

Matt must have heard the commotion and turned to glance into the kitchen. As soon as he saw her, his face lit up.

He looked over her shoulder at his mother and said something Anna couldn't hear then headed into the house.

He stopped in front of her, and a combination of warmth and comfort mixed with a wave of lust, making her want to press her body to his and kiss him. Thankfully, good sense prevailed, but barely.

"I need to go out and get my dad," Anna said, taking two sideways steps toward the door both in an effort to go out to her dad and self-preservation. She wasn't sure how long her self-control would last, which was very bad, given they had a bigger audience than two boys.

Maybe this was a bad idea. She should probably leave Toby here and take her father back home. Only now that he'd agreed to come, he'd acted a tiny bit excited.

"I'll help." Matt put a hand on the small of her back and ushered her toward the door. His hand sent another wave of desire through her as she felt his fingertips through the thin cotton fabric of her dress.

When she went outside, she realized her father had already opened his car door and had gotten out of the car. He was now leaning against the back passenger door.

"Dad!" she shouted, hurrying toward him. "Just wait there." She opened the trunk and got out his walker then set it up in front of him. "I told you I was coming right back."

Exhaustion and sorrow filled his eyes. "In another month, you're not gonna be here, Annaliese, and what am I gonna do then?"

Her heart broke. She knew what he would do, but now was not the time. "We'll talk about that later."

Matt walked up behind her. "Hello, Mr. Fischer. I'm happy you could make it."

Her father grabbed the handles of the walker and looked up at him. "You're not a kid anymore. Call me Albert."

"Yes, sir," Matt said with a smile. "Can I help you with anything?"

"If you've got a time machine and can go back to the day I decided it was a good idea to clean out my gutters, then yeah. Otherwise, I'm shuffling alone."

"Let's make a deal," Matt said. "If you need something done that puts you in danger, you give me a call and I'll take care of it."

Her father frowned as he lifted his walker and started toward the house. "Why would you do something like that for me? After all these years?"

"Because you're Anna's father and Anna is my friend. I take care of my friends. All you have to do is ask Tyler and Kevin once you get inside. Hell, I helped Kevin remodel his house. Cleaning a gutter or changing a lightbulb is nothing."

Anna stared at Matt, shocked by his offer, but her father had already walked several steps ahead with Matt beside him.

\* \* \*

Matt shadowed Anna's father until they were on the back patio, then he got Albert settled in a chair, but he was struggling to focus on the simple task because all he could think about was Anna's sexy bare legs. Her peach dress was simple and conservative, but he remembered every inch of what was underneath, and her legs were a reminder that he could only look and not touch.

*Get your shit together, Osborn.*

He glanced at his mother, who was sitting in one of the patio furniture love seats. "Mom, you remember Anna."

"Of course!" his mother said enthusiastically as she rose

from her chair and greeted Anna with a hug. "It's been too long," his mother said.

"Yes," Anna said. "It has."

"Kevin, Tyler, you remember Anna." His back muscles tensed while he waited for their response.

"Hey, Anna," Kevin said with a nod and a partial smile.

"Good to see you again," Tyler said, halfway sounding like he meant it.

Their wives gave each other conspiratorial glances and Matt never loved either of them more, certain they had coached their husbands to be civil.

He gestured to the blonde next to Kevin, then the brunette next to Tyler. "And this is Kevin's wife, Holly, and Tyler's wife, Lanie."

The blond woman waved. "Hi."

Lanie settled back in her chair and gave Anna an appraising glance and then smiled. "Holly and I have been *very* eager to meet you. We hear you knew these two way back when."

Anna laughed. "I can tell you college stories about both of your husbands."

Lanie's face lit up as she leaned forward and shot Holly a look. "I see a girls' night in our future."

Both of their husbands groaned, but Matt grinned. They had reason to worry. Anna had seen quite a bit.

He put a hand on Anna's father's shoulder. "Albert, can I get you something to drink? Mom fixed us some homemade lemonade."

Albert nodded, but he kept his eyes on the boys, who were playing with the dogs in the yard.

Matt turned to Anna, amazed anew that she was here. At this house. He watched her for a couple of awkward seconds, then realized everyone was staring at him. "Uh... Anna? Lemonade? Beer?"

But she'd been staring at him, too, and came to her senses when he had. "Lemonade sounds good."

His mother moved to the end of the love seat and patted the cushion next to her. "Have a seat, Anna. I want to hear about your adventures in England."

Matt went inside to get the drinks, and when he returned, Anna looked happy as she regaled the group about the differences between London and the Midwest. Holly and Lanie were rapt with attention, and he noticed Tyler and Kevin were listening, too. He was relieved they weren't being antagonistic. They had liked Anna in the past; they'd just held a grudge on his behalf, a grudge he could see they were softening.

He manned the grill at the other side of the patio, joining in the lively conversation, while the boys romped in the yard with the dogs. Just as he was taking the last piece of chicken off the grill, Anna's friend Ashley showed up, and Matt announced that it was time to eat. Everyone went inside to fill their plates, and Anna helped Matt man the food—making sure that all the sides had spoons, that there were enough plates, that everyone's drinks were refilled. She made sure both boys had plates of food, then took them out to get them settled and corral the dogs. When Matt returned to the patio, Anna was sitting in the love seat, but his mother had taken Matt's vacated seat. She had a sly look on her face when he glanced at her.

*Subtle, Mom.* Not that he was complaining...

Anna glanced up at him and smiled as he sat next to her. "The chicken is delicious," she said. "You'll have to tell me what you used in the marinade."

The group echoed Anna's statement as he sat down, and he absently thanked them, distracted by the bolt of heat that shot through him when his thigh touched her bare leg.

She cast a glance at him, and he could see she was just as affected as he was, which turned him on even more. He shifted in his seat to ease his discomfort. The last thing he needed was a very public display of his attraction.

The conversation turned to the outdoor kitchen Kevin and Holly were building in their backyard.

"Don't you ever want a yard to hang out in?" Kevin asked Tyler as he scooped up some potato salad.

Tyler shook his head. "No way. I cut enough yards when I was a kid to last me a lifetime."

"You can hire that out, you know," Matt said with a laugh. "Just like people hired you."

"Lanie and I love where we're at," Tyler said. "But if we want to cook out or hang out in a backyard, we'll just hit one of you two up. Why do you think I'm still friends with you? It's sure not because of the brotherhood."

"Brotherhood?" Anna asked, glancing from Tyler to Matt.

*Shit.* They *had* to bring up the brotherhood.

Kevin and Tyler laughed, cluing Matt into the fact that both men had been looking for an opportunity to slip it into the conversation.

Matt's mother sat up. "I remember your brotherhood. You fancied yourselves to be dragon slayers."

"That was when we were kids, Mrs. Osborn," Kevin said. "We came up with this one last summer after we realized we were all walking disasters when it came to anything to do with love. We vowed to avoid serious relationships and remain bachelors."

Matt groaned. "You lasted one day."

Kevin beamed. "What can I say? Holly's irresistible. Thank God for my weak willpower." Then he leaned over and gave his wife a lingering kiss.

The love in their eyes used to make Matt feel jealous,

but he cast a glance at Anna and she smiled at him with that same look. He knew he couldn't lose her, whether she went back to London or not. Anna hadn't had a man in her life since her ex. She might be open to a long-distance relationship. Both of them made enough money so they could afford the airfare to see each other several times a year. It wasn't ideal, but once Toby was old enough, Anna could move back, or when Ethan went to college or moved back in with his mother, he could even move to London.

Decision made, he felt truly hopeful for the future for the first time in years. Anna watched him with curiosity. Would she agree? He suspected she would. And if it eventually didn't work out, they'd deal with it then. There were no guarantees in life.

Thankfully, the conversation moved from the bachelor brotherhood to Lanie's cousin, Brittany, who had gotten married the summer before. All three men had gone to high school with her and her husband, Randy, and they had attended the wedding, which was how Lanie and Tyler met. Holly had been the wedding planner.

"Britt and Randy are very happy," Lanie said. "In fact, they just announced that Britt's pregnant. She's due next October."

"It was planned," Tyler said, shaking his head. "Can you believe it? They haven't even been married a year."

Kevin and Holly were strangely quiet.

"So when are you and Lanie planning on kids?" Matt asked.

They glanced at each other and Lanie said, "I'd like to wait at least a couple of years, which will be pushing the edge of a high-risk pregnancy, but I'm still getting my business consultant company off the ground. I want to be able to focus on both."

"And I'm in no hurry," Tyler said. "I'm content with it being just Lanie and me. Besides, my brother is kind of like having a kid—I just got to skip the baby, toddler, and whiny grade school age."

Matt's mother stared at Holly for a moment then said, "Some people love children and want to have them sooner. There's no one size fits all."

Holly glanced up at her, looking slightly less nervous.

"Oh, my God," Lanie said, covering her mouth with her hand. "Holly!"

Tyler glanced back and forth between both women. "What?"

"Is it true?" Lanie asked.

Holly gave a small nod.

Matt grasped what was happening and was surprised at the knife edge of jealousy that cut through him. But he quickly pushed it away. He was happy for Kevin and Holly. Besides, he had Ethan, and if Anna agreed to try to make this work long distance, he'd have Toby as well.

So why did it still hurt so much to realize that he might not ever have a child with Anna?

Lanie squealed and jumped out of her seat, then rushed over to her friend, pulling her to her feet and wrapping her in a tight hug. "When?"

"What the hell's going on?" Tyler asked, looking at Kevin in confusion.

"She's pregnant, you idiot," Lanie said over Holly's shoulder.

"What... *Oh, shit.* God, Kevin... Holly. Sometimes I really like the taste of shoe leather."

Matt buried his own disappointment and smiled at Kevin. "Congrats to you both. You'll be great parents."

"The baby's due in October. I don't know how I'm going

to handle the wedding planning *and* a baby," Holly said. "But with my grandmother's dementia starting to get worse...I wanted her to see our baby before she completely forgets who I am."

Kevin stood and wrapped an arm around Holly's back and pulled her close. "Not that we have to explain shit to *anyone*." He shot Tyler a dark look.

"You'll make it work," Anna said quietly, holding Holly's gaze. "Because you have a man who obviously loves you to the moon and back. You'll figure it out. *Together.* I did it as a single mother who worked insane hours, and I figured it out. Look at the beautiful boy God blessed me with. You'll be fine." She shook her head. "No, better than fine. You'll be wonderful."

Holly's eyes filled with tears. "Thank you, Anna. You have no idea how much I needed to hear that."

Lanie turned to Matt and pointed at him as she gave him a stern look. "I swear to God, Matt Osborn, if you let her get away, I'll kick your ass myself."

Matt put his hand on Anna's knee, the feel of her bare skin making him want to touch even more of her later. "We're friends again. Maybe we should leave it at that for now." He turned to look at her for confirmation. "We still need to work some things out." He hoped to God she'd agree to a long-distance relationship, but he couldn't assume she would. Her top priority was Toby—as it should be—and she was worried about confusing him. He had to admit he worried it would confuse both boys, but maybe they could put a lot of emphasis on their friendship.

He'd find a way to convince her, because life without her was unacceptable.

# Chapter Twenty-One

Anna had never wanted something so much. This was the life she wanted for her and her son—casual get-togethers with friends and family, just hanging out and talking, but mostly she wanted the man sitting next to her. She could have this if only she could convince Phillip. Would he be open to it?

It worried her that he'd called after so long. It worried her even more that he hadn't left a message. Should she have called him back? Chances were that he'd been drunk and called her with the same old crap.

But what if he'd found out that she'd left London?

Ashley, who had been quiet for the past ten minutes, blurted out, "I call bullshit. It's so obvious the two of you have the hots for each other, you might as well have a neon sign flashing over your heads."

"Ashley!" Anna gasped.

Lanie gave her a sly grin. "She's right. We can all see it. What's the problem?"

Matt wrapped an arm around her shoulders and tugged

her closer. Anna nearly pulled away, but everyone could see they were drawn to each other. Plus, it felt so right.

Matt held her tight, as though presenting a united front. "There are a lot of things to consider, it's not just us. We need to think about the boys."

Lanie motioned to the boys, who were playing in the yard with the dogs. "It looks like they're getting along great."

"That's how they got back together," Tyler said. "Because Anna's kid's on Ethan's team."

"But I'm only here for a short time," Anna said. "I'm helping my dad get back on his feet. And then I have to go back."

"Kevin says you're in banking," Holly said. "Surely you could get a job here."

"That's not the issue, dear," Matt's mother said, giving Anna a sympathetic look. "There are other factors to consider."

"Kevin and I had other factors to consider," Holly said. "Like the fact I worked for his mother. But everything worked out."

Anna gave her a tight smile. "Legally, I'm not allowed to move out of the country with Toby. Not until he's sixteen."

"But—" Lanie started to say.

Matt squeezed Anna tighter. "Anna's custody issues aren't up for debate."

Everyone was silent for several seconds then Ashley said in a cheery tone, "Hey! Long-distance relationships can be totally hot. You spend all that time missing each other, and then when you see each other, it's like tossing gasoline onto a bonfire."

"Ashley!" Anna protested in horror. "My father is here! And Matt's mom!"

"Give me a break," her dad grumped with a grin. "I know what sex is. How do you think you got here?"

Anna cringed. "Oh, my God. Dad!"

"I agree with Ashley," Matt's mom said with a smug look. "When Matt was little, his father's construction business had a major lull and we were desperate for money. He found a four-month construction project in Texas and came home a couple times. We couldn't keep our hands off each other. We had to send Matt to stay with his grandmother for the weekend..."

"Mom!" Matt shouted.

"How do you think I got pregnant with your sister? And I didn't even need yoga to help with my pelvic floor back then." She shook her head. "I tell you, that older woman who teaches yoga at the fitness place does wonders."

Tyler burst out laughing. "Kevin, isn't your gram teaching yoga at Blue Springs Fitness?"

Kevin's face turned red. "What of it?"

"I didn't tell you I was taking classes from her? She's amazing!" Lanie said to Kevin, then turned to Ashley. "Have you taken any of her tantric yoga classes? The things I learned..."

Tyler bolted upright in his seat, sloshing beer onto his shirt. "Oh. My. God. You learned that new...*thing* that you do"—he made a fist and then realized what he was doing and dropped his hand to his lap like it was on fire—"from Kevin's *grandmother*?"

"What difference does it make?" Lanie asked. "You definitely liked it."

Kevin stuck his fingers in his ears and started to sing loudly while scrunching his eyes shut. "La la la la la."

Anna laughed to see Kevin looking so horrified.

Shaking her head with a grin, Holly tugged down his hands.

"Have you heard about her upcoming class?" Ashley asked "I hear she's about to offer an Ohm class."

Kevin closed his eyes and scrunched up his shoulders to his ears like he was a turtle. "Do I want to know what that is?"

Ashley turned to him with a straight face. "It's an orgasm class. Your gram and her husband assist men or women help their female partners have an orgasm. Right there in class."

"Oh, my God," Kevin said, looking like he was about to throw up. "Is that *legal*?"

Ashley's mouth twisted to the side as she paused for a second, deep in thought. "I don't know. But she's not having it at the fitness center so maybe not."

Kevin rose from his seat. "I need another drink."

Everyone laughed as he disappeared into the house.

Anna was busy thinking about what Ashley had suggested. Should she consider a long-distance relationship? Would Matt be open to it? She could come back a few times a year and see Matt as well as her father. She wanted Toby to have a relationship with him, especially now that they were bonding.

Lanie turned to Anna. "Maybe we should bring you to an upcoming yoga class."

Anna forced a smile. She could picture herself fitting in with Matt's friends. Holly and Lanie were already including her, and Ashley fit right in, too. It made the thought of her mostly friendless life in London seem even sadder than usual. "We'll see what we can fit in before I head back to London in a month."

"That's so sad," Holly sighed, leaning her head on Kevin's shoulder when he sat down. "You two are a real-life love story."

Anna knew she should contradict her, but the words formed a lump in her throat.

"Hey," Kevin said, looking down at his wife. "What were we?"

She laughed. "We were a fairy tale."

Kevin seemed to ponder it for a moment then pulled her close and kissed her. "Okay."

"When you two get married, I want to plan your wedding," Holly said. "If you'll let me, of course."

Anna released a nervous laugh. "Whoa. You're making a few leaps. We didn't say anything about getting married."

Holly gave her a knowing look. "You will. It's your fate."

Lanie laughed. "*Someone's* planned too many weddings."

They teased each other about Holly's profession and how Lanie didn't seem to mind Holly's romantic tendencies when she planned Lanie and Tyler's wedding several months before.

Anna felt wistful as she watched them. Matt had told her that the two women had met last September and become fast friends. While Anna could come back to see Matt a few times a year, she'd never have *this*. Matt and his friends got together often. How would Matt feel about hanging out with the couples without her? Would he want to get married? She would love to marry him, but it seemed crazy when she would be living on the other side of the ocean for ten more years. Then there was the issue of kids. She hadn't missed Matt's reaction when he found out that Holly was pregnant. He'd never made any secret of the fact that he wanted children, and while he had Ethan, Abby would take back her son at some point. Sure, she could have Matt's children, but how realistic was that if they wouldn't be together full time? It would kill Matt to see his children only a few times a year, and she could never have children with him and leave them in the United States—which meant having children wasn't a realistic option. Anna wanted to give Matt everything he wanted—he deserved to be happy—but she felt like she was offering only half promises.

Everyone stayed another hour before Anna realized her father looked like he was about to fall asleep in his chair. She leaned into Matt's ear and whispered, "Dad's exhausted. I think I should take him home."

"He could lie down in my room if he wants to rest," Matt said quietly.

"He'll never lie down here. He's too proud."

"Then home it is," Matt said. "Do you want me to take him home or do you need to do it? Do you want to come back?"

Matt was a *good* man. He was the only man she'd ever loved, but he deserved more than she had to offer. "I think we should just go."

Disappointment washed over his face. "Okay, but I think we need to talk. Several things were suggested today, and I'd like to discuss them."

She hesitated. Was there more to say? But after their past, she wanted him to feel like she'd been completely honest and open with him. "Then let me take Dad home and I'll come back. He'll probably want to nap in his chair so that will buy me a couple of hours."

"At least let me help you get him in the car."

"I do this all the time. Can I leave Toby here? It would be a huge help."

"Consider it done."

Ten minutes later, Anna had her father in the car. He was usually quiet when they drove, so he surprised her when he said, "Today was good. I need to be with people more."

Her mouth dropped open. She never would have expected to hear him say that.

He chuckled. "Yeah, I know, but an old fart can change."

"Dad!"

"That's okay. I know I'm an old fart."

She laughed. "I was going to say you're already changing."

He turned serious. "We have some hard decisions to make, my girl."

*My girl.* He hadn't called her that since she was little. She found it ironic that he used that term of endearment when their roles were about to reverse. "I know."

"I know you're leaving, and you know I wish you weren't, but some things are out of our control. Instead of spending so much time and energy fighting it, sometimes a person needs to know when to let something go."

Her heart sank. "You think I should let Matt go?"

"No. The opposite. I never saw you happier than when you were with Matt. Today only proved it. You need to find a way to get that British weasel to let the boy go. He deserves someone like Matt Osborn in his life." He cleared his throat and shifted in his seat. "But there's something else we need to talk about, and I know it's eating at you."

She cast a quick glance toward him.

"I heard you talking to Dr. Martin at my last appointment. I know you've been spending your Saturdays looking at assisted living centers."

She swallowed, unsure how to proceed.

"It's okay, Annaliese. I know I can't live alone. The idea has taken some getting used to, and I'm sorry I've been a bear to live with, but I saw the handwriting on the wall, and I was having a hard time accepting it." He paused. "I'm not gonna fight you. I'm not gonna give you a hard time."

"Dad, I'm so sorry," she said, pulling into his driveway. "If I can figure out a way to stay, then you can stay in your house."

"No," he said with a hitch in his voice. "Even if you stay, I need to move. You need to build a life with Matt. I'll only get in the way."

"Dad—no. Don't say that."

"Have you found a place for me?"

She put the car in Park and took a deep breath. "Yeah."

"Make an appointment for me to see it. Hell, I'm due for a change."

"Dad. I'm so sorry."

"It's the seasons of life, my girl. I'm ready to accept it."

\* \* \*

Matt was eager for Anna to come back. She said she thought the round trip would take her thirty minutes, but it had been forty-five minutes and there was no sign of her.

"Relax," Kevin said. "That was always your problem. You never had any game."

Matt snorted as he cleaned up the counter containing the leftover sides. Tyler and Kevin were helping while the women sat on the patio watching the boys and the dogs.

"I never needed game."

"You mean you never needed game with *Anna*," Tyler piped up.

"True." He stopped scooping a bowl of leftovers into a plastic container. "So...let's talk about the elephant in the room. Anna."

"She's going back to England," Tyler said. "How's that going to work?"

"We'll figure it out."

Kevin shot Tyler a look then turned back to Matt. "We're worried you're going to get hurt again."

"Maybe I will, but I'm gonna try to convince her to give

this a shot anyway. If I don't, I'll regret it for the rest of my life."

"Then we wish you luck," Tyler said. "Anna's still just as great as she was back when we were at MU. You know, before she dumped you."

"Ha," Matt said, shaking his head. "Thanks."

Anna showed up shortly after they'd finished cleaning up the kitchen. As soon as Lanie and Holly saw her, they told their husbands it was time to go and dragged them to the front door.

"It was wonderful to meet you, Anna," Holly said as she pulled her into a hug. "I hope to see you again soon."

"Same here," Lanie said with a mischievous grin. "We need you to help us level out the testosterone."

After Matt's friends and Ashley left, Anna moved into the kitchen and watched Matt's mother with the boys and the dogs out the back windows.

Matt put his arm around her and pulled her to his side. "I want to try to work this out, Anna. I want to find a way for us to be together. Even if it's long distance."

"Is this fair to the boys? They won't understand all the time apart."

He turned her to stare into her worried eyes. "They're smart kids. Will they want it this way? Probably not, but neither do we. But it's better than you two leaving and never seeing you again. We'll adjust. We'll figure out how to make this work."

She took a step away from him, running her hand over her head. "I've been trying to imagine how this would work and I just don't know. I have to think."

"I can come see you three or four weeks a year. Kevin can cover for me. How much time can you get off?"

"Three weeks but—"

"That's seven weeks."

"Out of fifty-two, Matt," she said in exasperation. "About a month and a half out of twelve months."

"It's a month and a half we wouldn't have otherwise." He moved closer and reached for her hand. She let him link their fingers and tug her closer. His voice lowered. "There's only one woman for me, Anna, and that's you. I've spent twelve years looking, and no one else has even come close. I'll take what I can get, just give me *something*."

Tears filled her eyes. "Matt."

"I don't want to lose you again, Anna. Let's just try it, okay?"

"It's not fair to you."

"Let me be the judge of that," he insisted.

"It's not fair to the boys."

"Then let's spend the rest of the time you have left figuring it out. We won't tell the boys anything."

She loved this man with all her being. She had two options: stay away from him until she went back to London, or give herself a month of happiness. She might be miserable when she went back, but she'd be miserable anyway. "They can't know we're together."

His eyes widened. "*Are* we together?"

She nodded. "At least until I leave. I can't commit to a long-distance relationship yet, but we need to think about what that might look like." A mischievous grin spread across her face. "But then again, you might be sick of me by the time I leave."

He wrapped his arm around her and pulled her to his chest. "I'm willing to take my chances."

"Are you sure you want to consider a long-distance relationship?" she asked. "It's going to be hard. You'll get together with Kevin and Tyler and their wives, but you'll be alone, Matt. Until Toby's sixteen, and even then, I'm not sure I'll be able to come back. He'll still be in high school. Is that fair to ask him to move then? And then there's kids."

"What about kids?"

"Matt, you want kids."

His eyes widened in surprise. "You don't?"

"I do, but not if you're living on another continent. I've seen Toby struggle with wanting his father to be part of his life. I could never willingly have a child whose father only sees him or her six or seven weeks a year. Would *you* want that?"

His face fell. "No."

She leaned her cheek against his chest and sighed.

"If you didn't have to deal with Phillip, if you weren't legally bound to stay in the UK, what would you do?" Matt asked quietly.

She was quiet for a moment then said, "I'd move back. I'd move here. But Phillip *is* an issue. Maybe this is a bad idea."

She started to pull away but he held her close. "No. It's not. I only want you, Anna. I've always wanted you. I don't want to lose you again. We'll figure out kids later."

She reached up and kissed him. "I'm sorry," she said against his lips. "If only I had—"

"No," he said, taking her hand. "No regrets. Only forward."

# Chapter Twenty-Two

On Tuesday morning, Anna sat in Blair Hansen's conference room, feeling more confident as the attorney sat down next to her.

"Good morning, Anna," Blair said with a smile. "I hear we have multiple acquaintances, several of whom called, asking me to meet with you."

"I'm not surprised," Anna said apologetically. "I'm lucky enough to have several people eager to help me. I suspect my best friend Ashley is one of them."

"And Tyler Norris, Kevin Vandemeer, and Kevin's sister, Megan, who doesn't even know you." Blair laughed. "You have a lot of people in your corner. That's always a good sign. Why don't you fill me in on what's going on?"

While Blair took notes, Anna spent the next ten minutes telling Blair about her relationship with Phillip, and the divorce, the stipulation that she keep Toby in the UK, and how little Phillip was involved in Toby's life.

Blair finished writing and looked up at her. "I'm not

going to lie—the fact that your divorce was in the UK makes
things more difficult. Have you contacted your attorney in
England?"

"No, he died a couple of years ago."

Blair held her pen in midair. "I know a barrister who
helped me with a case a few years ago. If you can get me
a copy of the decree, I can have him take a look. You said
you've been here helping your elderly father?"

Anna explained her situation about caring for her father
and how she was supposed to return in four weeks, but he
couldn't be left alone and her employer wasn't sympathetic
to the situation.

"It sounds like perhaps you need an advocate with your
employer," Blair said as she wrote something on her legal
pad. "I'm not aware of the laws on the UK in regards
to family leave, but a large corporation should be able to
handle up to six months' leave especially if you're still
working."

"I hadn't considered that," Anna said.

Blair grinned. "That's why I get paid the big bucks. Now
tell me about your ex-husband. Will he agree to let your son
stay longer?"

"Phillip doesn't know we're here."

Blair glanced up with a blank expression. "And the
decree doesn't allow for you to take him out of the country?"

Anna's stomach twisted into a pretzel. "No."

"You realize that depending on the wording in your decree, you could be accused of kidnapping your son?"

She sucked in a breath.

Blair's expression softened. "Obviously, you hadn't."

"Phillip hasn't seen Toby or paid child support for three
years," Anna said, trying not to panic. "I called him before I

left, but I was frantic to get home to my dad, and there was so much to take care of before Toby and I left…I never called him again."

Blair reached out and covered Anna's hand. "Deep breath. If your ex-husband hasn't been part of your lives, then it sounds like he doesn't even know you're gone."

"He tried to call me." Anna's heart hammered against her rib cage. "On Saturday. It would have been late there—early hours of the morning—but I didn't get to the phone in time and he didn't leave a message."

"And you didn't call him back?"

Anna shook her head. "No. After Toby was born, he drunk-called me from the pubs off and on for about two years, telling me he was sorry and begging me to give him another chance. Before Saturday night, he hadn't called me in over a year. I wondered if he drunk-dialed me and figured it out when he heard my voice mail."

"Do you think he knows you're here?"

Anna twisted her hands in her lap, feeling like she was going to be sick. "I don't know. What if he does? What if he tries to take Toby?"

"If it should come to that—which I sincerely doubt it would—we could stress how emergent the situation was and that you made an attempt to contact your ex. Do you perhaps have a record of calling him?"

"Uh…" Anna's brain was still roiling with the news she could be accused of kidnapping Toby. "I called him from my cell phone." She reached for her purse with shaking hands. "I'm sure it's still listed in my call history."

"Anna."

She glanced up at Blair.

"Relax. I will make sure you're not arrested for bringing your son here. Okay?"

She nodded, still keyed up but feeling slightly relieved. "Okay."

"Why don't you get your phone out and take a screen shot of his number and the date?" Blair reached for the phone on the table and pushed a button to call her assistant. "Melissa, I need you to get me the number for Lyle Murphy, that London attorney I consulted on the Smeller case about two years ago."

"Will do, Blair," Melissa answered right away. "Do you want me to place the call?"

"Yes, please. But it's probably after hours so call his cell, and if he gets ticked, remind him that he owes me. We need to put Anna's mind at ease."

Fifteen minutes later when Blair hung up with the London attorney, Anna was no longer paranoid that the police were going arrest her as soon as she walked out the door, and Blair had given her hope.

"If your ex-husband hasn't been part of Toby's life up to this point," Blair said, "he might not put up a fight, but the fact he has the stipulation in the first place... Is Phillip vindictive?"

"Sometimes."

Blair pressed her lips together then said, "The best course of action is for you to call him and explain that you're here and why, then see how he reacts. If he handles that well, then broach the subject of making changes to the decree. The fact he's shown little interest bodes well for you, and it would be in your best interest for him to agree and avoid a long, drawn-out fight. It usually helps if you offer something in return. Perhaps agree to bring Toby back once a year to see your ex. It sounds like you can afford the trip so make it clear you'll foot the bill. Also, if you really are adamant about not collecting back-owed child maintenance, suggest that you'll forgive all the money he owes you if he'll agree. In fact," Blair said, tapping her pen on her legal pad. "Start with that. Save the visits as leverage in negotiating."

Anna nodded. "Good idea."

"Lyle's prepared to take action depending on how your conversation goes."

"Thank you, Blair."

Blair smiled. "Nothing makes me happier than helping women in difficult situations." She stood and grabbed a business card from a stack on a credenza against the wall, then picked up her pen and wrote a phone number on the back. "This is my cell phone number. Call me after your conversation with Phillip or for any reason."

"Oh..." Anna said, looking down at the card Blair handed her. "I'd hate to disturb you."

"That's what I'm here for, Anna." She grinned.

Anna walked out of the office, holding her cell phone in her hand, wondering when to make the call. She considered waiting until later, but decided now was best, especially with the newly gained confidence Blair had given her.

She stopped at a coffee shop on the first floor and ordered a drink, then sat down and looked at her phone.

*My whole future will be determined by this call.*

She shook her head in irritation. She wasn't prone to melodrama and now wasn't the time to start. Deciding to be pragmatic, she quickly pulled up Phillip's number and placed the call, wondering if he was still at his office. It had to be close to seven in the evening.

Her heartbeat picked up as the phone began to ring. After two rings she wasn't sure he'd answer, but then she heard his voice on the other end.

"Hello?"

"Phillip. It's Annaliese."

"Annaliese? This is a surprise."

"I called you nearly two months ago."

"Yeah, about that...Sorry I never called you back. I was busy."

"For two months?"

"Well...in my defense, we *are* divorced."

She almost countered that they had a son together, but considered that it might be best to hold off bringing up Toby. "You called me Saturday night."

"Yeah, well..."

When he didn't say anything else, she decided her drunk call theory was correct. "There was a reason for my call a couple of months ago." Only after the words came out of her mouth did she realize she sounded curt.

"Oh, Anna," he groaned. "I don't want to fight with you. Let's start this conversation over again."

Leaning her elbow on the table, she rested her forehead on her hand. "Okay."

"Annaliese, so lovely to hear from you," he said in the upper-crust voice he'd always reserved for when he was with his highbrow family.

She couldn't help grinning; there was no denying Phillip had always been a charmer and he could pour it on pretty thick. "Thank you, Phillip. What have you been up to?" She intentionally left off *for the last three years*.

"I got a new job. A grown-up one."

"Your previous jobs were grown-up jobs," she said without malice. "You just never treated them like you were a grown-up."

"I'll give you that." He paused and some of the playfulness left his voice. "I've been working on it."

"Have you met someone?" she asked. She thought she'd been that someone once.

"No," he said. "But my birthday's next week and something about hitting the big three-nine makes you do a lot of thinking."

The hairs on the back of her neck stood on end, worried about where this conversation was going. She also noticed that he hadn't commented on the fact that Toby's birthday was only a few days after his. "Well," she said, "it sounds like you're making steps in the right direction."

"I've been thinking about us."

*Shit.* "What in particular?"

"Where did we go wrong, Annaliese?"

She sighed. "You weren't ready to settle down. You weren't ready for a family."

"So how are you?" he asked, ignoring her statement. "Are you still with WorldCon Bank?"

"Um…yeah…and that's partially why I called."

"Are you having trouble with your job?" He paused. "You need money."

She expected him to sound pissed that she might be asking for money, but he sounded…guilty. This might work to her advantage. "Actually, the reason I called you a couple of months ago was to tell you that my father had an accident and broke his leg. He's in pretty bad shape."

"Oh, Anna. I'm sorry to hear that."

"Yeah…He needed help so I came here to take care of him."

He paused. "You're in the States now?"

"Yeah."

"What about Toby?" His tone was sharper.

Her back stiffened, and she prepared herself for an argument. "He's with me."

"You took him there without talking to me?" he asked, starting to sound combative.

"Phillip, I tried to call you."

"Still…"

"Still nothing. Why would you care?" Anna asked. "You haven't seen him in three years, not to mention you haven't paid a dime of child maintenance."

"So *that's* what this is about?" he asked, starting to get angry.

"No, Phillip," she said, forcing herself to keep her cool. "It's about my father. He was in the hospital and needed daily physical therapy. If I didn't come help him, he would have gone to a rehab center. It would have killed him. I got the call from the hospital and made arrangements to leave all within two days. Like I said, I tried to call you, but you didn't answer. And since you hadn't seen Toby in years, I didn't think coming to the States for three months would make any difference."

He was silent for several seconds, and Anna's blood pressure rose. What if he gave her trouble over this? "So you called me to tell me you're in the States."

"Actually, there's more." When he didn't respond, she said, "My father's not progressing as quickly as his doctor would like. He can't live alone anymore."

"You're wanting to stay longer?"

"Yes."

"Why do I get the feeling you're not calling to say you're staying for two more weeks?"

"You're right. I want to move back here permanently. My father's not getting any younger, and he and Toby are starting to get to know each other. Dad's teaching him how to play checkers." He was silent again. "I'd like to handle this amicably, Phillip."

"You're asking me to give him up?"

"Haven't you already done that?" she asked softly.

"I'm no good with babies, Annaliese. We both knew that. I was waiting until he got older."

"That's not how it works, Phillip. You can't just ignore your child until you think he's going to be fun, because guess what? That boy has been a delight his entire five—nearly six—years. You owed your son support—both emotional and financial."

"Ahh, the child maintenance...but it wasn't like I was seeing him."

"You think child maintenance is like a usage fee?" she asked in disbelief. "Since you don't see him, you don't have to pay for his expenses?"

"I never said that," he said defensively.

"No, it was just strongly inferred."

"I know I've screwed up, Annaliese. I told you I've been thinking things over, and I know I've fucked up. You want me to start paying maintenance?"

"Honestly, Phillip, I'll let every pound of maintenance go if you just agree to let me live in the States."

"So you *are* asking me to give him up?"

She took a breath to sound calm and rational. Better to play this a different way. "I don't want to shut you out of his life. Toby's beyond curious about you."

"I'm sure you gave him an earful," he retorted.

"No. I haven't vilified you. What purpose would it serve to make him bitter? I want better for him. I want him to be happy."

"Has he asked about me?"

"Occasionally," she answered truthfully. "I've told him that you have your own life and we have ours, but it's no reflection on him."

"He thinks I'm not there because he's done something wrong?"

"He's a small child, Phillip. He looks for answers. But he knows other children with absent parents, or no father at all. He's not traumatized by it." This was going off track. She really needed him to agree. "Like I said, you're welcome to see Toby. We can plan trips back to London so you can see him for days at a time." She paused. "I'd like your blessing to stay."

"So if I agree... what do you need from me?"

"I'll have my barrister draw up the paperwork for you to sign."

"I'll be giving him up."

"No," Anna said. "I promise you that you can see him."

"You'd do that even after I haven't contacted you for three years?"

"Toby is my priority, Phillip."

"I know," he said, sounding aggravated. "He always was."

She didn't dare touch that comment.

He cleared his throat. "I need to think about this."

"Of course," she said, even though she'd hoped to get his immediate agreement. "If you have any questions of concerns, feel free to call or text."

"It was really good to talk to you, Annaliese."

"Yeah, you, too."

"I'll let you know soon."

He hung up, and she was about to call Matt when her phone rang with Phillip's name on the screen. Was that a good or bad sign?

"Well, that was fast," she said as she answered the phone, trying to keep her tone light and breezy.

"There's no doubt I've been a wanker, and I'm trying to be a better person. It took me about three seconds to realize I needed to do the right thing."

Her breath caught in her chest. "Does that mean..."

"You can stay," Phillip said. "But I want to start seeing Toby."

She shook her head, trying to lodge her brain back into place and negotiate. "Yeah…of course. I can bring him back for a week over summer break."

"I want two weeks. I can take him to see my parents."

She almost protested, then realized Toby needed this connection to his father's family. "Okay."

"Okay…" Phillip paused. "I screwed us up, Annaliese. I'm sorry."

"Water under the bridge, Phillip."

"It really *was* good hearing from you."

She didn't want to talk about the past. She was too focused on the future. "I'll have my barrister send you the paperwork."

"All right. Good-bye, Annaliese."

"Bye."

Anna hung up and stomped her feet under the table in excitement. She called Blair and told her the news, and Blair said the barrister would have the paperwork sent out within the next few days.

"Does it usually move that quickly?" Anna asked.

"No," Blair admitted. "But the faster this is signed, sealed, and delivered, the better."

\* \* \*

Matt was on the jobsite talking to the electrical foreman about a setback on the outdoor shopping mall they were working on, trying to keep his mind off Anna.

He'd been anxious all morning knowing she was meeting with Blair, and had made enough screwups that he'd considered sending himself home until he heard from her. As the morning had gone on, he'd gotten more worried. She'd promised to call him after her appointment with Blair but now it was lunchtime. What did it mean that she hadn't called?

He was just about to pull out his phone and call her when he saw her father's car pull into the parking lot. She'd never visited him on a jobsite. This couldn't be good.

As Anna got out of the car, Matt held up a hand and said absently to the foreman, "Hold on, Dan. Give me a minute." By the time he'd finished the sentence, he was already several feet away.

She was in a white blouse and a black skirt that showed off her figure, and her three-inch heels reminded him of the night he'd seen her at the first soccer practice. Why hadn't she called him? Was she here to deliver bad news?

"Anna?" he asked, still several feet away but unable to read her face.

She saw him and started to cry.

"What happened?" he asked, trying not to panic. "Did you talk to Blair?"

She nodded, starting to sob. "I called Phillip."

"*What?* You did? What happened?"

She threw her arms around his neck and buried her face into his chest. "I can't believe it. I had to come tell you."

"Anna, you're scaring the shit out of me. Whatever happened, we'll work it out, okay? Just tell me."

She shook her head, trying to catch her breath. "No. That's not it. I'm sorry." She sucked in a breath and slowly pushed it out. "I can stay."

Sure he'd heard her wrong, he cupped the sides of her head and stared into her face. "*What?*"

She covered his hands with her own. "Phillip agreed. I can stay. I don't have go back."

"I need to hear this again," he said. "Say it again."

A watery smile spread across her face. "I can stay." She started to cry again.

He crushed her mouth with his and kissed her, and when he lifted his head, he blurted out, "Marry me."

"What?"

"I love you, Annaliese Fischer. We've wasted twelve damn years, and I don't want to wait another minute. Marry me."

She gasped. "But... don't you want to wait to be sure?"

"I *am* sure. I've never been so damn sure of anything in my life. You're still the same person I loved back then. We can wait five minutes, five months, or five years, and it's not going to change. I want you to be my wife." *Oh, shit.* "You want to wait." A new panic washed through him. Was she going to turn him down like she had twelve years ago? "We can wait. You can turn me down. I won't be upset this time."

Anna shook her head. "No. I want to marry you... it's just all happening so fast."

"But it feels right, doesn't it?" he asked.

She nodded, smiling up at him. "Yeah. It feels perfect."

He kissed her again, still wondering if he was dreaming. "I can't believe it." Then a new thought hit him. "I don't have a ring. Shit, I screwed this up, didn't I? Tyler proposed to Lanie with a marching band."

She smiled up at him then brushed her lips against his. "I have the ring. The one you gave me."

His heart skipped a beat, sure he'd heard her wrong. "You kept my ring?"

"I picked it up off the table. When I came home for Mom's funeral, I brought it with me. I was going to apologize and, if I'm honest, see if you'd forgive me. I think part of me hoped we could start again. But Ashley said you had a girlfriend, and I was devastated. Between losing my mom and knowing I'd lost you for good, I put it in the bag of her clothes to give to the thrift store. But Dad must have found it and kept it all this time. He put it in a box of photos he gave me last weekend."

He felt like he was going to be sick. So much fucking wasted time. "Anna, I didn't have a girlfriend six years ago."

"What?"

"Ashley was wrong. I didn't have a girlfriend when you came back for your mother's funeral."

"How do you know that?"

"Because I did the math in my head already. I wondered how many times our paths almost crossed and missed each other. I was single."

She started to cry again. "I'm sorry."

"No. No. No more tears over the past." He gave her a hard kiss. "Only happiness for us. We're due."

"Ask me again," she said, wiping her face. "Ask me to marry you again."

Matt got down on one knee and took her hand. "Anna, make me the happiest man alive and marry me."

"Yes," she said with tears in her eyes. "Yes. Forever, yes."

# Chapter Twenty-Three

Two weeks later, Anna stood on the sidelines of the soccer field, watching Matt practicing with ten five- and six-year-olds. She glanced down at the ring on her hand—not the one Matt had given her before. He'd declared it cursed and bought her a new one, giving it to her with the boys, who were shocked then ecstatic. They could have cared less about the oval one-carat stone surrounded by smaller diamonds; they were just excited that they were going to live together.

They were getting married in five days.

She'd expected some resistance from their family and friends. They were moving fast, but so far no one had put up a protest.

"Who am I to judge?" Holly had said when Anna and Matt called her to see if she'd plan their wedding. "Kevin and I knew each other a month before we got married. You two were together over a year before you broke up. You're the only ones who can decide whether it's too soon."

They decided to have a Sunday wedding because the first soccer game of the season was on Saturday and the boys were so excited Anna said there was no reason they had to miss it. They'd decided on an outdoor wedding in Matt's backyard, and Matt and Kevin had been building an arched trellis for them to get married under. Holly had a landscape designer come and plant a multitude of flowers the week before and she had found a minister to conduct the ceremony at sunset. They'd be surrounded by candles and Tiki lights. She'd quit her job, so she had plenty of time to help Holly prepare for the wedding... between packing up her father's house.

The simple reception would be in the backyard with cake and drinks and a playlist to dance to. Because it was a school night, they told the boys they could stay home from school the next day.

The men had ordered their tuxes and Anna had found an off-the-rack wedding dress. Everything was coming together perfectly—almost *too* perfectly—and Anna had a sinking feeling something would go wrong. Especially since Phillip hadn't signed the papers letting her stay in the States.

She'd sent him several texts over the last two weeks, asking him if he'd received them, and if there was a problem. Each time he'd texted back, saying not to worry. He'd do the "right thing."

But did the *right thing* mean he'd sign them? She was getting more and more nervous. Maybe she shouldn't have agreed to get married so soon, but they'd wasted so much time. She refused to let herself worry about it tonight.

Their wedding might be in five days, but tonight they were celebrating Toby's birthday.

The soccer team was having a practice scrimmage, and

Toby slipped around one of his teammates and kicked a ball into the goal.

"Did you see that, Mummy?" he shouted over to her.

"I saw it, birthday boy!"

He ran over to Matt, who affectionately rubbed the boy's head. Matt leaned down and said something that made a wide grin spread across Toby's face.

A car stopped on the side of the road, and a man looked out onto the field. He didn't have a child with him, so the fact he was so intently studying the field set Anna's nerves on edge.

Something about him getting out of the car looked familiar, but there was no way it could be *him*. Still, it made her nervous enough that she headed toward him.

He wore jeans and a button-down shirt. His loafers weren't faring so well as he made his way down the grassy hill. He took one look at Anna and broke into a warm smile. "Annaliese!" He held his hands out at his sides. "Surprise!"

She felt light-headed and she blinked, hoping to snap herself out of her stupor. "Phillip? What in the hell are you doing here?"

"I'm here to see my son. It's his birthday, isn't it?" His eyes narrowed. "I'm pretty sure it's today."

"Yes, it's today. But what are you doing *here*?" she repeated. Why hadn't he called before showing up? Had he shown up to sign the papers in person?

He grinned. "I told you, I've been doing a lot of thinking about you and me and what went wrong, so I came for Toby's birthday." He scanned the kids on the field. "Is he out there?"

He didn't even know what his son looked like. But how would he? He hadn't seen him since he was two.

"I don't know, Phillip. Why don't you tell me?"

He gave her a confused look. "Why are you so upset? I thought you'd think this was a good thing. You said I could see him over the summer."

"You should have called first. Summer break's only a month away." How would Toby react to this? She needed to prepare him to meet the father who hadn't given him the time of day. She needed to make sure he was emotionally ready. Leave it to Phillip to think only of himself.

"So, I'm early. Where is he?" He shielded his eyes from the sun and scanned the field. "Uh-oh," he said, looking amused. "Is this a closed practice? The coach is headed right for me."

Anna turned, and sure enough, Matt was headed their way.

Given Matt's animosity toward her ex-husband, this was bound to go badly.

\* \* \*

Matt had kept his eye on Anna most of the practice, but in his defense, he couldn't help himself. He still struggled to believe that she was here, let alone that they were getting married in less than a week. Part of him wanted to make sure she was really here and not some hallucination. Plus, she was sexy as hell and he couldn't seem to keep his eyes off her.

He'd noticed the unfamiliar car with the man he didn't recognize pull up to the curb before Anna seemed to. But when the man got out of the car and headed straight for Anna, Matt was on full alert and headed straight for him.

"Hey, Coach Matt," one of the kids protested as Matt strode through the middle of the scrimmage.

"I'll be right back," he responded, keeping his gaze on the man who was engaged in a conversation with Anna. A conversation that was not going well from the looks of it.

A ball hit Matt in the back of the head, but he ignored it and kept walking.

By the time Matt reached them, the man had turned his attention to Matt, wearing a smart-ass grin. Matt had the irrational urge to wipe it off his face.

"Anna?" Matt asked, still several feet away. "Are you all right?"

"Yeah," she said, looking anything but with her pale face and wide eyes.

He reached out a hand toward her, wanting to put himself between the two of them.

"Can I help you?" Matt asked.

The guy's smart-ass grin spread. "I'm here to see my son. Maybe you'll tell me which one of those kids is him since Annaliese isn't so forthcoming."

Matt's blood ran cold when he heard the first word uttered in a British accent.

*Oh, fuck.*

Was he here to cause trouble? The look on his face suggested that he was.

A swarm of emotions filled his head, choking out reasonable thought, but there were ten kids down on the field, one of which was his nephew and the other Anna's son—a boy this prick couldn't even recognize. But then again, he hadn't seen the boy for over three years. How *would* he recognize him?

Anna said to Matt with pleading eyes, "I can handle this."

"This doesn't concern you, Coach. Don't you have a bunch of kids to teach?" the asshole asked. "Or do you need someone to show them how to play *real* football?"

Matt took a step forward, but Anna stepped between them.

"*Matt.* I've got this."

This man had been out of their lives for three years. *Three years.* Why show up now?

Matt was torn over leaving her to deal with him, but Phillip was *her* ex, and she'd never been one to want someone else to fight her battles for her. As long as he didn't appear to be threatening her, Matt would back off...but he'd still be watching. "Let me know if you need me."

*   *   *

Anna watched Matt head back to the field, thankful there hadn't been an ugly confrontation between the two men.

"Really, Annaliese?" Phillip said in a sneer, "The football coach? So original."

"And screwing models and nineteen-year-olds *is*?"

"*I'm* changing."

"How long has it been since you screwed a woman who wouldn't be considered cliché."

His smile fell.

"Why are you here, Phillip?"

His dazzling hazel eyes turned to her. "I want us to try again."

Her mouth dropped open. "*What?* Are you kidding me? Try *again*? That would insinuate you tried in the first place, but just so we're clear, that ship sailed to the fucking middle of the Pacific Ocean and sank to the deep, murky depths the night you missed your son's birth because you were too busy screwing a woman you picked up in a pub."

He groaned. "I've apologized for it a hundred times, Annaliese."

"Actually, Phillip, you never *once* apologized. You made plenty of excuses, but no apologies."

"Well...I *am* sorry."

"And while I appreciate the sudden and strangely suspicious effort, it's *literally* six years too late—"

He gave her a triumphant smile. "I *knew* today was his birthday."

"Well, congratulations. You *guessed* the correct date of your son's birth."

"Annaliese," he groaned. "Come on. Don't you ever wonder how it could have been if we'd made it work?"

"There is no we. *We* ended before we were even married. *We* ended when I found out I was pregnant and you were still busy sleeping around. I was stupid enough to fall for the 'I've changed' word vomit before and look where that got me—pregnant and alone."

He frowned and took a step closer, lowering his voice. "I've screwed up, I won't deny it. I should have been there for you, but if we're honest, that's not the real reason we didn't work. It's because you never could get over that college boyfriend of yours. What was his name? Mike? Mitch?" He gasped and turned his gaze back to the field. "*Matt.* His name was Matt. And he lived in your home town."

*Shit.*

She shot him a glare. "My personal life is none of your business, Phillip. Not anymore."

"Actually, Annaliese, when you decide to move *my son* to the other side of the world because you're screwing your old college boyfriend, it *makes* it my business."

"*Your son?* You never showed one *minute* of interest in Toby until I called you two weeks ago."

"Not true," he said, getting pissed. "I told you I'd been thinking about us and what went wrong."

"And you decided to place the blame of our failed marriage on *me? Seriously?* Could you be any more delusional?"

He grimaced. "I suppose I'm partially to blame. But I'm taking an interest in him now." He pointed out to the field. "And I don't like my son being around *him*."

She wanted to kick Phillip's ass all the way back to London, but antagonism wasn't going to help her cause. And her cause was to get her ex-husband to sign the papers allowing her to stay in Blue Springs.

Her legs weakened as she realized what was at risk. What if Phillip decided not to sign?

She was handling this all wrong, but damned if it didn't burn to have to kiss his ass to protect her son—to finally have the life she'd always wished for.

"Okay," she said, trying to keep a civil tone. "So you want to be involved in your son's life . . . then tell me which one is your son."

"What?"

"Point out which child is your son."

His brow lowered as he scanned the field, then he pointed. "That one. The one on the end who just kicked the ball."

"The one with the bun?" she asked in disbelief. "That's a girl named Becca."

"Oh. Well she looks kind of like him and man buns are in."

"The bun aside, she looks *nothing* like him."

"Fine. One down. My odds of picking him out are getting better."

How would Toby react if he found out that his father showed up and not only didn't recognize him, but had considered it a game to guess which child was him? "Phillip, you need to go."

"I want to see my son, Annaliese."

"No. You want to use him as a tool to get whatever you

*think* you want." She'd spent the last six years protecting Toby from every imaginable danger—from cars in the street, to poisonous chemicals, to strangers. She never imagined that she'd have to protect him from his own father.

"I want you," he said. "I want you back."

She looked at him in horror. "Is this a *game* to you?"

"No, Annaliese. Is it so hard to imagine that I want you back? That I want us to be a family?"

"Yes. It *is* hard to imagine. You never loved me. You and I are not getting back together, and if you want to get to know your son, dropping out of nowhere on his birthday is a cruel and heartless way to do it. The fact you can't see that is alarming."

"I want to see my son, Annaliese," he repeated, sounding angrier and more insistent.

"Then call me and we'll make arrangements, but not today. You have no idea how much it will hurt him for you to show up like this. I won't let you ruin this for him. You need to go."

He turned to look out onto the field as though he was still trying to identify his son. "Fine," he finally said. "I'll go, but I'm not giving up on him or you."

That was what she was afraid of.

# Chapter Twenty-Four

T ake a deep breath," Blair said over the phone.

As soon as Phillip left, Anna had called Blair in a state of panic and told her what happened. "I can't lose Toby."

"You won't. We'll work this out."

"I think I've screwed up everything." She waved to Matt as he shot her another worried glance.

"No," Blair said. "You stood your ground and protected your son. You did the right thing. I know you're upset, but he can't do anything tonight, so as hard as this is, try to put it to the side and enjoy your son's birthday." She paused and her voice softened. "I know. Easier said than done, but the more upset you get, the more power you give him over you."

"I'm getting married, Blair."

Lawyer Blair was back. "What? When?"

"Sunday."

Blair hesitated. "You didn't mention you were engaged when you were in my office."

"I wasn't." Anna lifted a hand to her temple, feeling her panic start to bubble up again. "Matt proposed after I found out that Phillip agreed to let me move here, and we've been apart so long... We just want to be together. I've wasted so much time. I don't want to waste any more."

"What about your father?"

"He's still moving into the assisted living apartment. He actually wants to go there, but he's moving into Matt's house with us until it's available." She took a breath. "He's all for us getting married. Look, I know it's fast, but we were together before and—"

"Anna," Blair said in a soothing voice. "You don't have to explain yourself to me. I dated my husband in law school and then we broke up. When we met again, it was at his cousin's wedding and he was a groomsman. Oh, and the groom just happened to be *my fiancé*. It's a long, sordid tale, but bottom line is I, of all people, understand."

"Thank you."

"But"—her tone became sober—"the fact is that as far as we know, Phillip hasn't signed the new agreement. And if he *doesn't* sign, you *will* have to return to England... and *soon* unless he gives you permission to stay longer, which I highly suggest we get in writing."

"You mean I might have to go back to England after Matt and I are married."

"I don't want to alarm you, Anna, but if Phillip raises a stink, you might have to go back before you even make it to the altar."

Anna felt like she was going to vomit. "I have to cancel my wedding."

"Don't make any decisions tonight, but I want you to come to my office first thing tomorrow. And bring Matt if you like. This does pertain to the both of you."

"If I have to go back...I already quit my job, Blair." Oh, God. What was she going to do?

"Come in tomorrow and we'll work it out then."

\* \* \*

Matt was dying to know what happened with Anna's ex and even more worried when he saw her on the phone for at least ten minutes, pacing close to the road. He'd started to walk toward her, but she'd lifted her hand, telling him to hold off. Common sense told him that she'd called Blair, who was obviously more qualified to handle this than he was, but damn, Anna was upset and he wanted to be there for her, even if only for support.

He called practice early, and held a quick team meeting to make sure everyone knew when and where to be on Saturday for the game. "Any questions?" he asked.

He answered a few questions about snacks and what socks to wear, then told Ethan and Toby to gather all the equipment as he hurried over to Anna. She was off the phone and her arms were wrapped across her chest, but it was the expression on her face that scared him.

"So that was Phillip," he said in a matter-of-fact tone, trying to bury his anger at Anna's ex-husband. Outrage, no matter how justified, wouldn't help anything right now.

Her cheeks pinkened. "I'm so sorry. I should have never married him. I should have come back home to have Toby. I was stupid and now I'm paying for it."

"Jesus, Anna," he said, grabbing her upper arms. "I lived with a bank robber. I think I won the Worst Ex contest, so no guilt. Now what happened?"

Tears swam in her eyes. "It's bad."

He swallowed the bile rising in his throat. "How bad?"

She shook her head, only spiking his fear.

"What did he want?"

"To see Toby. To try to make *us* work again, but as you figured out, he doesn't even recognize his own son…" She bit her quivering lip. "I handled it all wrong. I think I made it worse."

He hauled her to his chest, burying a hand in her hair as he held her tight, scared he was going to lose her again. "Do you…" His voice broke and he started again. "Do you want to try again with him?"

She jerked out of his hold and stared up at him with fury in her eyes. "No! How can you ask that?"

"Because I'm scared, Anna. I just got you back. I can't handle…"

She lifted her hand to his face and gave him a sad smile. "I love you, Matt. I would rather live in a cardboard box than go back to him, but you have to believe me when I say there really is *nothing* to go back to with him. We weren't ever really together, not really. He moved a few things into my place, but he still had his apartment. We were married four months before Toby was born, and then I had the locks changed before I even went home from delivering him. That's not a marriage." Tears filled her eyes again. "But Blair—"

"We got everything, Uncle Matt," Ethan said, dragging a giant bag behind him stuffed with soccer balls. Toby followed behind hauling a bag of cones. "Can we go to Red Robin now? I want to give Toby his present."

Anna turned her back to the boys and wiped her face, then pivoted around with a bright smile. "Yes! We have to go to the restaurant named after Toby!"

"Anna…" Matt said, grabbing her wrist.

She gave him a gentle kiss, her lips lingering longer than

usual before she whispered, "Later. I refuse to let Phillip ruin Toby's birthday."

"Agreed." The asshole had already ruined it for him and Anna, he'd be damned if he stole it from Toby.

\* \* \*

An hour later, they were at the restaurant with Anna's father and Matt's mother, finishing their dinners and anticipating the waiters bringing out a sundae and singing "Happy Birthday." Anna choked down more of her food so she didn't look like she was upset, trying to put as much of the nightmare out of her head as she could. But it was hard to talk about the upcoming wedding when she wasn't sure there would be one. Instead she focused on the fact that Toby was surrounded by people who loved him—something he'd never had before—and the thought of having that snatched away from her ripped her soul to shreds.

Toby was the priority here, not her and her relationship with Matt. She needed to maintain her perspective.

The waitstaff emerged, singing their own version of a birthday song, and Toby beamed with happiness. Anna smiled at him, forcing her eyes to remain dry, and Matt grabbed her hand and squeezed.

"Make a wish," Ethan said.

Toby closed his eyes, then opened them and blew out the candle.

And that's when Anna saw him, sitting at the bar watching them with a smirk.

Her body stiffened and Matt noticed immediately, turning toward her with a worried expression. "Anna?"

She mutely shook her head, pushing him to get out of the

booth so she could stand. Phillip was on his way to their table, and she had to get Toby out of there.

But Matt realized the source of her panic and stood, moving to the side so Anna could get out.

"Toby, let's go to the bathroom." One look at the fury on Matt's face made her add, "Ethan, too." Surely Phillip wouldn't dare follow them into the women's bathroom.

Toby looked up at her like she'd lost her mind. "But I don't have to go."

"That's the man who showed up asking for directions to the soccer practice," Anna's father said. "He said he worked with you."

That explained how Phillip had found them at the field.

But Phillip was already at the table. Matt stood in front of him, looking slightly down at her ex. "This is a private party."

Anna tried to reach over and lift Toby from his seat, but he jerked out of her hands. "I don't have to go, and I want to eat my ice cream."

*Dammit.*

She let go of her son and turned to face Phillip. "Not now."

"It's his birthday."

"It's never mattered to you before," she said, trying to keep tears from her voice. "This is the first birthday he's had an actual party. I'm begging you, Phillip. Don't take this from him."

"Take this from him? I'm just trying to join it. Don't be so melodramatic, Annaliese." He grinned as he glanced at the ring on her finger. "It seems like being cordial would work in your best interest here. You're cordial..." He put his hand on his chest. "And then I'm cordial. I happen to have some papers you're very interested in, and they currently don't have a signature." He paused and lowered his voice. "I just want to meet him again, for fuck's sake."

Matt's hand rested on her shoulder. If she let him talk to Toby in exchange for him signing the agreement, was she selling out her son?

She was about to send Phillip away, but Toby stood behind her and tugged on her arm. "Mummy?"

A smile that looked genuine spread across Phillip's face as he squatted so he was eye level with her son. "Hi, you must be the birthday boy."

Anna put her hand on his head as Toby nodded.

"Do you know who I am?"

He shook his head, wide-eyed.

Phillip glanced up at Anna for two seconds then looked behind her at their now silent and confused party. "I'm a friend of your mom's."

"You talk like me," Toby said.

Phillip's grin spread. "That's right. We're more alike than you think. Anyway, I brought you a present for your birthday, but you have to come over here to get it." He held out a rectangular white box with a big red bow.

Anna's heart lurched in her chest, and she was torn when Toby glanced up at her, seeking permission.

Phillip wasn't going to let this go, and the sooner he left, the better. She bit her bottom lip and nodded.

Toby took a couple of tentative steps toward Phillip, then glanced back at Anna. She forced a smile as Matt's hand squeezed her shoulder.

Phillip studied Toby's face in awe. "You look like your mother." Toby studied the present, and Phillip laughed. "I guess you want this, don't you?" Toby nodded and Phillip handed it over. "You might already have one of these, so if you do, I'll take you to get something else."

Toby held the box with both hands. "I can't go with strangers."

Anna sucked in a breath, ready for Phillip to out himself.

Phillip laughed again. "I suppose I *am* a stranger, but I'd like to change that. Go sit down and open your present. I need to talk to your mother."

Toby turned to slide into his seat and Phillip stood. "He's beautiful, Annaliese."

"Yes, he is," she said. "Inside and out."

"I want to see him. Tomorrow. I want to be the one to tell him who I really am. I'll call you later to make the arrangements." He turned to Matt, his eyes hardening. "If you ever try to keep me from seeing my son again, I'll kick your ass. Got it?"

Matt stood his ground. "I'll do everything in my power to protect that boy, do *you* get it?"

Phillip didn't answer as he spun around and stomped out of the restaurant.

# Chapter Twenty-Five

The next night Anna stood in front of room 227 of the Hampton Inn, Toby's hand clinging to hers. She'd told him they were going to see her friend from the night before, and he seemed nervous. There was a good chance he was picking up on Anna's anxiety, but he'd already seemed to form his own opinion of Phillip, deeming him scary.

Phillip had wanted her to just drop Toby off, but she made it perfectly clear that she would be with her son the entire time on this visit.

Anna and Matt had gone to see Blair that morning. She'd told Anna that she had the London barrister filing a petition to let her stay in the United States until the court decided, but she ran the risk of losing the stay and would have to go back to England or let Phillip take her son.

"No. No way." She turned to Matt. "We should cancel the wedding. We can't take the risk of me having to leave."

Matt took her hands. "I'm willing to take the chance.

Even if we get married and you leave immediately to get on a plane to London, I want to do it. Nothing is changing my mind. No matter where we live."

"Matt...I can't—"

"If you don't want to marry me, I understand, but as far as I'm concerned, nothing has changed."

Now that she'd decided to marry him, the thought of calling off the wedding ripped her heart to shreds. "No. I still want to marry you."

So now, based on Blair's advice, Anna stood outside Phillip's hotel room, trying to look reasonable and cooperative, so if he didn't sign, she had established that she was more than willing to give Phillip access to their son.

The door swung open, and Phillip greeted them both with a smile. "No guard dog today?" he asked Anna.

"We don't have a dog," Toby said in a tone slightly louder than a whisper.

Phillip glanced down at him and chuckled. "I'd forgotten children were so literal."

Anna didn't respond.

Phillip stepped out of the way. "Come in. Have a seat."

They walked into the room and Phillip shut the door behind them. Anna sat in the chair in the corner next to the bed, and Toby stayed next to her, clinging to her leg with one hand and clutching his iPad in the other. She wrapped an arm around his back, and held him close to reassure him that she was there, but she wasn't feeling very reassured herself.

Phillip sat on the bed. "Do you like your iPad?"

Toby nodded. "I never had one before."

A pleased smile spread across Phillip's face. "Well, then I did good."

Toby didn't answer.

"Do you know who I am?" Phillip asked, leaning over to hold eye contact.

Toby nodded. "You're friends with Mummy."

"That's right. Do you know how we know each other?" When Toby shook his head, Phillip said, "We used to be married."

Toby narrowed his eyes. "You're not married anymore because Mummy is marrying Matt on Sunday."

Phillip's amused face rose to look at her, but she also saw anger in his eyes.

Matt had introduced the idea of coaching Toby on what to say and what not to say, but Anna had said it would only confuse him and suggested they had something to hide. She still stood by that belief, but there was no doubt Phillip would use everything at his disposal.

"But your mum and I used to be married, and we had a baby. Do you know who that is?"

Toby looked up at Anna with questions in her eyes, and she nodded. He turned back to Phillip. "Me."

"That's right. You're brilliant, aren't you? Your mum says you're in Year 1 at school."

"It's kindergarten here."

Phillip nodded, his smile fading. "So you've been living here for a while, huh?"

Toby nodded.

"Have you been living with your football coach?" he asked in a bitter tone.

"Phillip!" Anna scolded. "That is inappropriate."

"Is it, Annaliese?" he asked in a snide tone.

Toby glanced between the two of them. "We live with Grandpa, but we're moving to Matt's after Mummy and Matt get married. Ethan has two dogs, but he doesn't have guard dogs."

"Do you like Matt?" Phillip asked.

Toby nodded vigorously. "He teaches me how to play soccer."

"It's football," Phillip said curtly. "These bloody Americans call it something it's not."

Toby shrank back into Anna.

Phillip pushed out a sigh and ran his hand through his hair in frustration. "What have you been telling him about me?" he angrily demanded.

"I've told him absolutely nothing about you," Anna said, trying to keep her tone civil. Shouting at him would only scare Toby. "Every impression he has of you up to this point is what you've shown him yourself."

He looked frustrated by that, then turned to Toby. "You know I'm your dad, right?"

Toby hesitated, then gave one nod of affirmation.

"Do you have any questions?"

Toby glanced up at Anna again. When she nodded, he turned to Phillip and shook his head.

"So what do you want to do?" Phillip asked. "Are you hungry?"

Toby shook his head.

Phillip turned to Anna in frustration. "Is he always this quiet?"

"He is with people he doesn't know."

"I'm his father, for Christ sake."

"He still doesn't know you. You can't just show up three or four years later and expect him to know who you are."

"Why didn't you tell him about me?"

"I shouldn't have to, Phillip."

He groaned and leaned his head back. "Not that again."

She held her tongue.

Phillip stood. "I'm hungry. Want to come with me to

get something to eat?" He glanced over his shoulder at the
phone on the dresser. "I'd order room service, but they don't
have it here."

Blair had told her to make sure Phillip knew she was open
to Toby having a relationship with him. "We can go with
you," she said. When he looked surprised, she said, "He just
needs more time with you. Let's go eat, and he can get to
know you a bit."

There was a restaurant next door so they walked over
and ordered their food. Phillip asked Toby for his iPad then
downloaded several games and taught him how to play. By
the time they had finished dinner, it was slightly less awkward, but Toby was still reserved.

Phillip walked with them to the parking lot and stopped
next to Anna's car.

"I want to see him again," Phillip said.

Anna opened the back door for Toby to climb in, and
she motioned for Phillip to move to the back of the car
with her. "Right now, Toby and I are a package deal until
he's comfortable being alone with you. And as you saw, I'm
not doing anything to discourage him from getting to know
you."

"You're not encouraging it either, are you?"

She groaned. "*Phillip*..."

"I want to spend more time with you, too, Annaliese."

"I'm getting married on Sunday, Phillip."

"It's going to be really hard to make it work if you're living in England."

Her heart stopped a beat. "Why? Why would you do this?
I told you that you can see Toby. Do you want to see him
more often? I'll agree to bring him three times a year."

A derisive laugh bubbled over his lips. "You really are
desperate to marry the guy."

"What do you really want, Phillip, because I can't believe you are suddenly interested in an instant family."

"You're wrong. I want to see him tomorrow."

Fear washed through her. "Toby has soccer practice on Thursday."

"Then you can bring him by after."

She took a breath and decided she needed to know the truth, even if it hurt like hell. "You're not going to sign the papers, are you?"

"Honestly, Annaliese? I don't know. I haven't decided yet. But bring him back tomorrow, and maybe I'll have an answer then."

*  *  *

Matt stared out his living room window, feeling like Ethan had when he'd been watching for Toby weeks ago. Since they had no idea how long Anna and Toby would be gone, Matt had brought her father to his house. They were planning to move in the next week after the wedding anyway. If Anna and Toby were leaving, he wanted to spend as much time with them as he could.

Headlights appeared down the street and Matt breathed a sigh of relief as the car pulled into the driveway. Matt was out the door the minute she set foot on the driveway.

"How'd it go?" he asked as soon as he reached her.

"Okay." She turned to the back door as it opened, and Toby climbed out. But she didn't seem okay. She seemed distant and worried.

"Did you have fun?" Matt asked in a lighthearted tone as he scooped the boy up into his arms.

"It was okay." Toby gave Matt a solemn look. "Mummy's friend is my dad."

"I heard." Matt shifted Toby in his arms and snagged Anna's hand. "Let's go inside and your mom can have a glass of wine while I help you get ready for bed. You can tell me all about it."

"Is Ethan home from church with Grandma yet?" Toby asked.

Matt's heart warmed hearing the boy call his mother Grandma. "Not yet, but he should be home soon."

"I wanted to go to church with Ethan, too. Can I go next week?"

*If you're here*, but Matt couldn't tell him that. "If it works out next Wednesday, sure."

"Yay. Thanks, Matt."

"You bet." Matt put the boy down once they were in the house. "Why don't you go get your pajamas, and I'll start your bath after I get your mom settled, okay?"

"Okay."

Matt gave Anna a soft kiss. "Would you like that glass of wine?"

"Yeah, sounds great, but I'll get it. Thanks for taking care of Toby."

"I love him, Anna. I love taking care of you both."

Matt went into the bathroom and sat on the toilet lid as he turned on the water in the tub.

Albert shuffled down the hall to his room and stopped in the open doorway. "You're good to her."

Matt stared at him in surprise. This was not the cranky man he'd met when he'd dated Anna years ago. "I love her."

Albert nodded. "I love her, too."

He picked up his walker to head to his room.

"Albert."

Anna's father stopped.

"No matter what happens, we're family now. You're not alone."

Tears filled the older man's eyes. "I knew you were a good man."

Just then Toby walked into the bathroom with his dinosaur pajamas in his hand.

"Does your mom help you wash your hair?" Matt asked, checking the water temperature again.

"I'm not a baby anymore. I'm six now. I can do it myself."

Matt grinned. "You *are* a big boy. I'm pretty sure you got bigger last night while you were sleeping."

"Really?" Toby asked, wide-eyed.

"Yeah. Really."

Toby moved in front of Matt and got up on his lap. "Do I have to live with my dad?"

"No, why would you think that?"

"Because I heard him tell Mummy he wants us to live in London."

Matt's heart sank.

"I don't want to live in London. I want to live here with you and Ethan."

"We want that, too, but sometimes grown-ups do things and don't think about how it affects little kids. It's not right, but that's the way it is." He tilted Toby's face up to look at him. "But you need to know that I will do everything I can to protect you and keep you safe." *Even if that meant letting him go.* He lowered his voice. "Your mommy and I are getting married and that means I'll be your stepdad."

"I get two dads now?" he asked.

Matt grinned even though his heart was breaking. "Even if I'm not living with you, you need to know that I love you. If you ever need me, all you have to do is call me, okay?"

Toby nodded.

"Even if it's on the other side of the world."

"I wish you were my dad, Matt."

Matt pulled him close. "I wish I was your dad, too. I love you."

"I love you, too."

Ethan came home while Toby was getting into the bath. Matt got a play-by-play of Toby's time with his father when he told Ethan about his night.

"He let you play games on your iPad?" Ethan asked in awe.

"Yeah, but he wanted to talk to Mummy more than me."

Ethan told Toby about a kid who threw up at church, and as their conversation moved away from Toby's mother, Matt realized his suspicions had just been confirmed.

Phillip wasn't here to get to know his son. He was here to win back Anna. He was never going to sign that damn paper. He would use Toby as a bargaining chip to get Anna to do what he wanted.

He put the boys to bed, telling them it was too late for a story, but the real reason he'd skipped the nightly ritual was he needed to talk to Anna.

It was late enough that he expected to find Anna asleep on the sofa. Instead, he found her watching *Grey's Anatomy* and the half-empty wine bottle on the coffee table.

"Hey, beautiful," he said, sitting next to her on the sofa. He wrapped an arm around her, pulling her to his side, and she snuggled into him. Damn, he could get used to this.

"I owe you big time for putting Toby to bed."

"You don't owe me anything, Anna. I like spending time with him."

"Unlike Phillip."

"It didn't go well?"

She told him how Toby was shy and slow to come out of his shell. And how Phillip became frustrated that Toby didn't instantly open up to him. "He wants to see him again tomorrow."

Matt kissed the top of her head. "Anna, he doesn't want Toby. He wants you."

She was silent for a moment. "I know, but you know I don't want *him*."

"I know. But we both know he's not going to sign that paper. You don't need to ask how high when he tells you to jump." He leaned her back so he could see her face. "Toby comes first. Let's make it to the wedding and then we'll figure out where to go from there."

# Chapter Twenty-Six

On Saturday afternoon, Anna stood on the sidelines of the soccer field, watching Toby and Ethan on the field. Toby gave her a wave, a smile lighting up his face.

"Is he any good?" she heard Phillip say behind her.

"You showed up," she said. She'd told him about Toby's game, but she'd secretly hoped he'd forget.

Phillip shrugged. "There's nothing else to do in this town."

"What are you doing here, Robins?" her father demanded. "Why don't you just leave my daughter alone?"

"With all due respect, sir," Phillip said, "I just want to get to know my son."

"What's his number?" her father asked. "The number on his jersey?"

"Well, first of all," Phillip said, pointing toward the field. "That's not a jersey. And second, how would I know?"

"Because they got those jerseys last week, and the boy has been talking about it nonstop since." He leaned into his face. "He's number six. He thinks he's six because he just had a birthday. Even I know that. How come you don't?"

"Maybe it's because Annaliese kept him from me."

"Is that how you're gonna paint it?" her father asked. "Because that won't fly with not knowing what number is on his jersey. Not when you've been forcing both of them to spend time with you every day this week."

Phillip held up his hands. "No one forced anyone. It was always Anna's choice."

"Dad," Anna said, never loving her father more than she did right now. "It's okay."

"The hell it is."

Anna walked several feet away from the crowd as the whistle blew and the game started. "Phillip, you are welcome and even encouraged to come to Toby's game, but you need to go stand somewhere else. Toby's not with me, so there's absolutely no reason for you to be with me right now."

"Maybe I want the pleasure of your company."

She crossed her arms over her chest. "And you're full of shit."

"You're so cute when you act all American," he said with a grin. "And I don't think I told you how cute you look with your hair cut. You wore it longer when we were together."

He lifted a hand as though he planned to touch her short waves, but she took a step back.

"This is inappropriate, Phillip."

"Why? We were married once."

"Why are you doing this?" she asked in disgust. "I was always too tame for you. Too boring. And a wife and kid? Please…"

Frustration washed over his face. "Okay, you want to know the truth?"

"Yes, please. *The truth.*"

His suck-up smile faded. "I got a new job."

"I know. You told me," she said, gesturing with her hand. "A grown-up one, you said."

"Yeah, that's right. But they think I'm a family man. They specifically *wanted* a family man."

She sucked in a breath. "Oh, my God. You don't even want me. You just want the boring family to impress your boss." When he looked down at the ground and remained quiet, she said, "I'm right!"

He looked up. "Anna..."

"So they all think you have a family? And you used Toby and me. Do you have a photo of us in your office?"

He cringed.

"Oh, my God," she said. "You are unbelievable."

"I need this job, Annaliese. My grandfather's pissed that I haven't held a job for more than a year and he's threatening to cut me out of his will and take away my trust. But seeing all those men with their families makes me want one, too. Then I realized I have one. Sure, we're a bit rusty, but you and I cared for each other once."

"So you want to pretend to be some happy family?" she asked in disbelief. "You're insane."

"If you'd just give us a chance..."

"No," she whisper-shouted. "I will *not* give you a chance. If I had my way, I'd never see your face again. I'm only talking to you because you happen to be my son's father."

She started to walk away, but he called after her, "If you don't come back to London, then I'll tell the police you kidnapped Toby and take him back to England myself while you sit in jail."

She spun around to face him, her worst nightmare come true. "You can't be serious."

"I don't want to do it this way, Anna, but it's within my legal rights."

Tears stung her eyes. "Why are you doing this, Phillip? We're happy here. Toby's happy here, happier than I've ever seen him. And my father...I want my son to know his grandfather."

"And him," Phillip said. "You want *him*."

"Matt?"

He didn't answer then said, "I'm willing to negotiate."

She released a bitter laugh and turned toward the field. "Our son is playing his very first soccer match and you would rather work out the terms of blackmailing me into pretending to be your wife at an office picnic."

"Fine, forget the office parties and picnic. Hell, I'll even tell them you and I are separated, but I need Toby."

"You need your son as a prop?"

"I'll start spending more time with him, too. It wouldn't look right if he acts like he's scared of me."

"You would really use our son that way?"

"He's my son, too." When she didn't answer, he said, "It doesn't have to be this way, Annaliese."

"You can't do this. That's got to be the most selfish thing I've ever heard." She shook her head. "No. I'm going to fight you on this."

"I'll sue you for full custody and use this trip to Missouri as evidence that you tried to kidnap him."

"It will never work. The court will see that you haven't paid child maintenance or seen him in years."

"And I'll point out that I took a week off from work to see my son and talk reason into you before I resorted to pressing charges. Are you willing to take the chance?"

Matt had been right. Phillip was never going to sign the paper. Her next best step was to go back and throw herself on the mercy of the court.

"I'm flying home on Monday morning," Phillip said, "I

have two tickets. One for me and one for Toby. You are welcome to come with us, too, but make no mistake, Toby will come with me."

Anna stared at him in disbelief.

"I'm holding a ticket for you, Annaliese. They'll hold it until tonight, so let me know. Regardless, I'll see you at the Kansas City Airport at ten on Monday morning."

Then he turned and walked away.

Anna tried to hide her worry from her dad and Matt's mom, and although she did a poor job of it, they didn't ask questions.

The boys won their game, and Ethan scored a goal. Anna was happy to have this moment with them, but all she wanted to do was pull Matt away and tell him about Phillip. Once snacks were passed out and Matt gave the team a congratulatory speech, everyone scattered to the parking lot.

Matt had been giving her questioning glances. He knew something was wrong, so she wasn't surprised when he pulled her to the side, leaving the boys next to his mother. "Did I see Phillip here at the start of the game?"

She gave a slight nod. "Yes."

"He left early?"

"After he delivered his ultimatum, he had no reason to stay."

He scowled. "*Ultimatum?*"

She gathered her courage, then said. "You were right, Matt. He's not going to sign, and he's tired of waiting."

"What does that mean?"

She crossed her arms over her chest. "It means he purchased two tickets to London for him and Toby, leaving Monday morning. He's holding a ticket in my name until tonight." She took a breath. "Matt, he's taking Toby one way or the other," she said in a broken voice. "And if I try to stop him, he'll have me arrested for kidnapping."

"Okay," he said. She could see he was trying to stay calm, but she heard the panic in his voice. "We need to call Blair."

"I already did. She says short of talking Phillip out of it, there's nothing I can do."

He didn't respond.

Tears filled her eyes. "I'm so sorry."

"No," he said, wrapping her up in his arms. "No. You didn't do anything wrong."

"Mummy?" Toby asked in a small, scared voice. "Why are you crying?"

"I'm okay," she said, wiping her face. "Why don't you see where everyone wants to go for lunch. You can be in charge of taking the votes."

"Okay…" He wasn't buying her excuse, but at least did as she suggested.

"We have to tell everyone," she said as Toby walked away. "But not yet."

"Let's tell them after the wedding."

"Do you still want to get married?" she asked. "I know before you said you did regardless, but this is real, Matt. Consider the circumstances."

He kissed her. "You're not getting out of marrying me that easy, Anna Fischer." Then he sobered. "Tell Phillip that you're flying with him. We can't let him take Toby alone."

"Are you sure?" she asked.

"Toby is our number one priority. That hasn't changed."

# Chapter Twenty-Seven

"God is smiling on your wedding," Matt's mother said as she fluffed Anna's dress. "You couldn't pick a more beautiful day. The temperature is perfect, the sun is setting, and there's not a cloud in the sky."

"Yes," Anna said as she smiled at her reflection in the full-length mirror in Matt's bedroom. "It's perfect." Her A-line white silk dress was simple except for the sheer lace back and a scalloped lace neckline. Her blond hair hung in soft waves above her shoulders, and the pieces of hair that were constantly falling into her face were pinned back with a small sprig of baby's breath.

Matt's mother gave her a hug. "I'm so thankful you're back in Matt's life. I always knew you two were meant to be together."

"Let's hope so," Anna said.

"What?" his mother asked in confusion.

She and Matt had decided to keep the news of her and Toby's impending departure to themselves until after they had dinner and cake, and danced. They wanted their wedding to be a celebration and not a sorrowful occasion, but it was hard keeping such a monstrous secret to herself.

Anna pulled free and picked up her wildflower bouquet in an attempt to change the topic. "Surely it's about time to start."

The bedroom door opened and Holly poked her head in. "You must be a mind reader, Anna. I came to get you. It's time."

Matt's mother gave Anna a last kiss on the cheek, then left her alone with Holly.

"Any last-minute questions?" Holly asked, then grinned. "Any second thoughts?"

Should they have waited? Would it confuse the boys more if they were married and living apart? But as stupid as it felt, knowing that she was leaving as his wife made her feel like she was more likely to return to him. She didn't have her job, but at least she still had her flat. She had enough savings to see her and Toby through for several months before they'd start feeling the pinch of her lost income. Her father would stay with Matt until his room at the assisted living center was ready in another few weeks.

"Whoa..." Holly said, taking in the stack of suitcases in the open closet. "I was kidding about the second thoughts. Are you nervous?"

Anna smiled. "Not for the reason you think. I've never been more certain of anything in my life."

"Then everything else will work itself out."

Anna certainly hoped so.

Holly checked her makeup and hair, fluffed her dress even though Matt's mother had already done it, then opened the door and told her to walk down the hall.

A string quartet played outside, a group of high school orchestra students who were friends of Tyler's brother.

Toby was waiting for her in the hall, dressed in a black tux. Holly had pinned a yellow flower to his lapel and his hair was neater than usual, *probably Matt's doing*, she thought to herself.

He gasped when he saw her. "Mummy. You look so pretty."

"Thank you, baby, and *you* look so handsome," she said as she bent over to kiss his cheek. "Are you ready for us to marry Matt?" She studied his face. "You know Matt's marrying *us* and not just me, right?"

"I know, Mummy," Toby said solemnly. "Matt already told me."

"He did?" she asked in surprise.

He nodded.

The music changed to some classical piece Anna had heard a hundred times but couldn't name, and Holly moved to the back door. "Anna, it's time."

Anna smiled down at Toby. "Just like we practiced."

Holly opened the door and Anna walked out, holding hands with her son.

The sun had sunk lower in the sky, and the house cast long shadows in the yard, but the candles and torches spread around the arbor gave the backyard a romantic glow. The few people they had invited were sitting in folding chairs, but she only had eyes for the man in the black tux, waiting in front of the arbor. His eyes locked on hers and a huge smile spread across his face. Ethan stood next to him, wearing a black tux of his own. He reached up and slipped his hand into Matt's.

It seemed to take an eternity to walk across the yard to him, not because the twenty feet was too far, but because she'd waited for over a decade for this moment and she couldn't believe it was finally here.

*  *  *

When Anna walked out the back door with Toby, Matt was sure he'd never seen a more beautiful woman in his life. She hadn't let him see her dress, saying they couldn't afford to tempt fate, but now he was glad she'd hidden it from him. The lace bodice and full silk skirt were so perfectly *her*. Her eyes had locked on to his, and she smiled.

Toby clung to her hand, looking equally excited and scared. Before the wedding, he'd confessed he was nervous that so many people would be looking at him, but Matt had assured the little guy that all eyes would be on his beautiful mother, not to mention Toby knew everyone who'd be sitting in the chairs. But when Toby still looked scared, Matt had told him if he became too overwhelmed, to come stand next to Matt and he would keep him safe.

Right now, Toby was plastered to his mother's side. They had practiced Toby giving his mother's hand to Matt, but it was obvious he wanted no part of that plan now.

Anna looked down at her son and gave him a patient smile as she tried to pull her hand free, then gave Matt an apologetic look.

Matt grinned and reached for Toby's free hand, putting him between them.

Anna's eyes widened in surprise and it took everything in him to resist the urge to kiss her and tell her that this was their life now—love, reassurance, and compromise. Given their circumstances, this way seemed better.

Hand in hand, the four of them walked under the arbor

together, Toby between Anna and Matt, and Ethan on Matt's right side. The minister stared at them for a moment before he started the ceremony. Matt told himself to remember all of this, but the words floated past him. He could only focus on the woman next to him, afraid he would blink and realize it was all a dream.

When it came time for the vows, Matt pulled his hands free from both boys and reached into his pocket to pull out his vows, then stopped. They had been written to Anna, but now he realized they were incomplete.

He wrapped an arm around Ethan's back and said, "Anna and Toby, Ethan and I welcome you into our family. Our hearts are yours. Our home is yours. We want you to always feel welcome and loved."

Matt paused and took Toby's hand in his. "Toby."

The boy looked up at Matt with so much love and trust, Matt felt his heart break. How much time would he miss with him? What harm would his manipulative father cause? But today was about the blessings he was gaining, not what he was about to lose. "Toby, I'm marrying your mom, but I'm also making a promise to you. I promise to love and protect you, putting your safety and protection, putting your needs above my own." He paused, trying to swallow the lump in his throat. "And though I might not always be there in person, I will only be a phone call away, and I promise if you need me, I will come to you, no matter where you are, I will come. Today, I promise to love your mother forever, but I also promise to always love you."

Anna lifted her fingertips to her eye, patting a trailing tear.

Matt lifted his gaze to hers. "Annaliese."

Tears flooded her eyes.

He reached for her hand and grinned, his eyes stinging. "Only happy tears today, beautiful."

She gave him a watery smile. "The happiest."

He lifted his free hand to gently brush away another tear. "Anna, I knew you were the one the night of our first date." He smiled at her, his beautiful bride. "We were like two pieces of a puzzle that fit perfectly together. But it wasn't time, and I lost you." Her face blurred with his tears before he blinked and sent them rolling down his face. "And then I found you again."

Anna's chin quivered and more tears escaped.

"And despite my stubbornness and stupidity, I realized what a blessing I'd been given. How many people wish for a second chance and never get it? Anna." He grabbed both of her hands. "Every moment with you is a gift. Every. Moment. And I will take them when I can and be grateful that I was given this second chance. Maybe our separation is my penance for not fighting for you before, and I will gladly accept it now." His throat clogged with tears. "But I'm sorry you and Toby and Ethan have to pay the price."

Anna shook her head, her face with tears. "Only happy tears today, Matt. Only happy."

"Only happy." He smiled, more tears escaping. He pulled her hand and pressed her palm to his chest and covered it with his own. "There's an empty spot inside that only you can fill. When I'm with you, I feel like I can do anything, because you make me a better man. You make me believe I'm capable of more. So now..." His voice choked. "Now I realize I can't fix this, and I'm letting you down..."

She shook her head. "No, Matt. No."

"It's easy to feel like a good man when things are going

well, but your love…it makes it easier for me to handle life when things go south. Because you believe in me, Anna. When I see the love in your eyes, I see the man you see, and you make me want to be him."

She lifted a hand to his face, brushing away his tears. "Oh, Matt. You *are* him. I wish you could see what I see." She glanced down at Ethan and Toby then back up at him. "I see a man whose heart is so full of love, he gives it away freely and without conditions. I see a man who puts the needs of a child who is not his son above his own needs, even when it hurts so much…" She took a breath. "When I see you, I see a man who is a role model for my son. A man whose actions speak louder than inflated words and false promises. I see a man who is the true definition of a father." A tiny sob escaped.

Matt lifted his hands to her face and held her still as he searched her eyes. "No. Happy tears today. I chose this freely, Anna. I was so stupid before, but now I see it clearly. You are my everything. *You.*"

She nodded and took a breath. "My life has been so empty without you, and it's about to get empty again, but I will take every moment with you I can get, and thank God for what he gives. Because I'd rather have moments of perfection with you in exchange for a lifetime of emptiness." She released a tear-filled laugh as she glanced out into the shocked faces of the guests. "So much for waiting to tell them."

"I'm sorry," he said.

She shook her head, her eyes burning bright. "I'm not. This is the way it's supposed to be, especially now. The separation is part of us, it should be part of our vows, too."

He nodded. "Yeah."

"I knew you were the one, too. The night of our first date.

And when I let you go, I knew it was the stupidest thing I had ever done, but I also knew it was right. And if I had to do it all again, I would follow the same path, and that makes me feel so selfish, because of the pain I've caused you, and the pain I will still inflict. But without that path, I wouldn't have Toby, and life without him is inconceivable." Her face softened. "But the pain made me a better person, a more grateful person. I took your love for granted before, but now—because of the separation—I know what a *gift* I've been given. You, Matthew Michael Osborn, are a gift. I've never met a man who loves so deeply, so completely, so *selflessly*." Her voice choked again and she looked down at Toby then back into his eyes. "And so I will take the special moments—embrace them and be grateful—because there is only one man I have ever loved...It's always been you, Matt. Always and forever you."

Matt leaned over and kissed her, his tears blending with her own.

"We're not to that part yet," the minister said.

Matt pulled back and smiled at Anna before glancing over at the confused-looking man. "We don't seem to do things the typical way."

The minister grinned. "I can see that. Do you want to exchange the rings now?"

Matt looked at Anna, realizing he'd interrupted her vows, but she nodded. "Yes. Rings."

The boys each handed them their rings, and Matt and Anna stared into each other's eyes as they slipped them on their fingers and repeated more vows.

The minister held out his hands. "By the power vested in me by the State of Missouri, I now pronounce you man and wife. You may kiss the bride." He chuckled. "Again."

Matt kissed her with the love he offered today and the

promise of tomorrow while their family and friends clapped and cheered.

\*    \*    \*

The reception was a blur. Anna felt a strange blend of happiness and sorrow, but she told herself to get used to it. This would be her life for the next ten years.

They knew everyone was confused, so before they walked back down the aisle, Matt explained the situation. She glanced down at Toby and Ethan to see if they were upset, but they each clung to Matt and Anna's hands with a resigned stoicism.

*Matt had already told them.*

He hadn't wanted them to find out when everyone else did. He wanted to answer their questions and ease their fears. One more piece of evidence that marrying him was the right thing to do.

Despite their sorrow, they made the reception a celebration of their love. They danced and ate, and after everyone left, they put the boys to bed, tucking them in together. While Anna knew Matt and Ethan would come to London in June, a month and a half seemed like an eternity.

Matt grabbed her hand and tugged her into their room. He pressed her back to the door as he closed it, kissing her with tenderness and longing.

She lifted her hands to his face, drinking in everything she could so she could remember it all and replay it in her head when she lay in her lonely bed in London.

"I love you, Matt. I love you so much."

"I love you, too."

He picked her up and carried her to the bed. They undressed each other in a slow, unhurried pace, savoring every touch. Matt laid her gently on the bed and kissed her everywhere.

Soon she was pulling him on top of her. He watched her face as he entered her and they continued their wordless dance, their bodies expressing their love until they came together.

Matt rolled to his side, bringing her with him as he wrapped her up in his arms and his love.

# Chapter Twenty-Eight

Matt stared at a spreadsheet, working on a bid he planned to present the next day. He and Kevin were working through lunch to put the finishing touches on the proposal, and the numbers were starting to swim on the screen. Anna had been gone three weeks and two days, and it felt like she'd been gone three years.

"Are you sorry?" Kevin asked in a subdued voice.

Matt turned to look at him and blinked, sure he'd missed something. "What?"

"Are you sorry you married her?" He paused and leaned closer. "You're supposed to be happy when you get married, Matt, not depressed. I know it seemed like a good idea in the heat of the moment, but are you sorry?"

Anger billowed in his chest, pissed that his friend could suggest that marrying Anna was a mistake, but he knew Kevin only had his best interest in mind. Hell, after Matt had dropped Anna and Toby off at the security checkpoint at the airport, Kevin and Tyler had been outside on the sidewalk, waiting to help Matt pick up the pieces of his broken heart.

"I love her," Matt said quietly. "And I love that little boy." He sat back in his seat. "Don't worry, I'm not moping around at home. I wouldn't do that to Ethan."

"You shouldn't pretend either," Kevin said.

"I'm not. I love my life with Ethan and the dogs, even if it feels like half of me is missing. Ethan keeps my distracted. When I come to work, reality hits me."

Kevin grinned. "So you're saying I should act more like a five-year-old."

Matt shook his head and laughed. "Give it a shot." He turned serious. "Her attorney's working on changing her decree to let her move out of the country, but the odds aren't in Anna's favor. So we'll make do."

"Making do is making you miserable. I hate seeing you like this, Matt," Kevin said.

Matt didn't like it either, but as far as he was concerned, there was no other option.

His phone rang and he smiled. Anna usually let Toby call him after he came home from school. "I need to take this," Matt said.

Kevin nodded and moved back to his desk in the corner of their small office.

Matt answered his phone, happy to see it was a video call.

Anna's face appeared on the screen when he answered and his heart was happy, if only for a few moments.

"I know you're at work," Anna said. "I hope we're not interrupting."

"That's the beauty of being the boss," Matt said. "I can do whatever I want."

"Says you…" Kevin grumbled from the corner.

"Hi, Kevin," Anna called out. "From one money person

to another, we know the money person is the one in charge, even if the CEO thinks differently."

Kevin shook his head with a grin as he stood and headed for the bathroom. "Get that woman back here as soon as possible. I need someone on my side."

Anna heard him and frowned.

"Anna," Matt said, lowering his voice. "Ignore him."

"I spoke to the attorney today, Matt."

He studied her face and felt his heart sink. "Not good news, I take it?"

She shook her head. "He's still working on it, but he says the courts usually rule in favor of the country the child is currently living in. If only I had gone home to have him—"

"Anna, let it go. Ethan and I are coming in another month for two weeks. We can make it until then." He gave her a soft smile. "How's the job search going?"

She frowned. "So far nothing, but I have a head hunter working on it. She found a great job in the Netherlands but..."

"Phillip." Or Fucker, as Matt had begun referring to him in his head.

"I'll find something. In the meantime, I get to spend more time with Toby, and I'm getting the condo ready to put on the market."

Even though she hoped to find a new job in London, she had decided to be prepared to move outside of the city. Matt hated that she'd lost her job and would soon lose her condo, but she insisted everything was fine.

"I might have a buyer. I have a friend who knows a couple who want to move into this building. They're going to check it out tomorrow before I go to Toby's Family Day at school."

"Any word from Phillip if he's going to come to Family Day or not?"

"No."

"How's Toby handling that?"

"He refuses to talk about it."

Guilt nibbled at his conscience. "I'd come, Anna, I'd come in a heartbeat, but I have this presentation. We're not the only group bidding, and—"

"Matt," she said softly, leaning closer to the screen. "It's okay. It's just a silly school thing. In the grand scheme of life, Toby would rather have you here for two weeks instead of two days."

"I know, but still..."

Anna looked over her shoulder. "Matt, I have to go. The realtor's here to look around in case the deal with Darcy's friends falls through. Call me later, okay?"

"Okay. I love you."

"I love you, too." Matt put his phone on the desk, thinking about Toby's Family Day and his prick of a father.

Kevin emerged from the bathroom, and they went over their presentation, starting from the beginning. They had just finished when Matt's phone rang again, this time with a video call from Toby's iPad.

"Hey, little man," Matt said in a cheerful voice, then he saw the tears on the boy's face. "Toby, what's wrong?"

"He's not coming."

Matt had a good idea who he was referring to, but asked, "Who's not coming?"

"My dad. He's not coming. He says he has a business lunch."

Matt sat back in his seat. "Toby, I'm sorry."

"Why did he make me come back here?" Toby sobbed. "He never wants to see me. He says he'll come take me to play soccer, but he never comes."

"I'm sorry," Matt repeated, unsure what else to say. It

killed him to see Toby so upset. Especially when he knew there wasn't a damn thing he could do to make the little boy feel better. Matt had never felt so powerless in his life. He could only imagine how Toby and Anna were feeling.

"I want you to be my dad, Matt," Toby said through his tears. "Why can't you be my dad?"

"I'll be your dad," Matt said quietly. "I'll be your dad, too."

"But you're on the other side of the world," the boy wailed.

Matt felt like crying himself.

"Toby?" Anna's voice called out from off the screen. "Who are you talking to?" Her face appeared and she looked worried. "I'm so sorry he called you."

"No!" Matt protested, bolting upright in his seat. "I *want* him to call me. I want to be one of the people he turns to for help."

"There's nothing you can do," Anna said. "Short of dragging Phillip to this stupid Family Day lunch." She shook her head. "I have to get back to the realtor. Call me later."

And suddenly, Matt knew what he needed to do. He grabbed a piece of paper and scribbled *Ticket to London for one TODAY*, then held it up to his receptionist, out of the view of the screen. "Let me talk to Toby again before you hang up."

Carly's eyes widened, then turned to her computer.

Kevin frowned but remained silent.

The boy's face appeared again, covered in tears. "I'm sorry I bothered you at work, Matt."

Matt swallowed the lump in his throat. "I want you to call me. Even if I can't fix it, I want to know when you are hurting."

"I love you, Matt."

"I love you, too. I'll see you soon."

He hung up and stood. "Kevin, you have to give this presentation without me."

"What? Are you crazy?"

"No. Toby needs me, and I'm going to be there for him," Matt said as he packed his laptop in his bag.

"I found a flight, Matt," Carly said, sounding anxious. "It lands at ten a.m., but it leaves in less than two hours with a two-hour layover in Chicago. It's going to take you forty minutes to get to the airport."

"Book it and e-mail me the itinerary." Matt dug around in his desk. *Come on. Come on.* He was sure he'd left his passport in the office after his business trip to Toronto last fall. That would save him some time. He'd call his mother on the way to the airport and tell her he'd be gone a few days and ask her to stay with Ethan, Albert, and the dogs.

"What do you want me to put as your return date?"

"Make it one way." He found his passport buried under a stack of Post-it notes. He pulled it out and held it up triumphantly. "I can head straight to the airport." He looked up at Carly. "Did you book it?"

"Yeah."

"I'm out of here," he said as he bolted for the door.

\* \* \*

Matt stood outside Phillip's office, unsure if this stunt would get him arrested, but he decided it was worth the risk.

He knew he looked like shit as he marched up to the receptionist desk, but didn't really give a fuck at the moment, other than he hoped they wouldn't kick him out for looking like he'd slept in his clothes. "I need to speak to Phillip Robins."

The woman at the desk seemed appalled when she saw his hair, and he lifted his hand as he saw his reflection in the mirrored letters behind her. He had a serious case of bed head or, in his case, airplane seat head. "Do you have an appointment?" she asked.

"No, but *he* does. Is he here?"

"I'm afraid I'm not at liberty to discuss that."

"Then will you put a call through to him?"

"I'm afraid I can't…"

A door opened to the back and a man in a suit walked out. Matt took advantage of the opening and bolted for the door.

"You can't go back there!" the receptionist called after him.

Matt ignored her, realizing he didn't have much time before security showed up. But if he found the prick and knocked some sense into him, he estimated the fucker could make it to the lunch before it was over.

He started peeking into offices and looking at name plates. He stopped when he saw Phillip's name and nearly retched when he saw a photo of Anna and Toby on his credenza. Toby looked like he was two or three. The dickhead could have at least taken a selfie so he could have a current photo in his office. The fancy clock next to the photo read eleven thirty-five.

Dammit.

Matt needed to find Phillip. Stat. He had been counting on the asshole being here. Phillip had told Toby he had a lunch. What if he wasn't in the office?

He continued down the hall, looking in open offices until he was in a large area full of desks. Half the desks were empty, but several women glanced up at him, some with appreciation in their eyes. Matt hated to use his looks—

especially since he was looking pretty rough—but he was desperate.

"Can any of you ladies tell me where I can find Phillip Robins?" he asked, pouring on the charm.

"Oh..." one of the women said. She sat on the edge of a desk and bounced her crossed leg. She gave him a sexy grin. "You're an American."

"That's right," Matt said. "And I need to speak to Phillip Robins. Now."

Several women piped up that they didn't know where he was, but the first woman said, "You can find him in conference room two." Her grin spread. "Shagging Mary Beth."

Several of the women gasped.

Rage rushed through Matt's veins. The fucker couldn't go to his son's lunch because he had planned a fucking *nooner*. "And can you kindly show me the direction of conference room two. *Please*," he said through gritted teeth.

"I'll do better than that," she said as she hopped off the desk. "I'll take you there. I'm Dory, by the way."

"Matt." He followed her down the hall, reminding himself that he was here for Toby, not his need to exact revenge for the hell Phillip had put them through.

Dory stopped outside a door and gave him a mischievous grin. "Can I stay and watch?"

"That's a good idea," Matt said. "I suspect I might need a witness."

Her eyes danced, then she threw the door open.

Sure enough, Phillip's bare ass greeted them as he pounded into a woman lying on the conference table.

"Phillip..." the woman under him said.

"That's right, baby, call my name," Phillip said.

Dory covered her mouth to suppress a giggle. She had her phone in her hand, taking a video.

*Good idea.*

Several more people stood behind Dory.

"*Phillip,*" Mary Beth called out as she squirmed to get free.

"That's right, baby. Fight me."

"*Phillip!*"

Matt stomped inside the room and shoved Phillip to the side, sending him crashing to the floor.

The naked woman shrieked when she saw the small group gathered outside the door. Her blouse was spread open and her skirt was hiked up to her waist, exposing her lady bits for everyone to see. Matt turned his back to her, blocking the crowd's view.

Phillip scrambled to his feet, but fell over as he tried to pull his pants up from his ankles. "What the hell are *you* doing here?"

"I'm your fucking escort to your son's family lunch at his school."

"*What?*"

"You heard me. Your heartbroken son called me yesterday and told me you canceled on him because you had a business lunch. Unless I missed something before I walked in, you weren't eating anything."

"Who the hell do you think you are?" Phillip demanded, his face turning red.

"I'm the man who loves your son so much I jumped on a goddamned plane with no suitcase—which raises all kinds of flags with immigration, I might add—and traveled twelve hours to get here on time to drag your sorry ass to that boy's lunch. Now get to your feet and let's go."

Phillip scooted backward toward the corner. "I'm not going anywhere with you."

"I can assure you," Matt said, stomping across the room

and looming over him. "I am *not* leaving this office with-out you. You dragged that boy back to England, promising him that you would be involved in his life, and I'm go-ing to make sure you fucking keep your promise. Now let's go."

"Phillip?" a man said from the doorway. "Is that true?"

"Fuck," Phillip muttered under his breath. He tried to jerk his pants up, but his foot was caught on a pant leg, and he lost his balance and fell backward, hitting his head on the wall with a loud thud.

An older man walked into the room, looking down at Phillip in disgust. "Phillip, what is the meaning of this?"

He pointed up to Matt. "This man accosted me."

Matt held his hands up to his shoulders. "I admit to knocking him off the half-naked woman on the table, but in my defense, when a man tells a squirming woman to fight him, it looks like predatory behavior." He motioned toward the door. "Dory will back me up on that."

Dory held up her phone. "That's right. I have the whole thing on video."

"I wasn't raping her!" Phillip shouted. "It was consen-sual. We meet every Thursday to shag."

The older man lifted his eyebrows. "You have sex on the conference table every Thursday?"

"Sometimes we do it on the credenza," Mary Beth said behind him, then whispered to Matt, "or sometimes in Mr. Blankenship's chair."

From the look of disgust and nausea on the elderly man's face, not only had he heard her, but *he* was Mr. Blankenship.

"Pack your things and leave, Mr. Robins," Mr. Blanken-ship said. "You no longer work here."

"What?" Phillip called out in dismay. "It's not how it looks."

"I'm sure it's exactly how it looks," Mr. Blankenship said in a stern voice.

"Since you no longer work at the office that you lied to, saying you were a devoted husband and father," Matt said, "then I suppose you no longer have a reason to use your six-year-old son as leverage to keep your ex-wife separated from her husband."

"You're divorced?" Mr. Blankenship asked.

"You really need to do a better job of screening your employees," Matt grunted, then turned back to Phillip. "And since you no longer work here, then that means you're free to go eat lunch with your son," Matt said, then leaned over and pulled Phillip to his feet. His pants fell back to his ankles.

Matt scanned the doorway and found Dory, handing her his business card. "Can you send me a copy of that video?"

"Sure," she said with a sly grin. "After this, I'll even be the mother of your children."

"Thanks, but I've already got that covered."

# Chapter Twenty-Nine

Anna sat next to Toby, watching the door, willing Phillip to walk through it. Toby hated leaving Matt and Ethan, but at least if he had a relationship with his father, their separation would serve some purpose. When she found out Phillip had canceled on Toby—*again*—she'd tried every threat she could think of to get him to attend the lunch, but the sad truth was that Phillip held all the chess pieces, and she and Toby were his pawns.

Toby gave her a mournful look as he picked at the food on his tray. "He's not coming."

She wasn't sure whether to suggest he might show or accept his absence and destroy her son even more.

*Goddamn Phillip Robins.*

But her mind quickly turned to her conversation with Matt the day before. She'd tried calling him multiple times last night, and when she'd finally gotten ahold of him this morning, he'd sounded rushed and hung up saying he'd call her back soon. He still hadn't called.

They knew this wouldn't be easy, but maybe he was already tired of waiting for her...and the waiting had just begun. What would she do if he changed his mind about their marriage?

No, Matt loved her. He wouldn't change his mind. The devotion on his face every time they talked only proved she had nothing to worry about, and dodging her calls was so unlike him. But she wanted to share her good news: the couple had loved her condo and made an offer. When Matt and Ethan came in a month, they could help Anna and Toby pick out a new place. Maybe in Manchester since she'd gotten an e-mail this morning requesting an interview.

Out of reflex, she shot a glance to the door of the cafeteria, then nearly fell over.

Phillip was walking through the door...and Matt was marching behind him.

*Matt?* What in God's name was Matt doing here? Neither man looked happy, but rage covered Phillip's face while Matt's jaw was clenched with determination.

The two men stopped to scan the room. Matt's gaze landed on Anna and his expression softened when he saw her.

"Toby," she said as she pointed in their direction. "Look."

"*Matt!*" the boy shouted, jumping out of his seat and sprinting toward them.

Anna followed and gave a stern look to a teacher who said, "Slow down, Mr. Robins."

There was no slowing Toby down. He bolted for Matt, throwing himself with so much force, Matt stumbled and nearly fell before he dropped to a squat.

Toby threw his arms around Matt's neck, breaking out into a sob. "You came, I knew you'd come."

Matt pulled back, and looked confused. "I brought your dad, Toby. Just like you wanted."

Anna stared at the two of them in disbelief, then turned to Phillip, dying to know how the two men ended up walking in together.

Phillip looked pissed. "Let's get this over with."

"Not yet," Matt said in a gruff tone. He got to his feet, picking Toby up with him. "You have a few things to say first."

"Toby," Phillip said with an expression that suggested he was constipated. "I'm sorry for being..." He glanced at Matt.

Matt's eyes narrowed.

"I'm sorry for being a sorry excuse for a father."

Anna nearly fell over, sure she was hallucinating.

"Go on," Matt grunted.

Phillip cleared his throat. "And I'm sorry for putting my needs above your own. From now on, I will be the father you need me to be, no questions asked, which includes..." He looked like he wanted to strangle Matt, but continued. "Which includes letting you live in the States if that's where your mother wants to live."

"What?" Anna gasped. "*What?*"

"Go on," Matt said, letting Toby slide to the floor, but holding on to his hand.

"Anna." Phillip glanced away then back to her. "I'm sorry I wasn't..."

"Say it," Matt forced out through gritted teeth.

"I'm sorry I wasn't man enough to be there for you."

Anna's eyes flew open. There wasn't one ounce of sincerity in Phillip's words, but she couldn't deny there was still some justice in hearing him say them. It was obvious that Matt had coached Phillip in what to say, but what on earth had he held over Phillip's head?

"You're not done," Matt said.

Phillip swallowed, looking like he wanted to throw up. "I'm sorry I let you down and made your life hell. I'm sorry I played...that I toyed with our son's emotions. I'll..." He shot a look of pure hate at Matt.

Matt never blinked.

"I'll sign the paper letting you go to the States." He turned to Matt. "Am I done?"

"You need to ask your son if he wants you here. If he does, you stay. If he doesn't, you're free to go to your attorney's office and sign that paper. I expect to see it by five p.m. I would hate for there to be any misunderstanding here, so have I made myself clear?"

"Crystal," Phillip spit out.

"Toby?" Matt asked as he bent over to look the boy in the eye. "Do you want your dad here?"

"Yes."

Matt stood and nodded to Phillip. "You heard your son. Get your ass to your seat."

Toby moved in front of Phillip. "No. Not you." He pointed to Matt. "I want you. My real dad."

Tears filled Matt's eyes. "Robins, you are free to go."

Phillip didn't waste any time fleeing, but Anna was frozen in place.

She shook her head, unsure where to start. "How?"

"I flew," Matt said with a twinkle in his eyes.

"Why?"

"Because Toby needed me, and I told him I would come when he needed me, no matter what." He looked down at the boy. "Didn't I?"

"Toby, you asked him to come?" Anna asked in horror.

"No," Matt said, placing his hand on the boy's head. "But I knew he needed me."

Toby wrapped his arms around Matt's leg and squeezed.

Matt swallowed and forced a grin. "Toby wanted his father here so I was determined to give my boy what he wanted. Mom is staying with Ethan and your dad so I could come."

"But Phillip..."

"I thought he meant Phillip, so I went to his office to escort him here...as to the rest, let's just say there was a lot of divine intervention in play, which I will fill you in on later when no children are around."

Anna stared at him in disbelief. "I have never loved you more than I do right now."

"Good," he said with a nod then a grin spread across his face. "Because I've come to take you two home."

"Home?" she whispered.

"Home. Not your condo, although I'll stay here to get you packed up and organized, but then I'm taking my family *home*."

# *Epilogue*

M ummy!" Toby shouted from the living room. "Grandma's here with her boyfriend!"

The chorus of the two barking dogs confirmed they had guests.

A shudder went through Matt at the word "boyfriend," but Anna laughed.

"Your mother's allowed to have a man in her life, Matt."

"She already has *three* men in her life," he said as he pulled the plate of hamburger patties from the fridge. "Me and the two boys."

Anna wrapped a hand around the back of his head and pulled him down to kiss him. "It's not the same thing, and you know it."

A deep frown drew down his face. "I don't have to like it. But I know what will make me feel better." Then he pulled his wife into his arms and gave her a deep, passionate kiss.

"Oh," his mother teased behind him. "I see we've interrupted something."

Matt lifted his head and grinned. "Just taking advantage of you keeping Toby busy so I can kiss my beautiful bride."

"Ethan's not here yet," Toby said, sounding forlorn, and Anna walked over to him and wrapped an arm around his back.

"His mom will bring him soon."

Abby had been back for a little over a month and would be leaving in another month to go on a medical mission trip before she started her second year of med school. Ethan had been staying with Abby at Matt's mother's house, and Toby had missed him fiercely.

Matt's mother's boyfriend stood behind her holding a plastic container and a box of cupcakes.

"Where's Albert?" his mother asked.

"Anna's dad's already in the back with his pal Sugar. She's currently glued to his side."

Anna rushed over and took the box. "Thanks, Roger. These look delicious."

He laughed. "In full disclosure, I didn't make them."

Matt bit back a retort since Anna was shooting him a playful warning look, but he found it difficult when his mother gave her boyfriend a kiss.

The bell rang and Matt practically sprinted for the door to get away from more of his mother's PDA and greeted Kevin and Holly. Her pregnancy was beginning to show, and he was glad a surge of jealousy didn't wash through him when he saw her. Now that Anna and Toby were with him permanently, they'd been discussing when to add to their family. Both of them had agreed to wait another year or two, especially since Anna had just started her new part-time job in the local branch of a large bank's international department.

"You've got those ceiling fans hooked up, right?" Holly

asked as she walked past him. "I know it's pretty cool this year for the Fourth of July, but I'm hot."

Kevin followed her, holding a bag of chips and buns. "Please, God, tell me you do," he whispered to Matt. "She's hot all the time."

Holly glanced over her shoulder and shot him a dirty look. "I heard that."

A smile spread across Kevin's face. "I meant for you to hear. You've never been sexier."

The expression on her face suggested she didn't believe him. Kevin tossed the buns and chips at Matt, who made a quick save as Kevin swept his wife into his arms.

"I've obviously been slipping on telling you how beautiful you are, "Kevin said. "How can your body not be gorgeous when you're growing our baby?"

"Good save," she said with a snort.

He bent down and gave her a kiss. "It's not a save, Holly. It's true."

The door opened behind Matt, and Tyler, Lanie, and Eric were walking in. "I don't know if you two got fireworks," Tyler said. "But I stopped by the fireworks tent on Highway 7 and dropped a couple hundred dollars. I figured the little guys might like them."

Lanie laughed. "Don't let him fool you. He's using your children as a scapegoat."

Matt grinned and shook his head. "I got plenty of fireworks, too."

Holly shot her husband a devious look. "You better fess up to your extremely large purchase, too."

"So basically, we can put on a show for the neighborhood," Matt said. "I love it and so will the boys."

They all headed outside and Anna helped everyone get drinks and get settled while Matt started up the grill. Toby kept watching the door, and a half hour later, Abby walked in with Ethan. Toby nearly tackled him with a hug and the dogs quickly piled on.

When Abby walked over to Matt, he said, "Thanks for bringing him. I know your friends had other plans."

"Ethan needs family." Her chin quivered. "He needs *you*."

"He needs you, too, Abby. We're partners in raising him, and between all of us, he'll never doubt that he's loved."

She nodded. "He's started calling Toby his brother." Matt worried that would upset his sister, but she shrugged. "We're a nontraditional family. Who needs labels? They're close enough to be brothers."

"Thanks for understanding, Abs."

She pulled him into an unexpected hug. "Thank you for loving my son as though he was your own." Then she dropped her hold and shouted, "There's a beer somewhere with my name on it!"

Anna's friend Ashley arrived and hit it off with Abby. The two women realized they had multiple friends in common. Albert told everyone about his first two months in his new apartment. Getting around had gotten easier since he'd advanced from his walker to a four-footed cane.

"Hey, Albert," Kevin said. "You look like they're feeding you well there."

"That's just it," Anna said with a sly grin. "Meals aren't included. My father has suitors who flirt with food."

Albert chuckled and waved her off. "Only a few women bring me food."

Anna raised her eyebrows. "He hasn't prepared a dinner in over three weeks."

"Way to go, Albert," Eric said, holding up his fist to Albert, but when the older man didn't know what he was doing, Eric taught him how to do it. "You'll score even more ladies now."

"Don't encourage him," Anna teased.

Eric winked at her father. "We single guys need to stick together."

"Us, too?" Ethan asked.

"You bet," Eric said. "We can start our own bachelor club."

Matt and his two friends shouted "No!" at the same time, drawing questioning looks from everyone else.

Matt shook his head. "We started our bachelor brotherhood and a month later Kevin was married—all three of us were married in less than a year." He pointed his finger at Eric then swung it to point at Ethan, Toby, and Albert. "All four of you are too young to even think about getting married. You've got plenty of time to sow your wild oats."

Lanie grinned and gave Tyler a kiss. "Maybe they should be a little less enthusiastic about sowing their wild oats than you were."

"I'll say," Matt mumbled.

Lanie pointed at Albert. "And that goes for you too, mister."

Everyone laughed.

When the sun set, the men moved out front with the fireworks, and the women and the boys moved lawn chairs to the driveway.

Matt, Kevin, and Tyler lined up some of the fireworks and let Eric start lighting them. Matt glanced back at Anna and saw she was standing close to the house with Toby on her hip. He hurried over to make sure everything was okay, surprised to see tears on Toby's cheeks.

"Hey, what's going on, little guy?"

"The loud booms scare him," Anna said with a grimace. "This is his first Fourth of July."

Shit. He'd forgotten. "Do you want to go inside?"

"No." Toby kept his gaze on the display overhead, but he cringed and jumped whenever the next firework went off.

"I have an idea," Matt said. "I'll be right back." A couple minutes later he came back out, carrying his noise-canceling headphones and his phone. "You put these on and listen to music, then you can watch the fireworks and you don't have to hear them. Okay?"

"Okay."

Matt got them set up for him, and Toby let Anna move closer to the chairs.

Anna smiled up at Matt and gave him a lingering kiss. "Have I told you lately how much I love you?"

"Not in the last ten minutes." He laughed and kissed her back.

Someone tugged on his hand, and Matt had a pretty good idea who it was before he glanced down at Ethan.

"I want to see, too, Uncle Matt."

Matt almost told him that Anna wasn't holding Toby to give him a better view, but he picked up Ethan and set him on his shoulders.

Anna glanced over at him with a look so full of love, it sucked Matt's breath away. He wrapped an arm around her back and pulled her closer.

"Sometimes I feel like I'm dreaming," she said, her voice breaking. "Like this is too good to be true. Thank you for giving me everything I ever wanted. Thank you for waiting for me."

His heart was so full, he was surprised it didn't burst out of his chest. This was what he'd always wanted, too. "We made both our dreams come true." He reached for her hand and linked their fingers. "I would have waited forever for this. It was always you, Anna. Always you."

Ex-marine Kevin Vandemeer craves normalcy. Instead, he has a broken-down old house in need of a match and some gasoline, a meddling family, and the uncanny ability to attract the world's craziest women. At least that last one he can fix: he and his buddies have made a pact to swear off women, and this includes his sweetly sexy new neighbor...

See the next page for an excerpt from *Only You*.

# Chapter One

❧

This place is a piece of shit." Kevin Vandemeer stood in the front yard of the two-bedroom home he'd purchased sight unseen, running his hand over his head.

"Well, of course it is," his sister, Megan, said.

He turned to her, his mouth dropping open. "You purposely found me a piece-of-shit house? I know I was an asshole when we were kids, but this seems excessive for payback."

She shook her head in annoyance. "Stop being a drama queen. You said you wanted a flip house. This is a house to flip."

"That I could *live in*." He punctuated the last two words with his hand.

"*Noooo*, you said to find you a house that would make a good investment."

He swung his hand toward the two-story bungalow. The bright blue paint had peeled off in massive chunks. The covered front porch ran the length of the front of the house, although the right side dipped down, probably because the right pillar was missing. It had been replaced with several concrete blocks, then a few bricks, and finally, on top, a canned good. He took a step closer. "*Is that a can of pork and beans?*"

A grin spread across her face. "See? Your first dinner in your new home."

His gaze swung back to her. "Megan…"

She put her left hand on her small, rounded belly. He hadn't seen her since Christmas, and he'd had a hard enough time dealing with the wedding ring on her finger, much less the fact that she was pregnant.

"Kevin, look." The teasing tone was gone, seriousness replacing the merriment in her eyes. "I know it seems daunting, but you needed a project after everything…and this seemed like it would take up a lot of your time."

He ignored the *after everything* lead-in. He was starting to regret telling his sister about his latest breakup. "My new job is going to take up plenty of my time. *This* place is going to take the rest of my life. How did this even pass inspection?"

"Well…" She sounded insulted. "It didn't."

"What the hell are you talking about, Megan?"

"It's a flip house, Kevin. You take what you get and make the best of it."

"It looks like the whole place is about to fall into a sinkhole."

"It's not that bad."

"Let me be the judge of that. I want to see inside." He paused, horror washing through him. "Tell me you've been inside."

"Of course I've been inside." But she sounded unconvincing.

Well, shit. There was no telling what kind of mess he was going to find in there. Might as well find out what twenty-two thousand dollars in cash had bought him. Although in hindsight, that should have been a major clue. He'd chalked it up to the cheaper cost of living in the Midwest. Now he felt like an idiot.

Buying the house had seemed like a good idea at the time. He'd come back to his hometown because he needed a change. After twelve years in the marines, his second tour in Afghanistan had been enough to convince him he was ready for civilian life. So it had seemed fortuitous when his lifelong best friend practically begged Kevin to come work with him.

Kevin hesitantly took the executive contractor job even though he felt significantly underqualified. He'd protested that he didn't know the first thing about overseeing a construction project, let alone one as big as the shopping mall Matt had taken on.

"I need someone who can organize the financial end and watch the overspending. You may not have been a drill sergeant, but you sure as hell act like one. You're perfect," Matt had said.

Kevin had accepted the job for a variety of reasons. One, it was as different as he could get from trying to root out the Taliban in small Afghan villages. The horrors he had seen would haunt him to his dying day. And, two, he wanted to be part of his niece or nephew's life as well as have a chance to get closer to his sister.

After seeing the hellhole she'd bought him, he was reconsidering the second part of number two.

"Keys." He reached out his hand and she placed two keys in his palm.

"I'm not sure you need them, though. The lock on the front door doesn't exactly work."

"Then what exactly does it do?"

She gave him a hopeful grin. "Sits there and looks pretty."

This situation was going from bad to worse. "Am I going to find a homeless man sleeping in my basement?"

She cringed. "More like a family of squirrels in the attic."

Releasing a groan, he stomped across the front yard, tripping on an exposed tree root and nearly falling on his face.

"Be careful," she called after him. "The front yard is like a minefield."

"Thank you, Captain Obvious."

She laughed, and he made his way up the steps. At least they were made of concrete and looked fairly stable.

He paused, taking in the sight of the first house he'd ever owned. What the hell had he been thinking? His life had gone to shit—there was no denying that—but why had he trusted his sister to find him a place to live?

But, after *everything*, he'd wanted something familiar. Plus, his sister had recently moved back to Blue Springs, Missouri, after living in Seattle for years. After her entire wedding fiasco, he'd realized he barely knew her. Last summer, she'd shown up four days before her wedding with the man everyone presumed to be her fiancé. But he'd turned out to be a guy she'd met on the plane ride home. Kevin had kicked himself for months afterward, telling himself if he'd been more active in his sister's life, he would have known that the first guy was an asshole and the second was an imposter. She seemed happy now, but he planned to be around to see if it was really true.

Megan called after him. "Be careful on the…second board."

His foot fell through a porch slat and tossed him forward,

the front door breaking his fall, until it swung inward and he fell on his face flat on the floor.

"*Megan.*"

"Yeah...the porch has some wood rot. The boards need to be replaced."

"And my ankle?"

"God, I know men are babies, but you were a marine, Kevin Vandemeer. Isn't your motto Live free or die?"

"It's Semper fidelis. Always faithful. And you better be damn glad I'm faithful to not killing my only sister."

"In case you start to reconsider, just remember I'm giving you a niece or nephew in a few months."

"In the spirit of this sibling bonding time, I think it's fair to tell you that's the only thing saving your ass at the moment."

"Come on, Kevin. Don't be so cranky."

"*Cranky?*" He rolled to his side and glared back at her. "You think I'm *cranky*? You just pissed away over twenty thousand of my money!" He realized his voice was rising, but he didn't give a shit.

"Let's just go inside and I'll show you it's not as bad as you think it is, so stop being so cranky."

"I'm not cranky!" Somehow he suspected the inside was worse, but he was good and stuck now. And, speaking of stuck, he sat up and jerked his foot out of the hole, pulling off his shoe in the process. "*Goddamn it!*"

She grinned at him from the bottom of the steps. "Well, if the shoe fits..."

"Not funny." He crawled over to the hole and pulled his cell phone out of his jeans pocket, shining the flashlight down into the abyss. He found his shoe, but next to it was a pair of black beady eyes that shined back at him before whatever it was scurried for the corner. He jerked backward and pointed to the hole. "What the hell is *that*?"

She cocked her eyebrows. "It's a hole. I'm so glad all those years in the marines taught you some valuable discerning skills."

"There's something alive down there!"

She leaned back her head and groaned. "You are such a baby. It's probably a raccoon or a possum." Then she stomped up the steps and reached for his phone. "Give me that."

"I don't think you should be messing around with a wild animal in your condition. What if it attacks you?"

She knelt on the porch next to the hole. "I doubt it's going to jump out and chew off my face. And even if it does, I don't need my face to give birth. You'll just be stuck looking at the grisly scars during the holidays. Now give me your phone."

He knew that look from when they were kids. She wasn't budging until he caved, so he saved them both time and handed her his mobile. "Don't drop it. I've heard raccoons are like pack rats."

"But what if he needs to watch raccoon porn? I wonder what that's like...do they show lady raccoons doing the nasty in a trash can?" She leaned forward and shined the flashlight on his phone into the space, then she lay down on the porch and reached her arm down into the two-foot-wide space.

"What the hell are you doing, Megan?" he barked out in a panic. "You're going to get bitten!"

She sat up, holding a tiny gray kitten in her hand. "I think your data plan is safe." She held the now mewling animal in her hand and lifted it in front of her face. "What do you think, cutie? Do you want Kevin's phone?"

She cuddled it close to her chest and gave him the phone. "Get your shoe and I'll give you the grand tour after I pee."

"Does this place even have running water?"

"Ha. Ha," she said in dry tone. "People in Africa would call this a palace."

"Twenty-two-grand money pit is more like it."

He was totally screwed.

# ABOUT THE AUTHOR

Denise Grover Swank is a *New York Times* and *USA Today* bestselling author who was born in Kansas City, Missouri, and lived in the area until she was nineteen. Then she became a nomadic gypsy, living in five cities, four states, and ten houses over the course of ten years before she moved back to her roots. She speaks English and a smattering of Spanish and Chinese, which she learned through an intensive Nick Jr. immersion period. Her hobbies include witty (in her own mind) Facebook comments and dancing in her kitchen with her children (quite badly, if you believe her offspring). Hidden talents include the gift of justification and the ability to drink massive amounts of caffeine and still fall asleep within two minutes. Her lack of the sense of smell allows her to perform many unspeakable tasks. She has six children and hasn't lost her sanity. Or so she leads you to believe.

You can learn more at:
DeniseGroverSwank.com
Twitter @DeniseMSwank
Facebook.com/DeniseGroverSwank

Sign up for Denise's newsletter to get information on new releases and free reads!
http://DeniseGroverSwank.com/mailing-list/

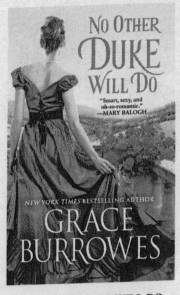

# Fall in Love with Forever Romance

## ALWAYS YOU
### By Denise Grover Swank

Matt Osborn had no idea coaching his five-year-old nephew's soccer team would get him so much attention from the mothers—attention he doesn't want now that he's given up on love and having a family of his own. Yep, Matt's the last of his bachelor buddies, and plans on staying that way. That is, until he finds himself face-to-face with the woman who broke his heart. The latest from *USA Today* bestselling author Denise Grover Swank is a winner!

# Fall in Love with Forever Romance

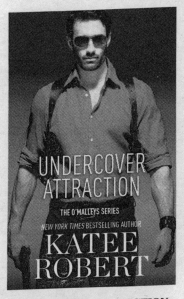

**UNDERCOVER ATTRACTION**
**By Katee Robert**

*New York Times* and *USA Today* bestselling author Katee Robert continues her smoking-hot O'Malleys series. Ex-cop Charlotte Finch used to think there was a clear line between right and wrong. Then her fellow officers betrayed her, and the world is no longer so black and white. Especially when it's Aiden O'Malley, one of the most dangerous men in Boston, who offers her a chance for justice. The only catch: She'll have to pretend to be his fiancée for his plan to work.

## Fall in Love with Forever Romance

### THE BACHELOR CONTRACT
**By Rachel Van Dyken**

Brant Wellington could have spent the rest of his life living under the magical spell of alcohol, women, and forgetting his problems. That is, until a certain bachelor auction forces him back on the family payroll and off to assess one of the Wellington resorts. Only no one warned him that his past would be there waiting for him...Don't miss the newest book from #1 *New York Times* bestselling author Rachel Van Dyken!

### WICKED INTENTIONS
**By Elizabeth Hoyt**

Don't miss *Wicked Intentions*, the *New York Times* bestseller that started Elizabeth Hoyt's classic Maiden Lane series!

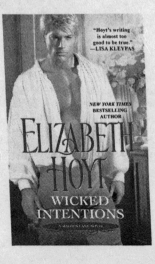